KEPLER

John Banville was born in Wexford, Ireland, in 1945. His first book, *Long Lankin*, was published in 1970. His other books are *Nightspawn*; *Birchwood*; *Dr Copernicus*, which won the James Tait Black Memorial Prize in 1976; *The Newton Letter*, which was filmed for Channel 4; *Mefisto*; and *The Book of Evidence*, which was shortlisted for the 1989 Booker Prize and won the 1989 GPA Book Award. *Kepler*, was awarded the Guardian Fiction Prize in 1981. John Banville is the literary editor of the *Irish Times* and lives in Dublin with his wife and two sons.

D1241035

JOHN BANVILLE

Kepler

Minerva

A Minerva Paperback

KEPLER

First published in Great Britain 1981
by Martin Secker & Warburg Limited
First paperback edition published 1983
by Granada Publishing Limited
This Minerva edition published 1990
by Mandarin Paperbacks
Michelin House, 81 Fulham Road, London SW3 6RB

Minerva is an imprint of the Octopus Publishing Group

Copyright © John Banville 1981

A CIP catalogue record for this book
is available from the British Library

ISBN 0 7493 9077 8

Printed in Great Britain
by Cox & Wyman Ltd, Reading

Preise dem Engel die Welt . . .

R.M. Rilke
Duino Elegies

I

Mysterium Cosmographicum

Johannes Kepler, asleep in his ruff, has dreamed the solution to the cosmic mystery. He holds it cupped in his mind as in his hands he would a precious something of unearthly frailty and splendour. O do not wake! But he will. Mistress Barbara, with a grain of grim satisfaction, shook him by his ill-shod foot, and at once the fabulous egg burst, leaving only a bit of glair and a few coordinates of broken shell.

And 0.00429.

He was cramped and cold, with a vile gum of sleep in his mouth. Opening an eye he spied his wife reaching for his dangling foot again, and dealt her a tiny kick to the knuckles. She looked at him, and under that fat flushed look he winced and made elaborate business with the brim of his borrowed hat. The child Regina, his stepdaughter, primly perched beside her mother, took in this little skirmish with her accustomed mild gaze. Young Tyge Brahe appeared then, leaning down from on high into the carriage window, a pale moist melanochroid, lean of limb, limp of paw, with a sly eye.

"We are arrived, sir," he said, smirking. That *sir*. Kepler, wiping his mouth discreetly on his sleeve, alighted on quaking legs from the carriage.

"Ah."

The castle of Benatek confronted him, grand and impassive in the sunlit February air, more vast even than the black bulk of woe that had lowered over him all the way from Graz. A bubble of gloom rose and broke in the mud of his fuddled wits.

Mästlin, even Mästlin had failed him: why expect more of Tycho the Dane? His vision swam as the tears welled. He was not yet thirty; he felt far older than that. But then, knuckling his eyes, he turned in time to witness the Junker Tengnagel, caparisoned blond brute, fall arse over tip off his rearing horse into the rutted slush of the road, and he marvelled again at the inexhaustible bounty of the world, that has always a little consolation to offer.

It was a further comfort that the grand serenity of Benatek was no more than a stony exterior: inside the gates, that gave into a cobbled courtyard, the quintet of travellers arrived in the midst of bedlam. Planks clattered, bricks crashed, masons whistled. An overburdened pack mule, ears back and muzzle turned inside out, brayed and brayed. Tyge waved a hand and said: "The new Uraniborg!" and laughed, and, as they stooped under a sagging granite lintel, a surge of excitement, tinged with the aftertaste of his dream, rose like warm gorge in Kepler's throat. Perhaps after all he had done right in coming to Bohemia? He might do great work here, at Brahe's castle, swaddled in the folds of a personality larger far and madder than his own.

They entered a second, smaller courtyard. There were no workings here. Patches of rust-stained snow clung in crevices and on window ledges. A beam of sunlight leaned against a tawny wall. All was calm, or was until, like a thing dropped into a still pool, a figure appeared from under the shadow of an arch, a dwarf it was, with enormous hands and head and little legs and a humped back. He smiled, essaying a curtsy as they went past. Frau Barbara took Regina's hand.

"God save you, gentles," the dwarf piped, in his miniature voice, and was ignored.

Through a studded door they entered a hall with an open fire. Figures moved to and fro in the reddish gloom. Kepler hung back, his wife behind him panting softly in his ear. They peered. Could it be they had been led into the servants' quarters? At a table by the fire sat a swarth man with a moustache, hugely eating. Kepler's heart thumped. He had heard tell of Tycho Brahe's eccentricities, and doubtless it was one of them to dine down here, and doubtless this was he, the great man at

4

last. It was not. The fellow looked up and said to Tycho's son: "Eh! you are returned." He was Italian. "How are things in Prague?"

"Chapped," young Tyge said, shrugging, "chapped, I would think."

The Italian frowned, and then: "Ah, I have you, I have you. Ha."

Kepler began to fidget. Surely there should have been some better reception than this. Was he being deliberately slighted, or was it just the way of aristocrats? And should he assert his presence? That might be a gross failure of tact. But Barbara would begin to nag him in a moment. Then something brushed against him and he twitched in fright. The dwarf had come quietly in, and planted himself now before the astronomer and examined with calm attention the troubled white face and myopic gaze, the frayed breeches, crumpled ruff, the hands clutching the plumed hat. "Sir Mathematicus, I venture," and bowed. "Welcome, welcome indeed," as if he were lord of the house.

"This," said young Brahe, "is Jeppe, my father's fool. It is a manner of sacred beast, I warn you, and can foretell the future."

The dwarf smiled, shaking his great smooth head. "Tut, master, I am but a poor maimed man, a nothing. But you are tardy. This long week past we have looked for you and your . . ." darting a glance at Kepler's wife ". . . baggage. Your dad is fretting."

Tyge frowned. "Remember, you," he said, "shit-eating toad, one day I will inherit you."

Jeppe glanced after Tengnagel, who had strode straight, glowering, to the fire. "What ails our broody friend?"

"A fall from his mount," Tyge said, and suddenly giggled.

"Yes? The trollops were so lively then, in town?"

Mistress Barbara bridled. Such talk, and in the child's hearing! She had been for some time silently totting up against Benatek a score of particulars that totalled now a general affront. "Johannes," she began, three semitones in ominous ascent, but just then the Italian rose and tapped a finger lightly on young Tyge's breastbone. "Tell him," he said, "your father, I regret this thing. He's angry still, and will not see me,

5

and I can wait no more. It was no fault of mine: the beast was drunk! So you tell him, yes? Now farewell." He went quickly out, flinging the wing of his heavy cloak across his shoulder and clamping his hat on his head. Kepler looked after him. "Johannes." Tyge had wandered off. Tengnagel brooded. "Come," said the dwarf, and showed again, like something swiftly shown before being palmed, his thin sly smile. He led them up dank flights of stairs, along endless stone corridors. The castle resounded with shouts, snatches of wild singing, a banging of doors. The guest rooms were cavernous and sparsely furnished. Barbara wrinkled her nose at the smell of damp. The baggage had not been brought up. Jeppe leaned in a doorway with his arms folded, watching. Kepler retreated to the mullioned window and on tiptoe peered down upon the courtyard and the workmen and a cloaked horseman cantering toward the gates. Despite misgivings he had in his heart expected something large and lavish of Benatek, gold rooms and spontaneous applause, the attention of magnificent serious people, light and space and ease: not this grey, these deformities, the clamour and confusion of other lives, this familiar—O familiar!—disorder.

Was Tycho Brahe himself not large, was he not lavish? When at noon the summons came, Kepler, who had fallen asleep again, stumbled down through the castle to find a fat bald man ranting about, of all things, his tame elk. They entered a high hall, and sat, and the Dane was suddenly silent, staring at his guest. And then Kepler, instead of lifting his spirit sufficiently up to meet this eminence, launched into an account of his troubles. The whining note even he could hear in his voice annoyed him, but he could not suppress it. There was cause for whining, after all. The Dane of course, Kepler gloomily supposed, knew nothing of money worries and all that, these squalid matters. His vast assurance was informed by centuries of patrician breeding. Even this room, high and light with a fine old ceiling, bespoke a stolid grandeur. Surely here disorder would not dare show its leering face. Tycho, with his silence and his stare, his gleaming dome of skull and metal nose, seemed more than human, seemed a great weighty engine whose imperceptible workings were holding firmly in their courses all the dis-

6

parate doings of the castle and its myriad lives.

"... And although in Graz," Kepler was saying, "I had many persons of influence on my side, even the Jesuits, yes, it was to no avail, the authorities continued to hound me without mercy, and would have me renounce my faith. You will not believe it, sir, I was forced to pay a fine of ten florins for the privilege, the *privilege*, mark you, of burying my poor children by the Lutheran rite."

Tycho stirred and dealt his moustaches a downward thrust of forefinger and thumb. Kepler with plaintive gaze stooped lower in his chair, as if the yoke of that finger and thumb had descended upon his thin neck.

"What is your philosophy, sir?" the Dane asked.

Italian oranges throbbed in a pewter bowl on the table between them. Kepler had not seen oranges before. Blazoned, big with ripeness, they were uncanny in their tense inexorable thereness.

"I hold the world to be a manifestation of the possibility of order," he said. Was this another fragment out of that morning's dream? Tycho Brahe was looking at him again, stonily. "That is," Kepler hastened, "I espouse the natural philosophy." He wished he had dressed differently. The ruff especially he regretted. He had intended it to make an impression, but it was too tight. His borrowed hat languished on the floor at his feet, another brave but ill-judged flourish, with a dent in the crown where he had inadvertently stepped on it. Tycho, considering a far corner of the ceiling, said:

"When I came first to Bohemia, the Emperor lodged us in Prague at the house of the late Vice Chancellor Curtius, where the infernal ringing of bells from the Capuchin monastery nearby was a torment night and day." He shrugged. "One has always to contend with disturbance."

Kepler nodded gravely. Bells, yes: bells indeed would seriously disturb the concentration, though not half so seriously, he fancied, as the cries of one's children dying in agony. They had, he and this Dane, much to learn about each other. He glanced around with a smile, admiring and envious. "But *here*, of course...?" The wall by which they sat was almost all a vast arched window of many leaded panes, that gave on to a prospect of vines and pasture lands rolling away into a blue pellucid distance. Winter sunlight blazed upon the Iser.

"The Emperor refers to Benatek as a castle," Tycho Brahe said, "but it is hardly that. I am making extensive alterations and enlargements; I intend that here will be my Bohemian Uraniborg. One is frustrated though at every turn. His majesty is sympathetic, but he cannot attend in person to every detail. The manager of the crown estates hereabouts, with whom I must chiefly deal, is not so well disposed towards me as I would wish. Mühlstein he is called, Kaspar von Mühlstein . . ." darkly measuring the name as a hangman would a neck. "I think he is a Jew."

A noontide bell clanged without, and the Dane wanted his breakfast. A servant brought in hot bread wrapped in napkins, and a jug from which he filled their cups with a steaming blackish stuff. Kepler peered at it and Tycho said: "You do not know this brew? It comes from Araby. I find it sharpens the brain wonderfully." It was casually said, but Kepler knew he was meant to be impressed. He drank, and smacked his lips appreciatively, and Tycho for the first time smiled. "You must forgive me, Herr Kepler, that I did not come myself to greet you on your arrival in Bohemia. As I mentioned in my letter, I seldom go to Prague, unless it is to call upon the Emperor; and besides, the opposition at this time of Mars and Jupiter, as you will appreciate, encouraged me not to interrupt my work. However, I trust you will understand that I receive you now less as a guest than as a friend and colleague."

This little speech, despite its seeming warmth, left them both obscurely dissatisfied. Tycho, about to proceed, instead looked sulkily away, to the window and the winter day outside. The servant knelt before the tiled stove feeding pine logs to the flames. The fellow had a cropped head and meaty hands, and raw red feet stuck into wooden clogs. Kepler sighed. He was, he realised, hopelessly of that class which notices the state of servants' feet. He drank more of the Arabian brew. It did clear the head, but it seemed also, alarmingly, to be giving him the shakes. He feared his fever was coming on again. It had dogged him now for six months and more, and led

8

him, in grey dawn hours, to believe he was consumptive. Still, he appeared to be putting on fat: this cursed ruff was choking him.

Tycho Brahe turned back and, looking at him hard, asked: "You work the metals?"

"Metals . . . ?" faintly. The Dane had produced a small lacquered ointment box, and was applying a dab of aromatic salve to the flesh surrounding the false bridge of silver and gold alloy set into his damaged nose, where as a young man he had been disfigured in a duel. Kepler stared. Was he to be asked perhaps to fashion a new and finer organ to adorn the Dane's great face? He was relieved when Tycho, with a trace of irritation, said:

"I mean the alembic and so forth. You claimed to be a natural philosopher, did you not?" He had an unsettling way of ranging back and forth in his talk, as if the subjects were marked on the counters of a game which he was idly playing in his head.

"No no, alchemy is not, I am not—"

"But you make horoscopes."

"Yes, that is, when I—"

"For payment?"

"Well, yes." He had begun to stammer. He felt he was being forced to confess to an essential meanness of spirit. Shaken, he gathered himself for a counter-move, but Tycho abruptly shifted the direction of play again.

"Your writings are of great interest. I have read your *Mysterium cosmographicum* with attention. I did not agree with the method, of course, but the conclusions reached I found . . . significant."

Kepler swallowed. "You are too kind."

"The flaw, I would suggest, is that you have based your theories upon the Copernican system."

Instead of on yours, that is. Well, at least they were touching on the real matter now. Kepler, his fists clenched in his lap to stop them trembling, sought feverishly for the best means of proceeding at once to the essential question. He found himself, to his annoyance, hesitating. He did not trust Tycho Brahe. The man was altogether too still and circumspect, like a species of large lazy predator hunting motionless from the sprung trap of his lair. (Yet he was, in his way, a great astronomer. That was

9

reassuring. Kepler believed in the brotherhood of science.) And besides, what *was* the essential question? He was seeking more than mere accommodation for himself and his family at Benatek. Life to him was a kind of miraculous being in itself, almost a living organism, of wonderful complexity and grace, but racked by a chronic wasting fever; he wished from Benatek and its master the granting of a perfect order and peace in which he might learn to contain his life, to still its fevered thrashings and set it to dancing the grave dance. Now, as he brooded in quiet dismay on these confusions, the moment eluded him. Tycho, pushing away the picked bones of his breakfast, began to rise. "Shall we see you at dinner, Herr Kepler?"

"But! . . ." The astronomer was scrabbling for his hat under the table.

"You will meet some other of my assistants then, and we can discuss a redistribution of tasks, now that we are one more. I had thought of setting you the lunar orbit. However, we must first consult my man Christian Longberg, who, as you will of course understand, has a say in these matters." They made a slow exit from the room. Tycho did not so much walk as sail, a stately ship. Kepler, pale, twisted the hat-brim in his trembling fingers. This was all mad. Friend and colleague indeed! He was being treated as if he were a raw apprentice. In the corridor Tycho Brahe bade him an absentminded farewell and cruised away. Frau Barbara was waiting for him in their rooms. She had an air always of seeming cruelly neglected, by his presence no less than by his absence. Sorrowing and expectant, she asked: "Well?"

Kepler selected a look of smiling abstraction and tested it gingerly. "Hmm?"

"Well," his wife insisted, "what happened?"

"O, we had breakfast. See, I brought you something," and produced from its hiding place in the crown of his hat, with a conjuror's flourish, an orange. "And I had coffee!"

Regina, who had been leaning out at the open window, turned now and advanced upon her stepfather with a faint smile. Under her candid gaze he felt always a little shy.

"There is a dead deer in the courtyard," she said. "If you lean out far you can see it, on a cart. It's very big."

10

"That is an elk," said Kepler gently. "It's called an elk. It got drunk, you know, and fell downstairs when . . ."

Their baggage had come up, and Barbara had been unpacking, and now with the glowing fruit cupped in her hands she sat down suddenly amidst the strewn wreckage of their belongings and began to weep. Kepler and the child stared at her.

"You settled nothing!" she wailed. "You didn't even *try*."

*   *   *

O familiar indeed: disorder had been the condition of his life from the beginning. If he managed, briefly, a little inward calm, then the world without was sure to turn on him. That was how it had been in Graz, at the end. And yet that final year, before he was forced to flee to Tycho Brahe in Bohemia, had begun so well. The Archduke had tired for the moment of hounding the Lutherans, Barbara was pregnant again, and, with the Stiftsschule closed, there was ample time for his private studies. He had even softened toward the house on Stempfergasse, which at first had filled him with a deep dislike the origins of which he did not care to investigate. It was the last year of the century, and there was the relieved sense that some old foul thing was finally, having wrought much mischief, dying.

In the spring, his heart full of hope, he had set himself again to the great task of formulating the laws of world harmony. His workroom was at the back of the house, a cubbyhole off the dank flagged passage leading to the kitchen. It had been a lumber room in Barbara's late husband's time. Kepler had spent a day clearing out the junk, papers and old boxes and broken furniture, which he had dumped unceremoniously through the window into the overgrown flowerbed outside. There it still lay, a mouldering heap of compost which put forth every spring clusters of wild gentian, in memory perhaps of the former master of the house, poor Marx Müller the pilfering paymaster, whose lugubrious ghost still loitered in his lost domain.

There were other, grander rooms he might have chosen, for

it was a large house, but Kepler preferred this one. It was out of the way. Barbara still had social pretensions then, and most afternoons the place was loud with the horse-faced wives of councillors and burghers, but the only sounds that disturbed the silence of his bolted lair were the querulous clucking of hens outside and the maidservant's song in the kitchen. The calm greenish light from the garden soothed his ailing eyes. Sometimes Regina came and sat with him. His work went well.

He was at last attracting some attention. Galileus the Italian had acknowledged his gift of a copy of the *Mysterium cosmographicum*. True, his letter had been disappointingly brief, and no more than civil. Tycho Brahe, however, had written to him warmly and at length about the book. Also, his correspondence with the Bavarian Chancellor Herwart von Hohenburg continued, despite the religious turmoil. All this allowed him to believe that he was becoming a person of consequence, for how many men of twenty-eight could claim such luminaries among their colleagues (he thought that not too strong a word)?

These crumbs might impress him, but others were harder to convince. He remembered the quarrel with his father-in-law, Jobst Müller. It marked in his memory, he was not sure why, the beginning of that critical period which was to end, nine months later, with his expulsion from Graz.

The spring had been bad that year, with rain and gales all through April. At the beginning of May there came an ugly calm. For days the sky was a dome of queer pale cloud, at night there was fog. Nothing stirred. It was as if the very air had congealed. The streets stank. Kepler feared this vampire weather, which affected the delicate balance of his constitution, making his brain ache and his veins to swell alarmingly. In Hungary, it was said, bloody stains were everywhere appearing on doors and walls and even in the fields. Here in Graz, an old woman, discovered one morning pissing behind the Jesuit church not far from the Stempfergasse, was stoned for a witch. Barbara, who was seven months gone, grew fretful. The time was ripe for an outbreak of plague. And it was, to Kepler, a kind of pestilence, when Jobst Müller came up from Gössendorf to stay three days.

He was a cheerless man, proud of his mill and his moneys and his Mühleck estate. Like Barbara, he too had social aspirations, he claimed noble birth and signed himself *zu Gössendorf*. Also like Barbara, though not so spectacularly as she, he was a user-up of spouses—his second wife was ailing. He accumulated wealth with a passion lacking elsewhere in his life. His daughter he looked on as a material possession, so it seemed, filched from him by the upstart Kepler.

But the visit at least served to cheer Barbara somewhat. She was glad to have an ally. Not that she ever, in Kepler's presence, complained openly about him. Silent suffering was her tactic. Kepler spent most of the three days of the visitation locked in his room. Regina kept him company. She too bore little love for Grandfather Müller. She was nine then, though small for her age, pale, with ash-blonde hair, that seemed always streaked with damp, pulled flat upon her narrow head. She was not pretty, she was too pinched and pale, but she had character. There was in her an air of completeness, of being, for herself, a precise sufficiency; Barbara was a little afraid of her. She sat in his workroom on a high stool, a toy forgotten in her lap, gazing at things—charts, chairs, the ragged garden, even at Kepler sometimes, when he coughed, or shuffled his feet, or let fall one of his involuntary little moans. Theirs was a strange sharing, but of what, he was not sure. He was the third father she had known in her short life, and she was waiting, he supposed, to see if he would prove more lasting than the previous two. Was that what they shared, then, a something held in store, for the future?

During these days she had more cause than usual to attend him. He was greatly agitated. He could not work, knowing that his wife and her father, that pair, were somewhere in the house, guzzling his breakfast wine and shaking their heads over his shortcomings. So he sat clenched at his jumbled desk, moaning and muttering, and scribbling wild calculations that were not so much mathematics as a kind of code expressing, in their violent irrationality, his otherwise mute fury and frustration.

It could not go on like that.

"We must have a talk, Johannes." Jobst Müller let spread like a kind of sickly custard over his face one of his rare smiles. It was seldom he addressed his son-in-law by name. Kepler tried to edge away from him.

"I—I am very busy."

That was the wrong thing to say. How could he be busy, with the school shut down? His astronomy was, to them, mere play, a mark of his base irresponsibility. Jobst Müller's smile grew sad. He was today without the wide-brimmed conical hat which he sported most times indoors and out, and he looked as if a part of his head were missing. He had lank grey hair and a bluish chin. He was something of a dandy, despite his years, and went in for velvet waistcoats and lace collars and blue knee-ribbons. Kepler would not look at him. They were on the gallery, above the entrance hall. Pale light of morning came in at the barred window behind them.

"But you might spare me an hour, perhaps?"

They went down the stairs, Jobst Müller's buckled shoes producing on the polished boards a dull descending scale of disapproval. The astronomer thought of his schooldays: now you are for it, Kepler. Barbara awaited them in the dining room. Johannes grimly noted the bright look in her eye. She knew the old boy had tackled him, they were in it together. She had been experimenting with her hair the night before (it had fallen out in great swatches after the birth of their first child), and now as they entered she whipped off the protective net, and a frizz of curls sprang up from her forehead. Johannes fancied he could hear them crackling.

"Good morning, my dear," he said, and showed her his teeth.

She touched her curls nervously. "Papa wants to speak to you."

Johannes took his place opposite her at the table. "I know." These chairs, old Italian pieces, part of Barbara's dowry, were too tall for him, he had to stretch to touch his toes to the floor. Still, he liked them, and the other pieces, the room itself; he was fond of carved wood and old brick and black ceiling beams, all suchlike sound things, which, even if they were not strictly his own, helped to hold his world together.

"Johannes has agreed to grant me an hour of his valuable

14

time," Jobst Müller said, filling himself a mug of small ale. Barbara bit her lip.

"Um," said Kepler. He knew what the subject would be. Ulrike the servant girl came paddling in with their breakfast on a vast tray. The guest from Mühleck partook of a boiled egg. Johannes was not hungry. His innards were in uproar this morning. It was a delicate engine, his gut, and the weather and Jobst Müller were affecting it. "Damned bread is stale," he muttered. Ulrike, in the doorway, threw him a look.

"Tell me," said his father-in-law, "is there sign of the Stiftsschule, ah, reopening?"

Johannes shrugged.

"The Archduke," he said vaguely; "you know."

Barbara thrust a smoking platter at him. "Take some bratwurst, Johann," she said. "Ulrike has made your favourite cream sauce." He stared at her, and she hastily withdrew the plate. Her belly was so big now she had to lean forward from the shoulders to reach the table. For a moment he was touched by her sad ungainly state. He had thought her beautiful when she was carrying their first. He said morosely:

"I doubt it will be opened while he still rules." He brightened. "They say he has the pox, mind; if that puts paid to him there will be hope."

"Johannes!"

Regina came in, effecting a small but palpable adjustment in the atmosphere. She shut the big oak door behind her with elaborate care, as if she were assembling part of the wall. The world was built on too large a scale for her. Johannes could sympathise.

"Hope of what?" Jobst Müller mildly enquired, scooping a last bit of white from his egg. He was all smoothness this morning, biding his time. The ale left a faint moustache of dried foam on his lip. He was to die within two years.

"Eh?" Kepler growled, determined to be difficult. Jobst Müller sighed.

"You said there would be hope if the Archduke were to . . . pass on. Hope of what, may we ask?"

"Hope of tolerance, and a little freedom in which folk may practise their faith as conscience bids them." Ha! that was

15

good. Jobst Müller had gone over to the papists in the last outbreak of Ferdinand's religious fervour, while Johannes had held fast and suffered temporary exile. The old boy's smoothness developed a ripple, it ran along his clenched jaw and tightened the bloodless lips. He said:

"Conscience, yes, conscience is fine for some, for those who imagine themselves so high and mighty they need not bother with common matters, and leave it to others to feed and house them and their families."

Johannes put down his cup with a tiny crash. It was franked with the Müller crest. Regina was watching him.

"I am still paid my salary." His face, which had been waxen with suppressed rage, reddened. Barbara made a pleading gesture, but he ignored her. "I am held in some regard in this town, you know. The councillors—aye and the Archduke himself—acknowledge my worth, even if others do not."

Jobst Müller shrugged. He had gathered himself into a crouch, a rat ready to fight. For all his dandified ways he gave off a faint tang of unwashed flesh.

"Fine manner they have of showing their appreciation, then," he said, "driving you out like a common criminal, eh?"

Johannes tore with his teeth at a crust of bread. "I ward addowed do—" he swallowed mightily "—I was allowed to return within the month. I was the only one of our people thus singled out."

Jobst Müller permitted himself another faint smile. "Perhaps," he said, with silky emphasis, "the others did not have the Jesuits to plead for them? Perhaps their *consciences* would not allow them to seek the help of that Romish guild?"

Kepler's brow coloured again. He said nothing, but sat, throbbing, and glared at the old man. There was a lull. Barbara sniffed. "Eat your sausage, Regina," she said softly, sorrowfully, as if the child's fastidious manner of eating were the secret cause of all this present distress. Regina pushed her plate away, carefully.

"Tell me," Jobst Müller said, still crouched, still smiling, "what *is* this salary that the councillors continue to pay you for not working?" As if he did not very well know.

"I do not see—"

"They have reduced it, papa," Barbara broke in eagerly. "It was two hundred florins, and now they have taken away twenty-five!" It was her way, when talking against the tide of her husband's rage, to close her eyes under fluttering lids so as not to see his twitches, that ferocious glare. Jobst Müller nodded, saying:

"That is not riches, no."

"Yes, papa."

"Still, you know, two hundred monthly . . ."

Barbara's eyes flew open.

"Monthly?" she shrieked. "But papa, that is *per annum*!"

"What!"

It was a fine playacting they were doing.

"Yes, papa, yes. And if it were not for my own small income, and what you send us from Mühleck, why—"

"*Be quiet!*" Johannes snarled.

Barbara jumped. "O!" A tear squeezed out and rolled upon her plump pink cheek. Jobst Müller looked narrowly at his son-in-law.

"I have a right, surely, to hear how matters stand?" he said. "It is my daughter, after all."

Johannes released through clenched teeth a high piercing sound that was half howl, half groan.

"I will not have it!" he cried, "I will not *have* this in my own house."

"Yours?" Jobst Müller oozed.

"O papa, stop," Barbara said.

Kepler pointed at them both a trembling finger. "You will kill me," he said, in the strained tone of one to whom a great and terrible knowledge has just come. "Yes, that's what you will do, you'll kill me, between you. It's what you want. To see my health broken. You would be happy. And then you and this your spawn, who plays at being my lady wife—" too far, you go too far "—can pack off back to Mühleck, *I* know."

"Calm yourself, sir," Jobst Müller said. "No one here wishes you harm. And pray do not sneer at Mühleck, nor the revenues it provides, which may yet prove your saving when the duke next sees fit to banish you, perhaps for good!"

Johannes gave a little jerk to the reins of his plunging rage.

Had he heard the hint of a deal there? Was the old goat working himself up to an offer to buy back his daughter? The idea made him angrier still. He laughed wildly.

"Listen to him, wife," he cried; "he is more jealous for his estates than he is for you! I may call *you* what I like, but I am not to soil the name of Mühleck by having it on my lips."

"I will defend my daughter, young man, by deeds, not words."

"Your daughter, *your daughter* let me tell you, needs no defending. She is seven-and-twenty and already she has put two husbands in their graves—*and* is working well on a third." O, too far!

"Sir!"

They surged from their chairs, on the point of blows, and stood with baleful glares locked like antlers. Into the heaving silence Barbara dropped a fat little giggle. She clapped a hand to her mouth. Regina watched her with interest. The men subsided, breathing heavily, surprised at themselves.

"He believes he is dying, you know, papa," Barbara said, with another gulp of manic laughter. "He says, he says he has the mark of a cross on his foot, at the place where the nails were driven into the Saviour, which comes and goes, and changes colour according to the time of day—isn't that so, Johannes?" She wrung her little hands, she could not stop. "Although *I* cannot see it, I suppose because I am not one of your elect, or I am not clever enough, as you . . . as you always . . ." She faded into silence. Johannes eyed her for a long moment. Jobst Müller waited. He turned to Barbara, but she looked away. He said to his son-in-law:

"What sickness is it that you think has afflicted you?" Johannes growled something under his breath. "Forgive me, I did not hear . . . ?"

"*Plague*, I said."

The old man started. "Plague? Is there plague in the city? Barbara?"

"Of course there is not, papa. He imagines it."

"But . . ."

Johannes looked up with a ghastly grin. "It must start with someone, must it not?"

18

Jobst Müller was relieved. "Really," he said, "this talk of . . . and with the child listening, really!"

Johannes turned on him again.

"How would I not worry," he said, "when I took my life in my hands by marrying this angel of death that you foisted on me?"

Barbara let out a wail and put her hands to her face. Johannes winced, and his fury drained all away, leaving him suddenly limp. He went to her. Here was real pain, after all. She would not let him touch her, and his hands fussed helplessly above her heaving shoulders, kneading an invisible projection of her grief. "I am a dog, Barbara, a rabid thing; forgive me," gnawing his knuckles. Jobst Müller watched them, this little person hovering over his big sobbing wife, and pursed his lips in distaste. Regina quietly left the room.

"O *Christ*," Kepler cried, and stamped his foot.

★   ★   ★

He was after the eternal laws that govern the harmony of the world. Through awful thickets, in darkest night, he stalked his fabulous prey. Only the stealthiest of hunters had been vouchsafed a shot at it, and he, grossly armed with the blunderbuss of his defective mathematics, what chance had he? crowded round by capering clowns hallooing and howling and banging their bells whose names were Paternity, and Responsibility, and Domestgoddamnedicity. Yet O, he had seen it once, briefly, that mythic bird, a speck, no more than a speck, soaring at an immense height. It was not to be forgotten, that glimpse.

The 19th of July, 1595, at 27 minutes precisely past 11 in the morning: that was the moment. He was then, if his calculations were accurate, 23 years, 6 months, 3 weeks, 1 day, 20 hours and 57 minutes, give or take a few tens of seconds, old.

Afterwards he spent much time poring over these figures, searching out hidden significances. The set of date and time, added together, gave a product 1,652. Nothing there that he could see. Combining the integers of that total he got 14, which

19

was twice 7, the mystical number. Or perhaps it was simply that 1652 was to be the year of his death. He would be eighty-one. (He laughed: with his health?) He turned to the second set, his age on that momentous July day. These figures were hardly more promising. Çombined, not counting the year, they made a quantity whose only significance seemed to be that it was divisible by 5, leaving him the product 22, the age at which he had left Tübingen. Well, that was not much. But if he halved 22 and subtracted 5 (that 5 again!), he got 6, and it was at six that he had been taken by his mother to the top of Gallows Hill to view the comet of 1577. And 5, what did that busy 5 signify? Why, it was the number of the intervals between the planets, the number of notes in the arpeggio of the spheres, the five-tone scale of the world's music! . . . if his calculations were accurate.

He had been working for six months on what was to become the *Mysterium cosmographicum*, his first book. His circum-stances were easier then. He was still unmarried, had not yet even heard Barbara's name, and was living at the Stiftsschule in a room that was cramped and cold, but his own. Astronomy at first had been a pastime merely, an extension of the mathemat-ical games he had liked to play as a student at Tübingen. As time went on, and his hopes for his new life in Graz turned sour, this exalted playing more and more obsessed him. It was a thing apart, a realm of order to set against the ramshackle real world in which he was imprisoned. For Graz was a kind of prison. Here in this town, which they were pleased to call a city, the Styrian capital, ruled over by narrow-minded merchants and a papist prince, Johannes Kepler's spirit was in chains, his talents manacled, his great speculative gift strapped upon the rack of schoolmastering—right! yes! laughing and snarling, mocking himself—endungeoned, by God! He was twenty-three.

It was a pretty enough town. He was impressed when first he glimpsed it, the river, the spires, the castle-crowned hill, all blurred and bright under a shower of April rain. There seemed a largeness here, a generosity, which he fancied he could see even in the breadth and balance of the buildings, so different from the beetling architecture of his native Württemberg towns. The people too appeared different. They were prome-naders much given to public discourse and dispute, and

Johannes was reminded that he had come a long way from home, that he was almost in Italy. But it was all an illusion. Presently, when he had examined more closely the teeming streets, he realised that the filth and the stench, the cripples and beggars and berserks, were the same here as anywhere else. True, they were Protestant loonies, it was Protestant filth, and a Protestant heaven those spires sought, hence the wider air hereabout: but the Archduke was a rabid Catholic, and the place was crawling with Jesuits, and even then at the Stifts-schule there was talk of disestablishment and closure.

He, who had been such a brilliant student, detested teaching. In his classes he experienced a weird frustration. The lessons he had to expound were always, always just somewhere off to the side of what really interested him, so that he was forever holding himself in check, as a boatman presses a skiff against the run of the river. The effort exhausted him, left him sweating and dazed. Frequently the rudder gave way, and he was swept off helplessly on the flood of his enthusiasm, while his poor dull students stood abandoned on the receding bank, waving weakly.

The Stiftsschule was run in the manner of a military academy. Any master who did not beat blood out of his boys was considered lax. (Johannes did his best, but on the one occasion when he could not avoid administering a flogging his victim was a great grinning fellow almost as old as he, and a head taller.) The standard of learning was high, sustained by the committee of supervisors and its phalanx of inspectors. Johannes greatly feared the inspectors. They dropped in on classes unannounced, often in pairs, and listened in silence from the back, while his handful of pupils sat with arms folded, hugging themselves, and gazed at him, gleefully attentive, waiting for him to make a fool of himself. Mostly he obliged, twitching and stammering as he wrestled with the tangled threads of his discourse.

"You must try to be calm," Rector Papius told him. "You tend to rush at things, I think, forgetting perhaps that your students do not have your quickness of mind. They cannot follow you, they become confused, and then they complain to me, or . . ." he smiled ". . . or their fathers do."

21

"I know, I know," Johannes said, looking at his hands. They sat in the rector's room overlooking the central courtyard of the school. It was raining. There was wind in the chimney, and balls of smoke rolled out of the fireplace and hung in the air around them, making his eyes sting. "I talk too quickly, and say things before I have had time to consider my words. Sometimes in the middle of a class I change my mind and begin to speak of some other subject, or realise that what I have been saying is imprecise and begin all over again to explain the matter in more detail." He shut his mouth, squirming; he was making it worse. Dr Papius frowned at the fire. "You see, Herr Rector, it is my *cupiditas speculandi* that leads me astray."

"Yes," the older man said mildly, scratching his chin, "there is in you perhaps too much . . . passion. But I would not wish to see a young man suppress his natural enthusiasm. Perhaps, Master Kepler, you were not meant for teaching?"

Johannes looked up in alarm, but the rector was regarding him only with concern, and a touch of amusement. He was a gentle, somewhat scattered person, a scholar and physician; no doubt he knew what it was to stand all day in class wishing to be elsewhere. He had always shown kindness to this strange little man from Tübingen, who at first had so appalled the more stately members of the staff with his frightful manners and disconcerting blend of friendliness, excitability and arrogance. Papius had more than once defended him to the supervisors.

"I am not a good teacher," Johannes mumbled, "I know. My gifts lie in other directions."

"Ah yes," said the rector, coughing; "your astronomy." He peered at the inspectors' report on the desk before him. "You teach *that* well, it seems?"

"But I have no students!"

"Not your fault—Pastor Zimmermann himself says here that astronomy is not everyone's meat. He recommends that you be put to teaching arithmetic and Latin rhetoric in the upper school, until we can find more pupils eager to become astronomers."

Johannes understood that he was being laughed at, albeit gently.

"They are ignorant barbarians!" he cried suddenly, and a log fell out of the fire. "All they care for is hunting and warring and looking for fat dowries for their heirs. They hate and despise philosophy and philosophers. They they they—they do not *deserve* . . ." He broke off, pale with rage and alarm. These mad outbursts must stop.

Rector Papius smiled the ghost of a smile. "The inspectors?"

"The . . . ?"

"I understood you to be describing our good Pastor Zimmermann and his fellow inspectors. It was of them we were speaking."

Johannes put a hand to his brow. "I—I meant of course those who will not send their sons for proper instruction."

"Ah. But I think, you know, there are many among our noble families, and among the merchants also, who would consider astronomy *not* a proper subject for their sons to study. They burn at the stake poor wretches who have had less dealings with the moon than you do in your classes. I am not defending this benighted attitude to your science, you understand, but only drawing it to your attention, as it is my—"

"But—"

"—As it is my *duty* to do."

They sat and eyed each other, Johannes sullen, the rector apologetically firm. Grey rain wept on the window, the smoke billowed. Johannes sighed. "You see, Herr Rector, I cannot—"

"But try, will you, Master Kepler: try?"

He tried, he tried, but how could he be calm? His brain teemed. A chaos of ideas and images churned within him. In class he fell silent more and more frequently, standing stock still, deaf to the sniggering of his students, like a crazed hierophant. He traipsed the streets in a daze, and more than once was nearly run down by horses. He wondered if he were ill. Yet it was more as if he were . . . in love! In love, that is, not with any individual object, but generally. The notion, when he hit on it, made him laugh.

At the beginning of 1595 he received a sign, if not from God himself then from a lesser deity surely, one of those whose task is to encourage the elect of this world. His post at the Stiftsschule carried with it the title of calendar maker for the province of Styria. The previous autumn, for a fee of twenty florins from the public coffers, he had drawn up an astrological calendar for the coming year, predicting great cold and an invasion by the Turks. In January there was such a frost that shepherds in the Alpine farms froze to death on the hillsides, while on the first day of the new year the Turk launched a campaign which, it was said, left the whole country from Neustadt to Vienna devastated. Johannes was charmed with this prompt vindication of his powers (and secretly astonished). O a sign, yes, surely. He set to work in earnest on the cosmic mystery.

He had not the solution, yet; he was still posing the questions. The first of these was: Why are there just six planets in the solar system? Why not five, or seven, or a thousand for that matter? No one, so far as he knew, had ever thought to ask it before. It became for him the fundamental mystery. Even the formulation of such a question struck him as a singular achievement.

He was a Copernican. At Tübingen his teacher Michael Mästlin had introduced him to that Polish master's world system. There was for Kepler something almost holy, something redemptive almost, in that vision of an ordered clockwork of sun-centred spheres. And yet he saw, from the beginning, that there was a defect, a basic flaw in it which had forced Copernicus into all manner of small tricks and evasions. For while the *idea* of the system, as outlined in the first part of *De revolutionibus*, was self-evidently an eternal truth, there was in the working out of the theory an ever increasing accumulation of paraphernalia—the epicycles, the equant point, all that—necessitated surely by some awful original accident. It was as if the master had let fall from trembling hands his marvellous model of the world's working, and on the ground it had picked up in its spokes and the fine-spun wire of its frame bits of dirt and dead leaves and the dried husks of worn-out concepts.

Copernicus was dead fifty years, but now for Johannes he rose again, a mournful angel that must be wrestled with before he could press on to found his own system. He might sneer at the epicycles and the equant point, but they were not to be discarded easily. The Canon from Ermland had been, he suspected, a greater mathematician than ever Styria's calendar

24

maker would be. Johannes raged against his own inadequacies. He might know there was a defect, and a grave one, in the Copernican system, but it was a different matter to find it. Nights he would start awake thinking he had heard the old man his adversary laughing at him, goading him.

And then he made a discovery. He realised that it was not so much in what he *had* done that Copernicus had erred: his sin had been one of omission. The great man, Johannes now understood, had been concerned only to see the nature of things demonstrated, not explained. Dissatisfied with the Ptolemaic conception of the world, Copernicus had devised a better, a more elegant system, which yet, for all its seeming radicalism, was intended only, in the schoolman's phrase, to save the phenomena, to set up a model which need not be empirically true, but only plausible according to the observations.

Then had Copernicus believed that his system was a picture of reality, or had he been satisfied that it agreed, more or less, with appearances? Or did the question arise? There was no sustained music in that old man's world, only chance airs and fragments, broken harmonies, scribbled cadences. It would be Kepler's task to draw it together, to make it sing. For truth was the missing music. He lifted his eyes to the bleak light of winter in the window and hugged himself. Was it not wonderful, the logic of things? Troubled by an inelegance in the Ptolemaic system, Copernicus had erected his great monument to the sun, in which there was embedded the flaw, the pearl, for Johannes Kepler to find.

But the world had not been created in order that it should sing. God was not frivolous. From the start he held to this, that the song was incidental, arising naturally from the harmonious relation of things. Truth itself was, in a way, incidental. Harmony was all. (Something wrong, something wrong! but he ignored it.) And harmony, as Pythagoras had shown, was the product of mathematics. Therefore the harmony of the spheres must conform to a mathematical pattern. That such a pattern existed Johannes had no doubt. It was his principal axiom that nothing in the world was created by God without a plan the basis of which is to be found in geometrical quantities. And man is godlike precisely, and only, because he can think in terms that mirror the divine pattern. He had written: The mind grasps a matter so much the more correctly the closer it approaches pure quantities as its source. Therefore his method for the task of identifying the cosmic design must be, like the design itself, founded in geometry.

Spring came to Graz and, as always, took him by surprise. He looked out one day and there it was in the flushed air, a quickening, a sense of vast sudden swooping, as if the earth had hurtled into a narrowing bend of space. The city sparkled, giving off light from throbbing window panes and polished stone, from blue and gold pools of rain in the muddied streets. Johannes kept much indoors. It disturbed him, how closely the season matched his present mood of restlessness and obscure longing. The Shrovetide carnival milled under his window unheeded, except when a comic bugle blast or the drunken singing of revellers shattered his concentration, and he bared his teeth in a soundless snarl.

Perhaps he was wrong, perhaps the world was not an ordered construct governed by immutable laws? Perhaps God, after all, like the creatures of his making, prefers the temporal to the eternal, the makeshift to the perfected, the toy bugles and bravos of misrule to the music of the spheres. But no, no, despite these doubts, no: his God was above all a god of order. The world works by geometry, for geometry is the earthly paradigm of divine thought.

Late into the nights he laboured, and stumbled through his days in a trance. Summer came. He had been working without cease for six months, and all he had achieved, if achievement it could be called, was the conviction that it was not with the planets themselves, their positions and velocities, that he must chiefly deal, but with the intervals between their orbits. The values for these distances were those set out by Copernicus, which were not much more reliable than Ptolemy's, but he had to assume, for his sanity's sake, that they were sound enough for his purpose. Time and time over he combined and recombined them, searching for the relation which they hid. Why are there just six planets? That was a question, yes. But a profounder asking was, why are there just these distances between them? He waited, listening for the whirr of wings. On that ordinary morning in July came the answering angel. He was in class. The day was warm and bright. A fly buzzed in the tall window, a rhomb of sunlight lay at his feet. His students, stunned with boredom, gazed over his head out of glazed eyes. He was demonstrating a theorem out of Euclid—afterwards, try as he might, he could not remember which —and had prepared on the blackboard an equilateral triangle. He took up the big wooden compass, and immediately, as it always contrived to do, the monstrous thing bit him. With his wounded thumb in his mouth he turned to the easel and began to trace two circles, one within the triangle touching it on its three sides, the second circumscribed and intersecting the vertices. He stepped back, into that box of dusty sunlight, and blinked, and suddenly something, his heart perhaps, dropped and bounced, like an athlete performing a miraculous feat upon a trampoline, and he thought, with rapturous inconsequence: I shall live forever. The ratio of the outer to the inner circle was identical with that of the orbits of Saturn and Jupiter, the furthermost planets, and here, within these circles, determining that ratio, was inscribed an equilateral triangle, the fundamental figure in geometry. Put therefore between the orbits of Jupiter and Mars a square, between Mars and earth a pentagon, between earth and Venus a . . . Yes. O yes. The diagram, the easel, the very walls of the room dissolved to a shimmering liquid, and young Master Kepler's lucky pupils were treated to the rare and gratifying spectacle of a teacher swabbing tears from his eyes and trumpeting juicily into a dirty handkerchief.

*   *   *

At dusk he rode out of the forest of Schönbuch. The bright March day had turned to storm, and a tawny light was sinking in the valley. The Neckar glimmered, slate-blue and cold. He stopped on the brow of a hill and stood in the stirrups to breathe deep the brave tempestuous air. He remembered Swabia not like this, strange and fierce: was it he, perhaps, that had changed? He had new gloves, twenty florins in his purse, leave of absence from the Stiftsschule, this dappled grey mare

27

lent him by his friend the district secretary of Styria, Stefan Speidel, and, safe in a satchel by his side, wrapped in oilskin, most precious of all, his manuscript. The book was done, he had come to Tübingen to publish it. Black rain was falling when he entered the narrow streets of the town, and lanterns flickered on the bastioned walls of Hohentübingen above him. After the annunciation of July, it had taken seven more months of labour, and the incorporation of a third dimension into his calculations, to round out his theory and complete the *Mysterium*. Night, storm, a solitary traveller, the muted magnificence of the world; a trickle of rain got under his collar, and his shoulder-blades quivered like nascent wings.

Presently he was sitting in a bed, in a low brown room at The Boar, with a filthy blanket pulled to his chin, eating oatcakes and drinking mulled wine. Rain drummed on the roof. From the tavern below there rose a raucous singing—fine hearty people, the Swabians, and prodigious topers. Many a skinful of Rhenish he himself as a student had puked up on that rush-strewn floor down there. It surprised him, how happy he was to be back in his homeland. He was downing the dregs of the jug in a final toast to Mistress Fame, that large and jaunty goddess, when the potboy banged on the door and summoned him forth. Bleared and grinning, half drunk, and still with the blanket clutched about him, he struggled down the rickety stairs. The aleroom had the look of a ship's cabin, the drinkers swaying, candlelight swinging, and, beyond the streaming windows, the heaving of the oceanic night. Michael Mästlin, his friend and sometime teacher, rose from a table to meet him. They shook hands, and found themselves grappling with an unexpected shyness. Johannes without preamble said: "I have written my book." He frowned at the filthy table and the leathern cups: why did things not quake at his news?

Professor Mästlin was eyeing the blanket. "Are you ill?"

"What? No; cold, wet. I have lately arrived. You had my message? But of course, since you are here. Ha. Though my piles, forgive my mentioning it, are terrible, after that journey."

"You don't mean to lodge here, surely?—no no, you shall stay with me. Come, lean on my arm, we must see to your bags."

"I am not—"

"Come now, I say. You are on fire, man, and your hands, look, they're shaking."

"I am not, I tell you, I am *not ill*."

The fever lasted for three days. He thought he might die. Supine on a couch in Mästlin's rooms he raved and prayed, plagued by visions of gaudy devastation and travail. His flesh oozed a noxious sweat: where did it come from, so much poison? Mästlin nursed him with a bachelor's unhandy tenderness, and on the fourth morning he woke, a delicate vessel lined with glass, and saw through an angle of window above him small clouds sailing in a patch of blue sky, and he was well.

Like a refining fire the fever had rinsed him clean. He went back to his book with new eyes. How could he have imagined it was finished? Squatting in a tangle of sheets he attacked the manuscript, scoring, cutting, splicing, taking the theory apart and reassembling it plane by plane until it seemed to him miraculous in its newfound elegance and strength. The window above him boomed, buffeted by gales, and when he raised himself on an elbow he could see the trees shuddering in the college yard. He imagined washes of that eminent exhilarated air sweeping through him also. Mästlin brought him his food, boiled fish, soups, stewed lights, but otherwise left him alone now; he was nervous of this excitable phenomenon, twenty years his junior, perched on the couch in a soiled nightshirt, like an animated doll, day after day, scribbling. He warned him that the sickness might not be gone, that the feeling of clarity he boasted of might be another phase of it. Johannes agreed, for what was this rage to work, this rapture of second thoughts, if not an ailment of a kind?

But he recovered from that too, and at the end of a week the old doubts and fears were back. He looked at his remade manuscript. Was it so much better than before? Had he not merely replaced the old flaws with new ones? He turned to Mästlin for reassurance. The Professor, shying under this intensity of need, frowned into a middle distance, as if surreptitiously spying out a hole down which to bolt. "Yes," he said, coughing, "yes, the idea is, ah, ingenious, certainly."

"But do you think it is *true*?"

Mästlin's frown deepened. It was a Sunday morning. They walked on the common behind the main hall of the university. The elms thrashed under a violent sky. The Professor had a grizzled beard and a drinker's nose. He weighed matters carefully before committing them to words. Europe considered him a great astronomer. "I am," he announced, "of the opinion that the mathematician has achieved his goal when he advances hypotheses to which the phenomena correspond as closely as possible. You yourself would also withdraw, I believe, if someone could offer still better principles than yours. It by no means follows that the reality immediately conforms to the detailed hypotheses of every master."

Johannes, debilitated and ill-tempered, scowled. This was the first time he had ventured out since the fever had abated. He felt transparent. There was a whirring high in the air, and then suddenly a crash of bells that made his nerves vibrate. "Why waste words?" he said, yelled, bells, *damn*. "Geometry existed before the Creation, is co-eternal with the mind of God, *is God himself . . .*"

Bang.

"O!" Mästlin stared at him.

". . . For what," smoothly, "exists in God that is not God himself?" A grey wind swarmed through the grass to meet him; he shivered. "But we are mouthing quotations merely: tell me what you truly think."

"I have said what I think," Mästlin snapped.

"But that, forgive me, magister, is scholastic shilly-shally."

"Well then, I am a schoolman!"

"You, who teaches his students—who taught *me*—the heliocentric doctrine of Copernicus, *you* a schoolman?" but turned on the professor all the same a thoughtful sidelong glance.

Mästlin pounced. "Aha, but that was also a schoolman, *and* a saver of the phenomena!"

"He only—"

"A schoolman, sir! Copernicus respected the ancients."

"Well then; but I do not?"

"It seems to me, young man, that you have not much respect

30

for anything!"

"I respect the past," Johannes said mildly. "But I wonder if it is the business of philosophers to follow slavishly the teaching of former masters?"

He did: he wondered: was it? Raindrops like conjured coins spattered the pavestones. They gained the porch of the Aula Maxima. The doors were shut and bolted within, but there was room enough for them to shelter under the stone Platonic seal. They stood in silence, gazing out. Mästlin breathed heavily, his annoyance working him like a bellows. Johannes, oblivious of the other's anger, idly noted a flock of sheep upon the common, their lugubriously noble heads, their calm eyes, how they champed the grass with such fastidiousness, as if they were not merely feeding but performing a delicate and onerous labour: God's mute meaningless creatures, so many and various. Sometimes like this the world bore in upon him suddenly, all that which is without apparent pattern or shape, but is simply *there*. The wind tossed a handful of rooks out of the great trees. Faintly there came the sound of singing, and up over the slope of the common a ragged file of young boys marched, wading against the gale. Their song, one of Luther's stolid hymns, quavered in the tumultuous air. Kepler with a pang recognised the shapeless tunic of the seminary: thus he, once. They passed by, a tenfold ghost, and, as the rain grew heavy, broke file and scampered the last few paces, yelling, into the shelter of St Anne's chapel under the elms. Mästlin was saying: ". . . to Stuttgart, where I have business at Duke Frederick's court." He paused, waiting for a response; his tone was conciliatory. "I have drawn up a calendar at the Duke's bidding, and must deliver it . . ." He tried again: "You have done similar work, of course."

"What? O, calendars, yes; it is all a necromantic monkey-shine, though."

Mästlin stared. "All . . . ?"

"Sortilege and star magic, all that. And yet," pausing, "yet I believe that the stars do influence our affairs . . ." He broke off and frowned. The past was marching through his head into a limitless future. Behind them the doors with a rattle opened a little way and a skeletal figure peered at them and immediately

31

withdrew. Mästlin sighed. "Will you go with me to Stuttgart or will you not!"

They set out early next day for the Württemberg capital. Kepler's humour was greatly improved, and by the time they reached the first stop, Mästlin was slumped speechless in a corner of the post coach, dazed by a three-hour disquisition on planets and periodicity and perfect forms. They intended staying in Stuttgart perhaps a week; Johannes was to remain there for six months.

He conceived a masterly plan to promote his theory of celestial geometry. "You see," he confided to his fellow diners at the *trippeltisch* in the Duke's palace, "I have designed a drinking cup, about this size, which shall be a model of the world according to my system, cast in silver, with the signs of the planets cut in precious stones—Saturn a diamond, the moon a pearl, and so on—and, mark this, with a mechanism to serve through seven little taps, from the seven planets, seven different kinds of beverage!"

The company gazed at him. He smiled, basking in their silent amaze. A portly man in a periwig, whose florid features and upright bearing bespoke a jovian imperium, extracted a bit of gristle from his mouth and asked:

"And who, pray, is to finance this wonderful project?"

"Why, sir, his grace the Duke. That is why I am here. For I know that princes like to play with clever toys."

"Indeed?"

A blowsy lady, with a lot of fine old lace at her throat and what looked suspiciously like a venereal herpes coming into bloom on her upper lip, leaned forward for a good look at this bizarre young man. "Well then you must," she said, nodding disconcertingly under the weight of her elaborate capuchon, "cultivate my husband," and let fall an unnerving shriek of laughter. "He is second secretary to the Bohemian ambassador, you know."

Johannes bobbed his head in what he felt would pass for a bow in this exalted company. "I should be most honoured to meet your husband," and, for a final flourish, "*madame.*"

The lady beamed, and extended a hand palm upward across the table, offering him, as if it were a dish of delicacies, the florid personage in the periwig, who looked down on him and suddenly showed, like a seal of office, a mouthful of gold teeth.

"Duke Frederick, young sir," he said, "let me assure you, is careful with his money."

They all laughed, as at a familiar joke, and returned to their plates. A young soldier with a moustache, dismembering a piece of chicken, eyed him thoughtfully. "Seven different kinds of beverage, you say?"

Johannes ignored the martial manner.

"Seven, yes," he said: "*aqua vitae* from the sun, brandy from Mercury, Venus mead, and water from the moon," busily ticking them off on his fingers, "Mars a vermouth, Jupiter a white wine, and from Saturn—" he tittered "—from Saturn will come only a bad old wine or beer, so that those ignorant of astronomy may be exposed to ridicule."

"How?" The chicken leg came asunder with a thwack. Kepler's answer was a smug smile. Tellus, the Duke's chief gardener, a jolly fat fellow with a smooth bald skull whose presence at this travellers' table was the result of a recent upheaval in protocol, laughed and said: "Caught, caught!" and the soldier reddened. He had oily brown curls that fell to the collar of his velvet surcoat. A bird-like person stuck his head on its stalk of neck from behind the shoulder of Kepler's neighbour and quacked: "O but, you mean to say, do you, do I understand you, that we are not to be as it were, not to be told your wonderful, ah, theory? Eh?" He laughed and laughed, mercurial and mad, waving his little hands.

"I intend," Johannes confided, "to recommend secrecy to the Duke. Each of the different parts of the cup shall be made by different silversmiths, and assembled later, ensuring that my *inventum* is not revealed before the proper time."

"Your what?" his neighbour grunted, turning abruptly, a swarthy saturnine fellow with a peasant's head—Johannes later learned he was a baron—who until now had sat as if deaf, consuming indiscriminately plate after plate of food.

"Latin," the periwig said shortly. "He means invention," and bent on Kepler a look of inordinately stern rebuke.

"I mean, yes, invention . . ." Johannes said meekly. All at once he was filled with misgiving. The table and these people, and the hall behind him with its jumbled hierarchy of other tables, the scurrying servants and the uproar of the crowd at feed, all of it was suddenly a manifestation of irremediable disorder. His heart sank. A breezy request for an audience with the Duke, dashed off on the day he arrived at court, had not been replied to; now, fully a week later, the icy blast of that silence struck him for the first time. How could he have been such a fool, and entertain such high hopes?

He packed up his designs for the cosmic cup and prepared to depart for Graz immediately. Mästlin, however, calling up a last reserve of patience, held him back, urging him to draft another, more carefully considered plea. Preening, he allowed himself to be convinced. His second letter came back with eerie promptness that same evening, bearing in the margin in a broad childish hand a note inviting him to make a model of his cup, *and when we see it and decide that it is worth being made in silver, the means shall not want.* Mästlin squeezed his arm, and he, beside himself, could only smile for bliss and breathe: "*We . . . !*"

It took him a week to build the model, sitting on the cold floor of his room at the top of a windy turret with scissors and paste and strips of coloured paper. It was a pretty thing, he thought, with the planets marked in red upon sky-blue orbits. He placed it lovingly into the complex channels that would carry it to the Duke and settled down to wait. More weeks went past, a month, another and yet another. Mästlin had long since returned to Tübingen to oversee the printing of the *Mysterium*. Johannes became a familiar figure in the dull life of the court, another of those poor demented supplicants who wandered like a belt of satellites around the invisible presence of the Duke. Then a letter came from Mästlin: Frederick had requested his expert opinion in the matter. An audience was granted. Kepler was indignant: expert opinion indeed!

He was received in a vast and splendid hall. The fireplace of Italian marble was taller than he. A gauze of pale light flowed down from enormous windows. On the ceiling, itself a pendant miracle of plaster garlands and moulded heads, an oval painting depicted a vertiginous scene of angels ascending about an angry bearded god enthroned on dark air. The room was

34

crowded, the milling courtiers at once aimless and intent, as if performing an intricate dance the pattern of which could be perceived only from above. A flunkey touched Kepler's elbow, he turned, and a delicate little man stepped up to him and said:

"You are Repleus?"

"No, yes, I—"

"Quite so. We have studied your model of the world," smiling tenderly; "it makes no sense."

Duke Frederick was marvellously got up in a cloth-of-gold tunic and velvet breeches. Jewels glittered on his tiny hands. He had close-cut grey curls like many small springs and on his chin a little horn of hair. He was smooth, soft, and Johannes thought of the sweet waxen flesh of a chestnut nestled snug within the lustrous cranium of its shell. He perceived the measure of the courtiers' saraband, for here was the centre of it. He began to babble an explanation of the geometry of his world system, but the Duke lifted a hand. "All that is very correct and interesting, no doubt, but wherein lies the significance in *general*?"

The paper model stood upon a lacquered table. Two of the orbits had come unstuck. Kepler suspected a ducal finger had been dabbling in its innards.

"There are, sir," he said, "only five regular perfect solids. also called the Platonic forms. They are perfect because all their sides are identical." Rector Papius would be impressed with his patience. "Of the countless forms in the world of three dimensions, only these five figures are perfect: the tetrahedron or pyramid, bounded by four equilateral triangles, the cube, with six squares, the octohedron with eight equilaterals, the dodecahedron, bounded by twelve pentagons, and the icosahedron, which has twenty equilateral triangles."

"Twenty," the Duke said, nodding.

"Yes. I hold, as you see here illustrated, that into the five intervals between the six planets of the world, these five regular solids may be . . ." He was jostled. It was the mercurial madman from the *trippeltisch*, trying to get past him to the Duke, laughing still and pursing his lips in silent apology. Johannes got an elbow into the creature's ribs and pushed. ". . . may be inscribed . . ." and *pushed* ". . . so as to satisfy

35

precisely," panting, "the intervallic quantities as measured and set down by the ancients." He smiled; that was prettily put.

The loony was pawing him again, and now he noticed that they were all here, the venereal lady, and Meister Tellus, Kaspar the soldier, and of course the periwig, and, way out at the edge of the dance, the gloomy baron. Well, what of it? He was putting them in their places. He was suddenly intensely aware of himself, young, brilliant, and somehow wonderfully fragile. "And so, as may be seen," he said airily, "between the orbits of Saturn and Jupiter I have placed the cube, between those of Jupiter and Mars the tetrahedron, Mars and earth the dodecahedron, earth and Venus the icosahedron, and, look, let me show you—" pulling the model asunder like a fruit to reveal its secret core: "between Venus and Mercury the octahedron. So!"

The Duke frowned.

"That is clear, yes," he said, "what you have done, and how; but, forgive me, may we ask *why*?"

"Why?" looking from the dismembered model to the little man before him; "well . . . well because . . ."

A froth of crazy laughter bubbled at his ear.

*   *   *

Nothing came of the project. The Duke did agree that the cup might be cast, but promptly lost interest. The court silversmith was sceptical, and there were cries of dismay from the Treasury. Johannes returned disheartened to Graz. He had squandered half a year on a craving for princely favour. It was a lesson he told himself he must remember. Presently, though, the whole humiliating affair was driven from his thoughts by a far weightier concern.

It was one of the school inspectors, the physician Oberdorfer, who first approached him, with a stealthy smile and—could it be?—a wink, and invited him to come on a certain day to the house of Herr Georg Hartmann von Stubenberg, a merchant of the town. He went, thinking he was to be asked to draw up a nativity or another of his famous calendars. But there was no commission. He did not even meet Herr Burghermeister Hartmann, and forever after that name was to echo in his memory like the reverberation of a past catastrophe. He loitered on a staircase for an hour, clutching a goblet of thin wine and trying to think of something to say to Dr Oberdorfer. In the wide hallway below groups of people came and went, overdressed women and fat businessmen, a bishop and attendant clerics, a herd of hip-booted horsemen from the Archduke's cavalry, clumsy as centaurs. One of Hartmann's children was being married. From a farther room a string band sent music arching through the house like aimless flights of fine bright arrows. Johannes grew agitated. He had not been officially invited, and he was troubled by images of challenge and ejection. What could Oberdorfer want with him? The doctor, a large pasty man with pendulous jowls and exceedingly small moist eyes, vibrated with nervous anticipation, scanning the passing throng below and wheezing under his breath in tuneless counterpoint to the rapt silvery slitherings of the minstrels. At last he touched a finger to Kepler's sleeve. A stout young woman in blue was approaching the foot of the stairs. Dr Oberdorfer leered. "She is handsome, yes?"

"Yes, yes," Johannes muttered, looking hard at a point in air, afraid that the lady below might hear; "quite, ah, handsome."

Oberdorfer, whispering sideways like a bad ventriloquist, inclined his great trembling head until it almost rested against Kepler's ear. "Also she is rich, so I am told." The young woman paused, leaning down to exclaim over a pale pursed little boy in velveteen, who turned a stony face away and tugged furiously at his nurse's hand. Kepler all his life would remember that surly Cupid. "Her father," the doctor hissed, "her father has estates, you know, to the south. They say he has settled a goodly fortune to her name." His voice sank lower still. "And of course, she is certain to have been provided for also by her . . ." faltering ". . . her late, ah, husbands."

"Her . . . ?"

"Husbands, yes." Dr Oberdorfer briefly shut his little eyes. "Most tragic, most tragic: she is twice a widow. And so young!"

37

It dawned on Johannes what was afoot. Blushing, he ascended a step in fright. The widow threw him a fraught look. The doctor said: "Her name is Barbara Müller—née, aha, Müller." Johannes stared at him, and he coughed. "A little joke, forgive me. Her family is Müller—Müller zu Gössendorf—which is also by coincidence the name of her latest, late, her *last* that is, husband . . ." trailing off to an unhappy hum.

"Yes?" Johannes said faintly, turning away from the other's aquatic eye, and then heard himself add: "She is somewhat fat, all the same."

Dr Oberdorfer winced, and then, grinning bravely, with elephantine roguishness he said:

"Plump, rather, Master Kepler, plump. And the winters are cold, eh? Ha. Ha ha."

And he took the young man firmly by the elbow and steered him up the stairs, into an alcove, where there waited a sleek grim dandified man who looked Johannes up and down without enthusiasm and said: "My dear sir," as if he had, Jobst Müller, been rehearsing it.

So began the long, involved and sordid business of his wiving. From the start he feared the prospect of the plump young widow. Women were a foreign country, he did not speak the language. One night four years previously, on a visit to Weilderstadt, flushed with ale and wanting to reassert himself after losing heavily at cards, he had consorted with a scrawny girl, a virgin, so he was assured. That was his sole experience of love. Afterwards the drab had laughed, and tested between her little yellow teeth the coin he had given her. Yet beyond the act itself, that frantic froglike swim to the cataract's edge, he had found something touching in her skinny flanks and her frail chest, that rank rose under its furred cap of bone. She had been *smaller* than he; not so Frau Müller. No, no, he was not enthusiastic. Was he not happy as he was? Happier at least than he suspected he would be with a wife. Later, when the marrige had come to grief, he blamed a large part of the disaster on the unseemly bartering that had sold him into it.

He discovered how small a place was Graz: everyone he knew seemed to have a hand in the turbulent making of this match. Sometimes he fancied he could detect a prurient leer on the face of the town itself. Dr Oberdorfer was the chief negotiator, assisted by Heinrich Osius, a former professor of the Stiftsschule. In September these two worthies went together down to Mühleck to hear Jobst Müller's terms. The miller opened the bidding coyly, declaring himself not at all eager to see his daughter wed again. This Kepler was a poor specimen, with small means and an unpromising future. And what of his birth? Was he not the son of a profligate soldier? Dr Oberdorfer countered with a speech in praise of the young man's industry and prodigious learning. Duke Frederick of Württemberg, no less, was his patron. Then Osius, who had been brought for the benefit of his bluntness, mentioned Mistress Barbara's state: so young, and twice a widow! Jobst Müller frowned, his jaw twitching. He was growing weary of that refrain.

The negotiators returned confident to Graz. Then an unexpected and serious obstacle arose, when Stefan Speidel the district secretary, Kepler's friend, declared himself opposed to the match. He knew the lady, and thought she should be better provided for. Besides, as he admitted in confidence to Kepler, he wished her to marry an acquaintance of his at court, a man of rising influence. He apologised, waving a hand; you will understand, of course, Johannes? Johannes found it hard to conceal his relief. "Well yes, Stefan, certainly, I understand, if it is a matter of your conscience, and court affairs, O completely, completely!"

The printing of the *Mysterium* progressed. Mästlin had secured the blessing of the Tübingen college senate for the work, and was supervising the setting at Gruppenbach the printers. He reported faithfully the completion of each chapter, grumbling over the expense in cash and energy. Kepler wrote him back a cheerful note pointing out that attendance at this birth would, after all, ensure the midwife's immortal fame.

Kepler was himself busy. The school authorities, incensed by his six-month absence at the Württemberg court, had followed their inspectors' advice and set him arithmetic and rhetoric classes in the upper school. These were a torment. Rector Papius, despite his half-hearted threats, had held off from increasing the young master's duties—but Papius had been summoned to the chair of medicine at Tübingen. His successor, Johannes Regius, was a stern lean Calvinist. He and Kepler were enemies from the first. Regius considered the young man disrespectful and ill-bred, and in need of taming: the pup should marry. Jobst Müller, with the sudden smack of a card player claiming a trump, agreed, for Speidel's scheme had come to nothing, and the miller of Mühleck still had a daughter on his hands. Kepler's heart sank. In February of 1597 the betrothal was signed, and on a windy day at the end of April, *sub calamitoso caelo*, Mistress Barbara Müller put off her widow's weeds and was married for the third and last time in her short life. Kepler was then aged twenty-five years, seven months and . . . but he had not the heart to compute the figures, nor the courage, considering the calamitous disposition of the stars.

The wedding feast took place, after a brief ceremony in the collegiate church, at Barbara's inherited house on the Stempfergasse. Jobst Müller, when the deal was closed and he could afford again the luxury of contempt, had declared that he would not see celebrated in his own home, before his tenants and his servants, this affront to his family's name. He had settled on Kepler a sum of cash, as well as the yield of a vineyard and an allowance for the child Regina's upbringing. Was not that enough? He sat in silence throughout the morning, scowling under the brim of his hat, morosely drunk on his own Mühleck wine. Kepler, seeing him in a sulk, squeezed a drop of bitter satisfaction from the day by calling on him repeatedly to propose a toast, to make a speech, throwing an arm about his shoulders and urging him to sing up, sing up, sir, a rousing chorus of some good old Gössendorf ballad.

Baiting his father-in-law was a way of avoiding his bride. They had hardly spoken, had hardly met, during the long months of negotiation, and today when by chance they found themselves confronting each other they were paralysed by embarrassment. She looked, he gloomily observed, radiant, that seemed the appropriate word. She was pretty, in a vacant way. She twittered. Yet when amid a chiming of uplifted glasses he pressed his palms awkwardly to her damp trembling back and kissed her for the benefit of the company, he suddenly found himself holding something unexpectedly vivid and exotic, a creature of another species, and, catching her warm spicy smell, he was excited. He began to swill in earnest then, and was soon deliriously drunk. But even that was not enough to stifle his fright.

Yet in the weeks and months that followed he was almost happy. In May the first copies of the *Mysterium* arrived from Tübingen. The slim volume pleased him enormously. His pleasure was a little tainted however by a small obscure shame, as if he had committed an indiscretion the awfulness of which had not yet been noticed by an inattentive public. This was the first blush of that patronising attitude to the book, which in later years was to make it seem the production of a heedless but inspired child that he but vaguely remembered having been. He distributed copies among selected astronomers and scholars, and a few influential Styrians that he knew, all of whom, to his indignation and dismay, proved less than deafening in their shouts of surprise and praise.

The number of volumes he had contracted to buy under the printer's terms cost him thirty-three florins. Before his marriage he could not have afforded it, but now, it seemed, he was rich. Besides the sum Jobst Müller had settled on him, his salary had been increased by fifty florins annually. That, however, was a trifle compared with his wife's fortune. He was never to succeed in her lifetime in finding out how much exactly she had inherited, but it was greater even than the most eager of matchmakers had imagined. Regina had a sum of ten thousand from her late father, Wolf Lorenz the cabinetmaker, Barbara's first casualty. If the child had that much, how much more must her mother have got? Kepler rubbed his hands, elated, and shocked at himself too.

There was another form of wealth, more palpable than cash and as quickly squandered, which was a kind of burgeoning fortune of the senses. Barbara, for all her twittering silliness, was flesh, a corporeal world, wherein he touched and found startlingly real, something that was wholly other and yet recognisable. He flared under her light, her smell, the faintly salt taste of her skin. It took time. Their first encounters were a failure. On the wedding night, in the vast four-poster in the bedroom overlooking Stempfergasse, they collided in the dark with a crunch. He felt as if he were grappling with a heavy hot corpse. She fell all over him, panting, got an elbow somehow into his chest and knocked the wind out of him, while the bed creaked and groaned like the ghost voice of its former tenant, poor dead Marx Müller, lamenting. When the union was consummated at last, she turned away and immediately fell asleep, her snores a raucous and monotonously repeated protest. It was not until many months later, when the summer was over and cold winds were blowing down from the Alps, that they at last found each other, briefly.

He remembered the evening. It was September, the trees were already beginning to turn. He had stood up from a good day's work and walked into their bedroom. Barbara was bathing in a tub before a fire of sea-coals, dreamily soaping an extended pink leg. He turned away hastily, but she looked up and smiled at him, dazed with heat. A narrow shaft of late sunlight, worn to the colour of old brass, lay aslant the bed. *Ouf!* she said, and rose in a cascade of suds and slithering water. It was the first time he had seen her entirely naked. Her head sat oddly upon this unfamiliar bare body. Aglow and faintly steaming she displayed herself, big-bummed, her stout legs braced as if to leap, a strongman's shovel-shaped beard glistening in her lap. Her breasts stared, wall-eyed and startled, the dark tips pursed. He advanced on her, his clothes falling away like flakes of shell. She rose on tiptoe to peer past him down into the street, biting her lip and laughing softly. "Someone will *see* us, Johannes." Her shoulder-blades left a damp print of wings upon the sheet. The brazen sword of sunlight smote them.

It was at once too much and not enough. They had surrendered their most intimate textures to a mere conspiracy of the flesh. It took him a long time to understand it; Barbara never did. They had so little in common. She might have tried to understand something of his work, but it was beyond her, for which she hated it. He could have tried also, could have asked her about the past, about Wolf Lorenz the wealthy tradesman, about the rumours that Marx Müller the district paymaster had embezzled state funds, but from the start these were a forbidden topic, jealously guarded by the sentinels of the dead. And so, two intimate strangers lashed together by bonds not of their making, they began to hate each other, as if it were the most natural thing in the world. Kepler turned, hesitantly, shyly, to Regina, offering her all the surplus left over from his marriage, for she represented, frozen in prototype, that very stage of knowing and regard which he had managed to miss in her mother. And Barbara, seeing everything and understanding nothing, grew fitful and began to complain, and sometimes beat the child. She demanded more and more of Kepler's time, engaged him in frantic incoherent conversations, was subject to sudden storms of weeping. One night he found her crouched in the kitchen, gorging herself on pickled fish. The following morning she fainted in his arms, nearly knocking him down. She was pregnant.

She fulfilled her term as she did everything, lavishly, with many alarms and copious tears. She became eerily beautiful, for all her bulk. It was as if she had been designed for just this state, ancient and elemental; with that great belly, those pendant breasts, she achieved a kind of ideal harmony. Kepler began to avoid her: she frightened him now more than ever. He spent the days locked in his study, tinkering with work, writing letters, going over yet again his hopelessly unbalanced accounts, lifting his head now and then to listen for the heavy tread of the goddess.

She went early into labour, blundered into it one morning with shrill cries. The waves of her pain crashed through the house, wave upon wave. Dr Oberdorfer arrived, puffing and mumbling, and heaved himself up the stairs on his black stick like a weary oarsman plying a foundering craft. It struck Kepler that the man was embarrassed, as if he had caught indulging in some base frolic this couple whose troubled destinies he had helped to entangle. Her labour lasted for two days. The rain of February fell, clouding the world without, so that there was only this house throbbing around its core of pain. Kepler trotted up and down in a fever of excitement and dismay, wringing his hands. The child was born at noon, a boy. A great blossom of heedless happiness opened up in Kepler's heart. He held the softly pulsing mite in his hands and understood that he was multiplied. "We shall call him Heinrich," he said, "after my brother—but you will be a better, a finer Heinrich, won't you, yes." Barbara, pale in her bloodied bed, stared at him emptily through a film of pain.

He drew up a horoscope. It promised all possible good, after a few adjustments. The child would be nimble and bright, apt in mathematical and mechanical skills, imaginative, diligent, charming, O, charming! For sixty days Kepler's happiness endured, then the house was pierced again by screams, miniature echoes of Barbara's lusty howls, and Oberdorfer again sculled himself up the stairs and Kepler snatched the infant in his arms and commanded it not, not to die! He turned on Barbara, she had known, all that pain had told her all was wrong, yet she had said nothing, not a word to warn him, spiteful bitch! The doctor clicked his tongue, for shame, sir, for shame. Kepler rounded on him. And you ... you ...! In tears, his vision splintering, he turned away, clasping the creature to him, and felt it twitch, and cough, and suddenly, as if starting in amazement, die: his son. The damp hot head lolled in his hand. What pitiless player had tossed him this tender ball of woe? He was to know other losses, but never again quite like this, like a part of himself crawling blind and mewling into death.

*   *   *

Now his days darkened. The child's fall had torn a hole in the fabric of things, and through this tiny rent the blackness seeped. Barbara would not be consoled. She took to hiding in shuttered rooms, in cubbyholes, even under the bedclothes, nibbling in private her bit of anguish, making not a sound except for now and then a faint dry sobbing, like the scratching of claws, that made Kepler's hair stand on end. He let her be, crouching in his own hiding, watching for what would come next. The game, which they had not realised was a game, had ended; suddenly life was taking them seriously. He remembered the first real beating he had got as a child, his mother a gigantic stranger red with rage, her fists, the startling vividness of pain, the world abruptly shifting into a new version of reality. Yes, and this was worse, he was an adult now, and the game was up.

44

The year turned, and winter ended. Spring would not this year fool him with false hopes. Something was being surreptitiously arranged, he could sense it, the storm assembling its ingredients from breezes and little clouds and the thrush's song. In April the young Archduke Ferdinand, ruler of all Austria, made a pilgrimage to Italy where at the shrine of Loreto, in a rapture of piety, he swore to suppress the heresy of Protestantism in his realm. The Lutheran province of Styria trembled. All summer there were threats and alarms. Troops were mobilised. By the end of September the churches and the schools had been shut down. At last the edict, long expected, was issued: Lutheran clergy and teachers must quit Austria within a week or face inquisition and possible death.

Jobst Müller hurried up from Mühleck. He had gone over to the Catholics, and expected his son-in-law to follow him without delay. Kepler snorted. I shall do nothing of the kind, sir; mine is the reformed Church, I recognise no other, and stopped himself from adding: *Here I stand!* which would have been to overdo it. And anyway, he was not so brave as his bold words would have it. The prospect of exile terrified him. Where would he go? To Tübingen? To his mother's house in Weilderstadt? Barbara with unwonted vehemence had declared she would not leave Graz. He would lose Regina then also; he would lose everything. No, no, it was unthinkable. Yet it was being thought: his bag was packed, Speidel's mare was borrowed. He would go to Mästlin in Tübingen, welcome or not. Farewell! Barbara's kiss, juicy with grief, landed in his ear. She pressed into his trembling hands little packets of florins and food and clean linen. Regina tentatively came to him, and, her face buried in his cloak, whispered something which he did not catch, which she would not repeat, which was to be forever, forever, a small gold link missing from his life. Floundering in a wash of tears he stumbled back and forth between house and horse, not quite knowing how, finally, to go, beating his pockets in search of a handkerchief to stanch his streaming nose and uttering faint phlegmy cries of distress. At last, dumped like a wet sack in the saddle, he was borne out of the city into a tactlessly glorious gold and blue October afternoon.

He rode north along the valley of the Mur, eyeing apprehensively the glittering snowcapped crags of the Alps looming higher the nearer he approached. The roads were busy. He fell in with another traveller, whose name was Wincklemann. He was a Jew, a lens-grinder by trade, and a citizen of Linz: a sallow wedge of face, a bit of beard and a dark ironic eye. When they came down into Linz it was raining, the Danube pock-marked steel, and Kepler was sick. The Jew, taking pity on this mournful wayfarer with his cough and his quiver and his blue fingernails, invited Kepler to come home with him and rest a day or two before turning westward for Tübingen.

The Jew's house was in a narrow street near the river. Wincklemann showed his guest the workshop, a long low room with a furnace at the back tended by a fat boy. The floor and the workbenches were a disorder of broken moulds and spilt sand and wads of oily rag, all blurred under a bluish film of grinding flour. Dropped tears of glass glittered in the gloom about their feet. A low window, giving on to damp cobbles and timbered gables and a glimpse of wharf, let in a grainy whitish light that seemed itself a process of the work conducted here. Kepler squinted at a shelf of books: Nostradamus, Paracelsus, the *Magia naturalis*. Wincklemann watched him, and smiling held aloft in a leaf-brown hand a gobbet of clouded crystal.

"Here is transmutation," he said, "a comprehensible magic."

Behind them the boy bent to the bellows, and the red mouth of the furnace roared. Kepler, his head humming with fever, felt something sweep softly down on him, a shadow, vast and winged.

They climbed to the upper floor, a warren of small dim rooms where the Jew and his family lived. Wincklemann's shy young wife, pale and plump as a pigeon and half his age, served them a supper of sausage and black bread and ale. The air was weighted with a strange sweetish smell. The sons of the house, pale boys with oiled plaits, came forward solemnly to greet their father and his guest. To Kepler it seemed he had strayed into the midst of some ancient attenuated ceremony. After the meal Wincklemann brought out his tobacco pipes. It was Kepler's first smoke; a green sensation, not wholly unpleasant,

46

spread along his veins. He was given wine lightly laced with a distillate of poppy and mandragora. Sleep that night was a plunging steed carrying him headlong through the tumultuous dark, but when he woke in the morning, a thrown rider, the fever was gone. He was puzzled and yet calm, as if some benign but enigmatic potential were being unfurled about him.

Wincklemann demonstrated the implements of his craft, the fine-honed lapstones and the grinding burrs of blued steel. He brought out examples of the glass in all its forms, from sand to polished prism. In return Kepler described his world system, the theory of the five perfect solids. They sat at the long bench under the cobwebbed window with the furnace gasping behind them, and Kepler experienced again that excitement and faintly embarrassed pleasure which he had not known since his student days at Tübingen and the first long discussions with Michael Mästlin.

The Jew had read von Lauchen's *Narratio prima* on the Copernican cosmology. The new theories puzzled and amused him.

"But do you think they are *true*?" said Kepler; the old question.

Wincklemann shrugged. "True? This is a word I have trouble with." He never looked so much the Jew as when he smiled. "Maybe yes, the sun is the centre, the visible god, as Trismegistus says; but when Dr Copernic shows it so in his famous system, what I ask you do we know that is more wonderful than what we knew before?"

Kepler did not understand. "But science," he said, frowning, "science is a method of knowing."

"Of knowing, yes: but of understanding? I tell you now the difference between the Christian and the Jew, listen. You think nothing is real until it has been spoken. Everything is words with you. Your Jesus Christ is the word made flesh!"

Kepler smiled. Was he being mocked? "And the Jew?" he said.

"An old joke there is, that at the beginning God told his chosen people everything, everything, so now we know it all—and understand nothing. Only I think it is not such a joke. There are things in our religion which may not be spoken, because to speak such ultimate things is to . . . to damage them.

47

Perhaps it is the same with your science?"

"But . . . damage?"

"I do not know." He shrugged. "I am only a maker of lenses, I do not understand these theories, these systems, and I am too old to study them. But you, my friend," and smiled again, and Kepler knew that he was being laughed at, "you will do great things, that's plain."

It was in Linz, under Wincklemann's amused dark gaze, that he first heard faintly the hum of that great five-note chord from which the world's music is made. Everywhere he began to see world-forming relationships, in the rules of architecture and painting, in poetic metre, in the complexities of rhythm, even in colours, in smells and tastes, in the proportions of the human figure. A fine silver string of excitement was tightening steadily within him. In the evenings he sat with his friend in the rooms above the workshop, drinking and smoking, and talking endlessly. He was well enough to travel on to Tübingen, yet made no move to go, though he was still in Austria and the Archduke's men might seize him any time. The Jew watched him out of a peculiar stillness and intensity, and sometimes Kepler, bleared with tobacco and wine, fancied that something was being slowly, lovingly drained from him, a precious impalpable fluid, by that gaze, that intent, patient watching. He thought of those volumes of Nostradamus and Albertus Magnus on the Jew's shelves, of certain silences, of murmurings behind closed doors, of the grey blurred forms in their sealed jars he had glimpsed in a cupboard in the workshop. Was he being magicked? The notion stirred in him a confused and guilty warmth, a kind of embarrassment, like that which made him turn away from the uxorious smile the Jew sometimes wore in the presence of his young wife. Yes this, *this* was exile.

It ended. One day a messenger from Stefan Speidel came galloping to Wincklemann's door out of a stormy dawn. Kepler, barefoot and shivering, still stuffed with sleep, stood in a damp gust and with trembling fingers broke the familiar seal of the secretariat. A fleck of foam from the horse's champing jaws settled on his eyebrow. The Archduke had consented that an exception be made to the order of general banishment. He could go home again.

Later he had time to consider the ravelled mesh of influence that had saved him. The Jesuits, for their own shady reasons, were sympathetic to his work. It was through a Jesuit, Fr Grienberger of Graz, that the Bavarian Chancellor Herwart von Hohenburg, a Catholic and an amateur scholar, had first consulted him on questions of cosmology in certain ancient texts. They corresponded via the Bavarian ambassador at Prague and the Archduke Ferdinand's secretary, the Capuchin Peter Casal. And then, Herwart was the servant of Duke Maximilian, Ferdinand's cousin, and those two noblemen had studied together at Ingolstadt under Johann Fickler, a firm friend of the Jesuits and a native of Kepler's own Weilderstadt. Thus the strands of the web radiated. Why, when he thought about it, he had advocates everywhere! It worried him, obscurely.

He returned secretly disappointed. Given time, he might have made something of exile. The Stiftsschule was still closed, and he was free, there was that at least. But Graz was finished for him, used up. Things were not so bad as they had been, and other exiles had quietly begun to trickle back, but still he thought it prudent to stay indoors. Barbara in November announced another pregnancy, and he retired to the innermost sanctuary of his workroom.

He began to study in earnest, consuming ancients and moderns, Plato and Aristotle, Nicholas of Cues, the Florence academicians. Wincklemann had given him a volume by the cabalist Cornelius Agrippa, whose thinking was so odd and yet so like Kepler's own. He went back to his mathematics, and honed to a fine edge that instrument which up to now he had wielded like a club. He turned to music with a new intensity; Pythagoras's laws of harmony obsessed him. As he had asked why there should be just six planets in the solar system, now he pondered the mystery of musical relationships: why does for instance the ratio 3:5 produce a harmony, but not 5:7? Even astrology, which for so long he had despised, assumed a new significance in its theory of aspects. The world abounded for him now in signature and form. He brooded in consternation on the complexities of the honeycomb, the structure of flowers, the eerie perfection of snowflakes. What had begun in

Linz as an intellectual frolic was now his deepest concern.

The new year began well. At the core of this sudden rush of speculations he was at peace. Then, however, gradually, a fearful momentum gathered. The religious turmoil boiled up again, fiercer than ever. Edict followed edict, each one more severe than its predecessor. Lutheran worship in any form was banned. Children were to be baptised only by the Catholic rite and must attend only Jesuit schools. Then they moved on the books. Lutheran writings were rooted out and burned. A pall of smoke hung over the city. Threats whirred in the air, and Kepler shivered. After the burning of the books, what would there be for them but to burn the authors? Things were out of control. He felt as if, head and shoulders back and eyes starting in mortal fright, he were strapped to an uncontrollable machine hurtling faster and faster toward a precipice. The child, a girl, was born in June. She was called Susanna. He dreamed of the ocean. He had never seen it in waking life. It appeared an immense milky calm, silent, immutable and terrifying, the horizon a line of unearthly fineness, a hairline crack in the shell of the world. There was no sound, no movement, not a living creature in sight, unless the ocean itself were living. The dread of that vision polluted his mind for weeks. On a July evening, the air pale and still as that phantom sea, he returned to the Stempfergasse after one of his rare ventures abroad in the frightened town, and paused before the house. There was a child playing in the street with a hoop, an old woman with a basket on her arm limping away from him on the other side, a dog in the gutter gnawing a knuckle of bone. Something in the scene chilled him, the careful innocence with which it was arranged in that limitless light, as if to give him a sly nudge. Dr Oberdorfer waited in the hall, regarding him with a lugubrious stricken stare. The infant had died. It was a fever of the brain, the same that had killed little Heinrich. Kepler stood by the bedroom window and watched the day fade, hearing vaguely Barbara's anguished cries behind him and listening in awe to his mind, of its own volition, thinking: My work will be interrupted. He carried the tiny coffin himself to the grave, besieged by visions of conflict and desolation. There were reports from the south that the Turk had massed six hundred thousand men below Vienna. The Catholic council fined him ten florins for having the funeral conducted in the Lutheran rite. He wrote to Mästlin: *No day can soothe my wife's yearning, and the word is close to my heart: O vanity . . .*

Jobst Müller came up again to Graz, demanding that Kepler convert: convert or go, and this time stay away, and he would take his daughter and Regina back with him to Mühleck. Kepler did not deign even to answer. Stefan Speidel was another visitor, a thin, cold, tight-mouthed man in black. His news from court was grim: there would be no exceptions this time. Kepler was beside himself.

"What shall I do, Stefan, what shall I *do*? And my family!" He touched his friend's chill hand. "You were right to oppose the marriage, I do not blame you for it, you were right—"

"I know that."

"No, Stefan, I insist . . ." He paused, letting it sink in, and distinctly heard the tiny *ping* of another cord breaking. Speidel had lent him a copy of Plato's *Timaeus* on the day they first met, in Rector Papius's rooms; he must remember to return it. "Yes, well . . ." wearily. "O God, what am I to do."

"There is Tycho Brahe?" Stefan Speidel said, picking a speck of lint from his cloak and turning away, out of Kepler's life forever.

Yes, there was Tycho. Since June he had been installed at Prague, imperial mathematician to the Emperor Rudolph, at a salary of three thousand florins. Kepler had letters from the Dane urging him to come and share in the royal beneficence. But Prague! A world away! And yet where was the alternative? Mästlin had written to him: there was no hope of a post at Tübingen. The century approached its end. Baron Johann Friedrich Hoffmann, a councillor to the Emperor and Kepler's sometime patron, on a visit to Graz, invited the young astronomer to join his suite for the journey back to Prague. Kepler packed his bags and his wife and her daughter into a broken-down carriage, and on the first day of the new century, not unamused by the date, he set out for his new world.

It was a frightful journey. They lodged at leaky fortresses and rat-infested military outposts. His fever came on him again, and he endured the miles in a dazed semi-sleep from

51

which Barbara in a panic would shake him, looming down like a form out of his dreams, fearing him dead. He ground his teeth. "Madam, if you continue to disturb me like this, by God I will box your ears." And then she wept, and he groaned, cursing himself for a mangy dog.

It was February when they arrived in Prague. Baron Hoffmann settled them at his house, fed them, advanced them monies, and even lent Kepler a hat and a decent cloak for the meeting with Tycho Brahe. But there was no sign of Tycho. Kepler detested Prague. The buildings were crooked and ill-kept, thrown together from mud and straw and undressed planks. The streets were awash with slops, the air putrid. At the end of a week Tycho's son appeared, in company with Frans Gransneb Tengnagel, drunk, the two of them, and sullen. They carried a letter from the Dane, at once formal and fulsome, expressing greasy sentiments of regret that he had not come himself to greet his visitor. Tyge and the Junker were to conduct him to Benatek, but delayed a further week for their pleasure. It was snowing when at last they set out. The castle lay twenty miles to the north of the city, in the midst of a flat flooded countryside. Kepler waited in the guest rooms through a fretful morning, and when the summons came at noon he was asleep. He descended the stony fastness of the castle in a stupor of fever and fright. Tycho Brahe was magisterial. He frowned upon the shivering figure before him and said:

"My elk, sir, my tame elk, for which I had a great love, has been destroyed through the carelessness of an Italian lout." With a wave of a brocaded arm he swept his guest before him into the high wall where they would breakfast. They sat. "... Fell down a staircase at Wandsbeck Castle where they had stopped for the night, having drunk a pot of beer, he says, and broke a leg and died. My elk!"

The vast window, sunlight on the river and the flooded fields, and beyond that the blue distance, and Kepler smiled and nodded, like a clockwork toy, thinking of his dishevelled past and perilous future, and 0.00 something something 9.

52

II

Astronomia Nova

Enough is enough. He plunged down the steep steps and stopped, glaring about the courtyard in angry confusion. A lame groom trundling a handcart hawked and spat, two scullery maids upended a tub of suds. They would make him a clerk, by God, a helper's helper! "Herr Kepler, Herr Kepler please, a moment..." Baron Hoffmann, panting unhappily, hurried down to him. Tycho Brahe remained atop the steps, strenuously indifferent, considering a far-off prospect.

"Well?" said Kepler.

The baron, rheum-eyed grey little man, displayed a pair of empty hands. "You must give him time, you know, allow him to consider your requests."

"*He*," raising his voice against a sudden clamour of hounds, "he has had a month already, more. I have stated my conditions; I ask the merest consideration. He does nothing." And, louder again, turning to fling it up the steps: "Nothing!" Tycho Brahe, still gazing off, lifted his eyebrows a fraction and sighed. The pack of hounds with an ululant cheer burst through a low gate from the kennels and surged across the courtyard, avid brutes with stunted legs and lunatic grins and tiny tight puce scrotums. Kepler scuttled for the steps in fright, but faltered halfway up, prevented by Tycho the Terrible. The Dane glanced down on him with malicious satisfaction, pulling on his gauntlets. Baron Hoffmann turned up to the master of Schloss Benatek a last enquiring glance and then, shrugging, to Kepler:

"You will not stay, sir?"

"I will not stay." But his voice was unsteady.

Tengnagel and young Tyge came out, squinting in the light, sodden with the dregs of last night's drinking. They brightened, seeing Kepler in a dither. The grooms were bringing up the horses. The dogs, which had quietened, hunched with busy tongues over their parts or ruminatively cocked against the walls, were thrown into a frenzy again by the goitrous blare of a hunting horn. A haze of silvery dust unfurled its sails to the breeze and drifted lazily gatewards, a woman leaned down from a balcony, laughing, and in the sky a panel slid open and spilled upon Benatek a wash of April sunlight that turned the drifting dust to gold.

The baron went away to fetch his carriage. Kepler considered. What was left if he refused Tycho's grudging patronage? The past was gone, Tübingen, Graz, all that, gone. The Dane, thumbs hitched on his belt and fat fingers drumming the taut slope of his underbelly, launched himself down the steps. Baron Hoffmann alighted from the carriage, and Kepler mumbling plucked at his sleeve, "I want to, I want . . ." mumbling.

The baron cupped an ear. "The noise, I did not quite . . ?"

"I *want*—" a shriek "—to *apologise*." He closed his eyes briefly. "Forgive me, I—"

"O but there is no need, I assure you."

"What?"

The old man beamed. "I am happy to help, Herr Professor, in any way that I can."

"No, no, I mean to *him*, to *him*." And this was Bohemia, my God, repository of his highest hopes! Tycho was laboriously mounting up with the help of two straining footmen. Baron Hoffmann and the astronomer considered him doubtfully as with a grunt he toppled forward across the horse's braced back, flourishing in their faces his large leather-clad arse. The baron sighed and stepped forward to speak to him. Tycho, upright now and puffing, listened impatiently. Tengnagel and the younger Dane, downing their stirrup cups, looked on in high amusement. The squabble between Tycho and his latest collaborator had been the chief diversion of the castle since Kepler's arrival a month ago. The bugle sounded, and the hunt with Tycho in its midst moved off like a great rowdy engine, leaving behind it a brown taste of dust. Baron Hoffmann would not meet Kepler's hungry gaze. "I will take you into Prague," he muttered, and fairly dived into the sanctuary of his carriage. Kepler nodded dully, an ashen awfulness opening around him in the swirling air. *What have I done?*

They rattled down the narrow hill road. The sky over Benatek bore a livid smear of cloud, but the hunt, straggling away across the fields, was still in sunlight. Kepler silently wished them all a wasted day, and for the Dane with luck a broken neck. Barbara, wedged beside him on the narrow seat, pulsated in speechless anger and accusation (*What have you done?*). He did not wish to look at her, but neither could he watch for long the joggling view beyond the carriage window. This country roundabout of countless small lakes and perennially flooded lowlands (which Tycho in his letters had dubbed *Bohemian Venice!*) pained his poor eyesight with its fractured perspectives of quicksilver glitter and tremulous blue-grey distances.

". . . That he will of course," the baron was saying, "accept an apology, only he, ah, he suggests that it be in writing."

Kepler stared. "He wants . . ." and eye and an elbow setting up together a devil's dance of twitches ". . . he wants a *written apology* of me?"

"That is, yes, what he indicated." The baron swallowed, and looked away with a sickly smile. Regina at his side watched him intently, as she watched all big people, as if he might suddenly do something marvellous and inexplicable, burst into tears, or throw back his head and howl like an ape. Kepler regarded him too, thinking sadly that this man was a direct link with Copernicus: in his youth the baron had hired Valentine Otho, disciple of von Lauchen, to instruct him in mathematics. "Also, he will require a declaration of secrecy, that is, that you will swear an oath not to reveal to . . . to others, any astronomical data he may provide you with in the course of your work. He is especially jealous, I believe, for the Mars observations. In return he will guarantee lodgings for you and your family, and will undertake to press the Emperor either to ensure the con-

57

tinuation of your Styrian salary, or else to grant you an allowance himself. These are his terms, Herr Kepler; I would advise you—"

"To accept? Yes, yes, I will, of course." Why not? He was weary of standing on his dignity. The baron stared at him, and Kepler blinked: was that contempt in those watery eyes? Damn it, Hoffmann knew nothing of what it was to be poor and an outcast, he had his lands and title and his place at court. Sometimes these bland patricians sickened him.

"But what," said Barbara, choking on it, "what of *our* conditions, *our* demands?" No one replied. How was it, Kepler wondered, with a twinge of guilt, that her most impassioned outbursts were met always by the same glassy-eyed, throatclearing silence. The carriage lurched into a pothole with a mighty jolt, and from without they heard the driver address a string of lush obscenities to his horse. Kepler sighed. His world was patched together from the wreckage of an infinitely finer, immemorial dwelling place; the pieces were precious and lovely, enough to break his heart, but they did not fit.

The baron's house stood on Hradcany hill hard by the imperial palace, looking down over Kleinseit to the river and the Jewish quarter, and, farther out, the suburbs of the old town. There was a garden with poplars and shaded walkways and a fishpond brimming with indolent carp. On the north, the palace side, the windows gave on to pavonian lawns and a fawn wall, sudden skies pierced by a spire, and purple pennons undulating in a cowed immensity. Once, from those windows, Kepler had been vouchsafed an unforgettable glimpse of a prancing horse and a hound rampant, ermine and emerald, black beard, pale hand, a dark disconsolate eye. That was as near as he was to come to the Emperor for a long time.

In the library the baron's wife sat at an escritoire, sprinkling chalk from an ivory horn upon a piece of parchment. She rose as they entered, and, blowing lightly on the page, glanced at them with the distant relation of a smile. "Why Doctor—and Frau Kepler—you have returned to us," a faded eagle, taller than her husband but as gaunt as he, in a satin gown of metallic blue, her attention divided equally between her visitors and the letter in her hand.

58

"My dear," the baron murmured, with a jaded bow.

There was a brief silence, and then that smile again. "And Dr Brahe, is he not with you?"

"Madam," Kepler burst out, "I have been cruelly used by that man. He it was urged me, *pleaded* with me to come here to Bohemia; I came, and he treats me as he would a mere apprentice!"

"You have had a falling out with our good Dane?" the baroness said, suddenly giving the Keplers all her attention; "that is unfortunate," and Regina, catching the rustle of that silkily ominous tone, leaned forward past her mother for a good look at this impressive large blue lady.

"I set before him," said Kepler, "I set before him a list of some few conditions which he must meet if I was to remain and work with him, for example I deman—I asked that is for separate quarters for my family and myself (that place out there, I swear it, is a madhouse), and that a certain quantity of food—"

Barbara darted forward—"And firewood!"

"And firewood, to be set aside expressly—"

"For our use, that's right."

"—For our, yes, use," blaring furiously down his nostrils. He pictured himself hitting her, felt in the roots of his teeth the sweet smack of his palm on a fat forearm. "I asked let me see I asked, yes, that he procure me a salary from the Emperor—"

"His majesty," the baron said hastily, "his majesty is . . . difficult."

"See, my lady," Barbara warbled, "see what we are reduced to, begging for our food. And you were so kind when we first arrived here, accommodating us . . . ."

"Yes," the baroness said thoughtfully.

"But," cried Kepler, "I ask you, sir, madam, are these unreasonable demands?"

Baron Hoffmann slowly sat down. "We met upon the matter yesterday," he said, looking at the hem of his wife's gown, "Dr Brahe, Dr Kepler and myself."

"Yes?" said the baroness, growing more aquiline by the moment. "And?"

"This!" cried Barbara, a very quack; "look at us, thrown out on the roadside!"

The baron pursed his lips. "Hardly, *gnädige Frau*, hardly so
. . . so . . . Yet it is true, the Dane is angry."

"Ah," the baroness murmured; "why so?"

Drops of rain fingered the sunlit window. Kepler shrugged.
"*I* do not know." Barbara looked at him. ". . . I never said," he
said, "that the Tychonic system is misconceived, as he charges!
I . . . I merely observed of one or two weaknesses in it, caused I
believe by a too hasty acceptance of doubtful premises, that a
bitch in a hurry will produce blind pups." The baroness put a
hand up quickly to trap a cough, which, had he not known her
to be a noble lady fully conscious of the gravity of the moment,
he might have taken for a snigger. "And anyway, it *is* misconceived, a monstrous thing sired on Ptolemy out of Egyptian
Herakleides. He puts the earth, you see, madam, at the centre of
the world, but makes the five remaining planets circle upon the
sun! It works, of course, so far as appearances are concerned—
but then you could put any one of the planets at the centre and
still save the phenomena."

"Save the . . ?" She turned to the baron to enlighten her. He
looked away, fingering his chin.

"The phenomena, yes," said Kepler. "But it's all a trick our
Dane is playing, aimed at pleasing the schoolmen without entirely denying Copernicus—he knows it as well as I do, and I'm
damned before I will apologise for speaking the plain truth!"
He surged to his feet, choking on a sudden bubble of rage. "The
thing, excuse me, the thing is simple: he is jealous of me, my
grasp of our science—yes, yes," rounding on Barbara violent-
ly, though she had made no protest, "yes, jealous. And further-
more he is growing old, he's more than fifty—" the baroness's
left eyebrow snapped into a startled arc "—and is worried for
his future reputation, would have me ratify his worthless
theory by forcing me to make it the basis of my work.
But . . ." But there he faltered, and turned, listening. Music
came from afar, the tune made small and quaintly merry by the
distance. He walked slowly to the window, as if stalking some
rare prize. The rain shower had passed, and the garden
brimmed with light. Clasping his hands behind him and
swaying gently on heel and toe he gazed out at the poplars and
the dazzled pond, the drenched clouds of flowers, that jigsaw of

60

lawn trying to reassemble itself between the stone balusters of a balcony. How innocent, how inanely lovely, the surface of the world! The mystery of simple things assailed him. A festive swallow swooped through a tumbling flaw of lavender smoke. It would rain again. Tumty tum. He smiled, listening: was it the music of the spheres? Then he turned, and was surprised to find the others as he had left them, attending him with mild expectancy. Barbara moaned softly in dismay. She knew, O she knew that look, that empty, amiably grinning mask with the burning eyes of a busy madman staring through it. She began rapidly to explain to the baron and his pernous lady that our chief worry, our chief worry is, you see . . . and Kepler sighed, wishing she would not prattle thus, like a halfwit, her tiny mouth wobbling. He rubbed his hands and advanced from the window, all business now. "I shall," blithely drowning Barbara's babbling, which ran on even as it sank, a flurry of bubbles out of a surprised fish-mouth—"I shall write a letter, apologise, make my peace," beaming from face to face as if inviting applause. The music came again, nearer now, a wind band playing in the palace grounds. "He will summon me back, I think, yes; he will understand," for what did any of that squabbling matter, after all? "A new start!—may I borrow a pen, madam?"

By nightfall he had returned to Benatek. He delivered his apology, and swore an oath of secrecy, and Tycho gave a banquet, music and manic revels and the fatted calf hissing on a spit. The noise in the dining hall was a steady roar punctuated by the crimson crash of a dropped platter or the shriek of a tickled serving girl. The spring storm that had threatened all day blundered suddenly against the windows, shivering the reflected candlelight. Tycho was in capital form, shouting and swilling and banging his tankard, nose aglitter and the tips of his straw-coloured moustaches dripping. To his left Tengnagel sat with a proprietory arm about the waist of the Dane's daughter Elizabeth, a rabbity girl with close-cropped ashen hair and pink nostrils. Her mother, Mistress Christine, was a fat fussy woman whose twenty years of concubinage to the Dane no longer outraged anyone save her. Young Tyge was there too, sneering, and the Dane's chief assistant Christian

Longberg, a priestly pustular young person, haggard with ambition and self-abuse. Kepler was angry again. He wanted not this mindless carousing, but simply to get his hands on—right away, now, tonight—Tycho's treasure store of planet observations. "You set me the orbit of Mars, no let me speak, you set me this orbit, a most intractable problem, yet you give me no readings for the planet; how, I ask, let me speak please, how I ask am I to solve it, do you imagine?"

Tycho shrugged elaborately. "*De Tydske Karle,*" he remarked to the table in general, "*ere allesammen halv gale,*" and Jeppe the dwarf, squatting at his master's feet under the table, tittered.

"My father," said Mistress Christine suddenly, "my father went blind, you know, from swilling all his life like a pig. Take another cup of wine, Brahe dear."

Christian Longberg clasped his hands as if about to pray. "You expect to solve the problem of Mars, do you, Herr Kepler?" smiling thinly at the idea. Kepler realised who it was this creature reminded him of: Stefan Speidel, another treacherous prig.

"You do not think me capable of it, sir? Will you take a wager—let us say, a hundred florins?"

"O splendid," cried young Tyge. "An hundred florins, by Laertes!"

"Hold hard, Longberg," Tengnagel growled. "Best set him a certain time to do it in, or you'll wait forever for your winnings."

"Seven days!" said Kepler promptly, all swagger and smile without while his innards cringed. Seven days, my God. "Yes, give me seven days free of all other tasks, and I shall do it—provided, wait," and nervously licked his lips, "provided I am guaranteed free and unhindered access to the observations, all of them, everything."

Tycho scowled, seeing the trick. He had let it go too far, all the table was watching him, and besides he was drunk. Yet he hesitated. Those observations were his immortality. Twenty years of painstaking labour had gone into the amassing of them. Posterity might forget his books, ridicule his world system, laugh at his outlandish life, but not even the most heartless future imaginable would fail to honour him as a genius of exactitude. And now must he hand over everything to this young upstart? He nodded, and then shrugged again, and called for more wine, making the best of it. Kepler pitied him, briefly.

"Well then, sir," said Longberg, his look a blade, "we have a wager."

A troupe of itinerant acrobats tumbled into the hall, whizzing and bouncing and clapping their hands. Seven days! A hundred florins! Hoop la.

*   *   *

Seven days became seven weeks, and the enterprise exploded in his face. It had seemed so small a task, merely a matter of selecting three positions for Mars and from them defining by simple geometry the circle of the planet's orbit. He delved in Tycho's treasures, rolled in them, uttering little yelps of doggy joy. He selected three observations, taken by the Dane on the island of Hveen over a period of ten years, and went to work. Before he knew what had hit him he was staggering backwards out of a cloud of sulphurous smoke, coughing, his ears ringing, with bits of smashed calculations sticking in his hair.

All of Benatek was charmed. The castle hugged itself for glee at the spectacle of this irritating little man struck full in the face with his own boast. Even Barbara could not hide her satisfaction, wondering sweetly where they were to find the hundred florins, if you please, which Christian Longberg was howling for? Only Tycho Brahe said nothing. Kepler squirmed, asked Longberg for another week, pleaded penury and his poor health, denied that he had made any wager. Deep down he cared nothing for the insults and the laughter. He was busy.

Of course he had lied to himself, for the sake of that bet and the tricking of Tycho: Mars was not simple. It had kept its secret through millenniums, defeating finer minds than his. What was to be made of a planet, the plane of whose orbit, according to Copernicus, oscillates in space, the value for the oscillation to depend not on the sun, but on the position of the earth? a planet which, moving in a perfect circle at uniform speed, takes varying periods of time to complete identical portions of its journey? He had thought that these and other strangenesses were merely rough edges to be sheared away before he tackled the problem of defining the orbit itself; now he knew that, on the contrary, he was a blind man who must reconstruct a smooth and infinitely complex design out of a few scattered prominences that gave themselves up, with deceptive innocence, under his fingertips. And seven weeks became seven months.

Early in 1601, at the end of their first turbulent year in Bohemia, a message came from Graz that Jobst Müller was dying, and asking for his daughter. Kepler welcomed the excuse to interrupt his work. He detached its fangs carefully from his wrist—wait there, don't howl—and walked away from it calm in the illusion of that sleek tensed thing crouching in wait, ready at the turn of a key to leap forth with the solution to the riddle of Mars clasped in its claws. By the time they reached Graz, Jobst Müller was dead.

His death provoked in Barbara a queer melancholy lassitude. She shrank into herself, curled herself up in some secret inner chamber from which there issued now and then a querulous babbling, so that Kepler feared for her sanity. The question of the inheritance obsessed her. She harped on it with ghoulish insistence, as if it were the corpse itself she was nosing at. Not that there were not grounds for her worst fears. The Archduke's interdicts against Lutherans were still in force, and when Kepler moved to convert his wife's properties into cash the Catholic authorities threatened and cheated him. Yet it was with trumpetings of acclaim that these same authorities welcomed him as a mathematician and cosmologist. In May, when it seemed the entire inheritance might be confiscated, he was invited to set up in the city's market place an apparatus of his own making through which to view a solar eclipse which he had predicted. A numerous and respectful crowd gathered to gape at the magus and his machine. The occasion was a grand success. The burghers of Graz, lifting a puzzled and watering eye from the shimmering image in his *camera obscura*, bumped him indulgently with their big bellies and told him what a brilliant fellow he was, and only afterwards did he discover that a cutpurse, taking advantage of the ecliptic gloom at noonday, had relieved him of thirty florins. It was a paltry loss compared to what was thieved from him in Styrian taxes, but it seemed to sum up best the whole bad business of their leavetaking of Barbara's homeland.

She burst into a torrent of tears on the day of their departure. She would not be comforted, would not let him touch her, but simply stood and wound out of her quivering mouth a long dark ribbon of anguish. He hovered beside her, heart raw with pity, his ape arms helplessly enfolding hoops of empty air. Graz had meant little to him in the end, Jobst Müller even less, but still he recognised well enough that grief which, under a grey sky on the Stempfergasse, ennobled for a moment his poor fat foolish wife.

Returning to Bohemia, they found Tycho and his circus in temporary quarters at the Golden Griffin inn, about to move back into the Curtius house on the Hradcany, which the Emperor had purchased for them from the vice chancellor's widow. Kepler could not credit it. What of the Capuchins' famous bells? And what of Benatek, the work and the expense that had been lavished on those reconstructions? Tycho shrugged; he thrived on waste, the majestic squandering of fortunes. His carriage awaited him under the sign of the griffin. There would be a seat in it for Barbara and the child. Kepler must walk. He panted up the steep hill of the Hradcany, talking to himself and shaking his troubled head. A troupe of imperial cavalry almost trampled him. When he gained the summit he realised he had forgotten where the house was, and when he asked the way he was given wrong directions. The sentries at the palace gate watched him suspiciously as he trotted past for the third time. The evening was hot, the sun a fat eye fixed on him with malicious glee, and he kept looking over his shoulder in the hope of catching a familiar street in the act of taking down hurriedly the elaborate scenery it had erected in order to fox him. He might have sought help at Baron Hoffmann's, but the thought of the baroness's steely gaze was not inviting. Then he turned a corner and suddenly he had arrived. A cart was drawn up before the door, and heroically encumbered figures with splayed knees were staggering up the steps. Mistress Christine leaned out of an upstairs window and shouted something in Danish, and everyone stopped for a moment and gazed up at her in a kind of stupefied, inexpectant wonder. The house had a forlorn and puzzled air. Kepler wandered through the hugely empty rooms. They led him back, as if gently to tell him something, to the entrance hall. The summer evening hesitated in the doorway, and in a big mirror a parallelogram of sunlit wall leaned at a breathless tilt, with a paler patch in it where a picture had been removed. The sunset was a flourish of gold, and in the palace gardens an enraptured blackbird was singing. Outside on the step the child Regina stood at gaze like a gilded figure in a frieze. Kepler paused in shadow, listening to his own pulse-beat. What could she see, that so engrossed her? She might have been a tiny bride watching from a window on her wedding morning. Footsteps clattered on the stairs behind him, and Mistress Christine came hurrying down clutching her skirts in one hand and brandishing a fire iron in the other. "I will not have that man in my house!" Kepler stared at her, Regina with her head down walked swiftly past him into the house, and he turned to see a figure on a brokendown mule stop at the foot of the steps outside. He was in rags, with a bandaged arm pressed to his side like a beggar's filthy bundle of belongings. He dismounted and plodded up the steps. Mistress Christine planted herself in the doorway, but he pushed past her, looking about him distractedly. "I went first to Benatek," he muttered, "the castle. No one there anymore!" The idea amused him. He sat down on a chair by the mirror and began slowly to unpack his wounded arm, lowering to the floor loop upon loop of bandage with a regularly repeated, steadily swelling bloodstain in the shape of a copper crab with a wet red ruby in its heart. The wound, a deep sword-cut, was grossly infected. He studied it with distaste, pressing gingerly upon the livid surround. "*Porco Dio*," he said, and spat on the floor. Mistress Christine threw up her hands and went away, talking to herself.

"My wife, perhaps," said Kepler, "would dress that for you?"

The Italian brought out from a pocket of his leather jerkin a bit of grimy rag, tore it with his teeth and wrapped the wound

66

in it. He held up the ends to be tied. Kepler leaning down could feel the heat of the festering flesh and smell its gamey stink.

"So, they have not hanged you yet," the Italian said. Kepler stared at him, and then, slowly lifting his eyes to the mirror, saw Jeppe standing behind him.

"Not yet, master, no," the dwarf said, grinning. "But what of you?"

Kepler turned to him. "He is hurt, see: this arm . . ."

The Italian laughed, and leaning back against the mirror he fainted quietly into his own reflection.

Felix was the name he went by. His histories were various. He had been a soldier against the Turks, had sailed with the Neapolitan fleet. There was not a cardinal in Rome, so he said, that he had not pimped for. He had first encountered the Dane at Leipzig two years before, when Tycho was meandering southward towards Prague. The Italian was on the run, there had been a fight over a whore and a Vatican guard had died. He was starving, and Tycho, displaying an unwonted sense of humour, had hired him to escort his household animals to Bohemia. But the joke misfired. Tycho had never forgiven him the loss of the elk. Now, alerted by Mistress Christine, he came roaring into the hall in search of the fellow to throw him out. Kepler and the dwarf, however, had already spirited him away upstairs.

It seemed that he must die. For days he lay on a pallet in one of the big empty rooms at the top of the house, raving and cursing, mad with fever and the loss of blood. Tycho, fearing a scandal if the renegade should die in his house, summoned Michael Maier, the imperial physician, a discreet and careful man. He applied leeches and administered a purgative, and toyed wistfully with the idea of amputating the poisoned arm. The weather was hot and still, the room an oven; Maier ordered the windows sealed and draped against the unwholesome influence of fresh air. Kepler spent long hours by the sickbed, mopping the Italian's streaming forehead, or holding him by the shoulders while he puked the green dregs of his life into a copper basin, which each evening was delivered to the haruspex Maier at the palace. And sometimes at night, working at his desk, he would suddenly lift his head and listen, fancying

67

that he had heard a cry, or not even that, but a flexure of pain shooting like a crack across the delicate dome of candlelight wherein he sat, and he would climb through the silent house and stand for a while beside the restless figure on the bed. He experienced, in that fetid gloom, a vivid and uncanny sense of his own presence, as if he had been given back for a brief moment a dimension of himself which daylight and other lives would not allow him. Often the dwarf was there before him, squatting on the floor with not a sound save the rapid unmistakable beat of his breathing. They did not speak, but bided together, like attendants at the shrine of a demented oracle.

Young Tyge came up one morning, sidled round the door with his offal-eating grin, the tip of a pink tongue showing. "Well, here's a merry trio." He sauntered to the bed and peered down at the Italian tangled in the sheets. "Not dead yet?"

"He is sleeping, young master," said Jeppe.

Tyge coughed. "By God, he stinks." He moved to the window, and twitching open the drapes looked out upon the great blue day. The birds were singing in the palace grounds. Tyge turned, laughing softly.

"Well, doctor," he said, "what is *your* prognosis?"

"The poison has spread from the arm," Kepler answered, shrugging. He wished the fellow would go away. "He may not live."

"You know the saying: those who live by the sword..." The rest was smothered by a guffaw. "Ah me, how cruel is life," putting a hand to his heart. "Look at it, dying like a dog in a foreign land!" He turned to the dwarf. "Tell me, monster, is it not enough to make even you weep?"

Jeppe smiled. "You are a wit, master."

Tyge looked at him. "Yes, I am." He turned away sulkily and considered the sick man again. "I met him in Rome once, you know. He was a great whoremaster there. Although they say he prefers boys, himself. But then the Italians all are that way." He glanced at Kepler. "You would be somewhat too ripe for him, I think; perhaps the frog here would be more to his taste." He went out, but paused in the doorway. "My father, by the way, wants him well, so he may have the pleasure of kicking him down the Hradcany. You are a fine pair of little nurses. Look to it."

He recovered. One day Kepler found him leaning by the window in a dirty shirt. He would not speak, nor even turn, as if he did not dare break off this rapt attendance upon the world that he had almost lost, the hazy distance, those clouds, the light of summer feeding on his upturned face. Kepler crept away, and when he returned that evening the Italian looked at him as if he had never seen him before, and waved him aside when he attempted to change the crusted bandage on his arm. He wanted food and drink. "And where is the *nano*? You tell him to come, eh?"

The days that followed were for Kepler an ashen awakening from a dream. The Italian continued to look through him with blank unrecognition. What had he expected? Not love, certainly not friendship, nothing so insipid as these. Perhaps, then, a kind of awful comradeship, by which he might gain entry to that world of action and intensity, that Italy of the spirit, of which this renegade was an envoy. Life, life, that was it! In the Italian he seemed to know at last, however vicariously, the splendid and exhilarating sordidness of real life.

The Brahes, with that casual hypocrisy which Kepler knew so well, celebrated Felix's recovery as if he were the first hope of the house. He was brought down from his bare room and given a new suit, and led out, grinning, into the garden, where the family was at feed at a long table in the shade of poplar trees. The Dane sat him down at his right hand. But though the occasion started off with toasts and a slapping of backs, it began before long to ooze a drunken rancour. Tycho, ill and half drunk, brought up again the sore subject of his lost elk, but in the midst of loud vituperation fell suddenly asleep into his plate. The Italian ate like a dog, jealously and with circumspect hurry: he also knew well these capricious Danes. His arm was in a black silk sling that Tycho's daughter Elizabeth had fashioned for him. Tengnagel threatened to call him out with rapiers if he did not stay away from her, and then stood up, overturning his chair, and stalked away from the table. Felix laughed; the Junker did not know, what everyone else knew, that he had ploughed the wench already, long before, at Benatek. It was not for her that he had come back. The court at

Prague was rich, presided over by a halfwit, so he had heard. Perhaps Rudolph might have use for a man of his peculiar talents? The dwarf consulted Kepler, and Kepler responded with wry amusement. "Why, I had to wait a year myself before your master would arrange an audience for me, and I have been to the palace only twice again. What influence have I?"

"But you will have, soon," Jeppe whispered, "sooner than you would guess."

Kepler said nothing, and looked away. The dwarf's prophetic powers unnerved him. Tycho Brahe suddenly woke up. "You are wanted, sir," said Jeppe softly.

"Yes, I want you," Tycho growled, wiping bleared eyes.

"Well, here I am."

But Tycho only looked at him wearily, with a kind of hapless resentment. "Bah." He was unmistakably a sick man. Kepler was aware of the dwarf behind him, smiling. What was it the creature saw in their collective future? A warm gale was blowing out of the sky, and the evening sunlight had an umber tinge, as if the wind had bruised it. The poplars shook. Suddenly everything seemed to him to tremble on the brink of revelation, as if these contingencies of light and weather and human doings had stumbled upon a form of almost speech. Felix was whispering to Elizabeth Brahe, making the tips of her translucent ears glow with excitement. He was to leave, this time forever, before the year was out, no longer interested in imperial patronage, though by then Jeppe's prophecy would be fulfilled, and the astronomer would have become indeed a man of influence.

*　　*　　*

Kepler turned again now to his work on Mars. Conditions around him had improved. Christian Longberg, tired of squabbling, had gone back to Denmark, and there was no more talk of their wager. Tycho Brahe too was seldom seen. There were rumours of plague and Turkish advances, and the stars needed a frequent looking to. The Emperor Rudolph, growing ever more nervous, had moved his imperial mathematician in

70

from Benatek, but even the Curtius house was not close enough, and the Dane was at the palace constantly. The weather was fine, days the colour of Mosel wine, enormous glassy nights. Kepler sometimes sat with Barbara in the garden, or with Regina idly roamed the Hradcany, admiring the houses of the rich and watching the imperial cavalry on parade. But by August the talk of plague had closed the great houses for the season, and even the cavalry found an excuse to be elsewhere. The Emperor decamped to his country seat at Belvedere, taking Tycho Brahe with him. The sweet sadness of summer settled on the deserted hill, and Kepler thought of how as a child, at the end of one of his frequent bouts of illness, he would venture forth on tender limbs into a town made magical by the simple absence of his schoolfellows from its streets.

Mars suddenly yielded up a gift, when with startling ease he refuted Copernicus on oscillation, showing by means of Tycho's data that the planet's orbit intersects the sun at a fixed angle to the orbit of the earth. There were other, smaller victories. At every advance, however, he found himself confronted again by the puzzle of the apparent variation in orbital velocity. He turned to the past for guidance. Ptolemy had saved the principle of uniform speed by means of the *punctum equans*, a point on the diameter of the orbit from which the velocity will appear invariable to an imaginary observer (whom it amused Kepler to imagine, a crusty old fellow, with his brass triquetrum and watering eye and smug, deluded certainty). Copernicus, shocked by Ptolemy's sleight of hand, had rejected the equant point as blasphemously inelegant, but yet had found nothing to put in its place except a clumsy combination of five uniform epicyclic motions superimposed one upon another. These were, all the same, clever and sophisticated manoeuvres, and saved the phenomena admirably. But had his great predecessors taken them, Kepler wondered, to represent the real state of things? The question troubled him. Was there an innate nobility, lacking in him, which set one above the merely empirical? Was his pursuit of the forms of physical reality irredeemably vulgar?

In a tavern on Kleinseit one Saturday night he met Jeppe and the Italian. They had fallen in with a couple of kitchen-hands from the palace, a giant Serb with one eye and a low ferrety fellow from Württemberg, who claimed to have soldiered with Kepler's brother in the Hungarian campaigns. His name was Krump. The Serb rooted in his codpiece and brought out a florin to buy a round of schnapps. Someone struck up on a fiddle, and a trio of whores sang a bawdy song and danced. Krump squinted at them and spat. "Riddled with it, them are," he said, "I know them." But the Serb was charmed, ogling the capering drabs out of his one oystrous eye and banging his fist on the table in time to the jig. Kepler ordered up another round. "Ah," said Jeppe. "Sir Mathematicus is flush tonight; has my master forgot himself and paid your wages?" "Something of that," Kepler answered, and thought himself a gay dog. They played a hand of cards, and there was more drink. The Italian was dressed in a suit of black velvet, with a slouch hat. Kepler spotted him palming a knave. He won the hand and grinned at Kepler, and then, calling for another jig, got up and with a low bow invited the whores to dance. The candles on the tavern counter shook to the thumping of their feet. "A merry fellow," said Jeppe, and Kepler nodded, grinning blearily. The dance became a general rout, and somehow they were suddenly outside in the lane. One of the whores fell down and lay there laughing, kicking her stout legs in the air. Kepler propped himself against the wall and watched the goatish dancers circling in a puddle of light from the tavern window, and all at once out of nowhere, out of everywhere, out of the fiddle music and the flickering light and the pounding of heels, the circling dance and the Italian's drunken eye, there came to him the ragged fragment of a thought. False. What false? That principle. One of the whores was pawing him. Yes, he had it. *The principle of uniform velocity is false*. He found it very funny, and smiling turned aside and vomited absent-mindedly into a drain. Krump laid a hand on his shoulder. "Listen, friend, if you puke up a little ring don't spit it out, it'll be your arsehole." Somewhere behind him the Italian laughed. False, by Jesus, yes!

They went on to another tavern, and another. The Serb got lost along the way, and then Felix and the dwarf reeled off arm in arm with the bawds into the darkness, and Krump and the astronomer were left to stagger home up the Hradcany, falling and shouting and singing tearful songs of Württemberg their native land. In the small hours, his elusive quarters located at last, Kepler, a smouldering red eye in his mind fixed on the image of a romping whore, attempted with much shushing and chuckling to negotiate Barbara's rigid form into an exotic posture, for what precise purpose he had forgotten when he woke into a parched and anguished morning, though something of the abandoned experiment was still there in the line of her large hip and the spicy tang of her water in the earthen pot under the bed. She would not speak to him for a week.

Later that day, when the fumes of the charnel house had dispersed in his head, he brought out and contemplated, like a penniless collector with a purloined treasure, the understanding that had been given to him that the principle of uniform orbital velocity was a false dogma. It was the only, the obvious answer to the problem of Mars, of all the planets probably, and yet for two thousand years and more it had resisted the greatest of astronomy's inquisitors. And why had this annunciation been made to him, what heaven-hurled angel had whispered in his ear? He marvelled at the process, how a part of his mind had worked away in secret and in silence while the rest of him swilled and capered and lusted after poxed whores. He experienced an unwonted humility. He must be better now, behave himself, talk to Barbara and listen to her complaints, be patient with the Dane, and say his prayers, at least until the advent of new problems.

They were not long in coming. His rejection of uniform velocity threw everything into disarray, and he had to begin all over again. He was not discouraged. Here was real work, after all, fully worthy of him. Where before, in the *Mysterium*, there had been abstract speculation, was now reality itself. These were precise observations of a visible planet, coordinates fixed in time and space. They were events. It was not by chance he had been assigned the study of Mars. Christian Longberg, that jealous fool, had insisted on keeping the lunar orbit; Kepler laughed, glimpsing there too the quivering tips of angelic wings, the uplifted finger. For he knew now that Mars was the key to the secret of the workings of the world. He felt himself suspended in tensed bright air, a celestial swimmer. And seven months were becoming seventeen.

Tycho told him he was mad: uniform velocity was a principle beyond question. Next he would be claiming that the planets do not move in perfect circles! Kepler shrugged. It was the Dane's own observations that had shown the principle to be false. No no *no*, and Tycho shook his great bald head, there must be some other explanation. But Kepler was puzzled. Why should he seek another answer, when he had the correct one? There stood at the hatch of his mind an invoice clerk with a pencil and slate and a bad liver, who would allow no second thoughts. Tycho Brahe turned away; what little chance there had been that this Swabian lunatic would solve Mars for him was gone now. Kepler plucked at him, wait, look—where is my compass, I have lost my compass—the thing was as good as done! Even assuming a variable rate of speed, to define the orbit he had only to determine the radius of its circle, the direction relative to the fixed stars of the axis connecting aphelion and perihelion, and the position on that axis of the sun, the orbital centre, and the *punctum equans*, which for the moment he would retain, as a calculating device. Of course all this could only be done by a process of trial and error, but ... but wait! And Tycho swept away, muttering.

He made seventy attempts. At the end, out of nine hundred pages of closely-written calculations, came a set of values which gave, with an error of only two minutes of arc, the correct position of Mars according to the Tychonic readings. He clambered up out of dreadful depths and announced his success to anyone who would listen. He wrote to Longberg in Denmark, demanding settlement of their wager. The fever which he had held at bay with promises and prayers took hold of him now like a demented lover. When it had spent itself, he returned to his calculations to make a final test. It was only play, really, a kind of revelling in his triumph. He chose another handful of observations and applied them to his model. They did not fit. Arrange matters as he would, there was always an error of eight minutes of arc. He plodded away from his desk, thinking of daggers, the poison cup, a launching into empty air from a high wall of the Hradcany. And yet, in a secret recess of his heart, a crazy happiness was stirring at the prospect of throwing away all he had done so far and starting over again. It was the joy of the zealot in his cell, the scourge clasped in his hand. And seventeen months were to become seven years before the thing was done.

His overloaded brain began to throw off sparks of surplus energy, and he conceived all kinds of quaint ingenious enterprises. He developed a method of measuring the volume of wine casks by conic section. The keeper of the Emperor's cellars was charmed. He tested his own eyesight and made for himself an elaborate pair of spectacles from lenses ground in Linz by his old friend Wincklemann. The prosaic miracle of water had always fascinated him; he set up water clocks, and designed a new kind of pump which impressed the imperial engineers. Others of his projects caused much hilarity among the Brahes. There was his design for an automatic floor-sweeper, worked by suction power from a double-valved bellows attached to the implement's ratcheted wheels. He consulted the scullery maids on a plan for a laundry machine, a huge tub with paddles operated by a treadle. They ran away from him, giggling. These were amusing pastimes, but at the end of the day always there was the old problem of Mars waiting for him.

He liked to work at night, savouring the silence and the candleglow and the somehow attentive darkness, and then the dawn that always surprised him with that sense of being given a glimpse of the still new and unsullied other end of things. In the Curtius house he had burrowed into a little room on the top floor where he could lock himself away. The summer passed. Early one October morning he heard a step outside his door, and peering out spied Tycho Brahe standing in the corridor, his arms folded, gazing down pensively at his large bare feet. He was in his nightshirt, with a cloak thrown over his shoulders. Behind him, by the far wall, Jeppe the dwarf was creeping. They had the air of weary and discouraged searchers after some hopelessly lost small thing. Tycho looked up at Kepler without surprise.

"Sleep," said the Dane, "I do not sleep."

As if at a signal, there arose in the sky outside a vehement clanging. Kepler turned an ear to it and smiled. "Bells," he said. Tycho frowned.

Kepler's room was a cramped brown box with a pallet and a stool, and a rickety table aswarm with his papers. Tycho sat down heavily, fussing at his cloak; Jeppe scuttled under the table. Rain spoke suddenly at the window: the sky was coming apart and falling on the city in undulant swathes. Kepler scratched his head and absently inspected his fingernails. He had lice again.

"You progress?" said Tycho, nodding at the jumbled papers by his elbow.

"O yes, a little."

"And you still hold to the Copernican system?"

"It is a useful basis of computation . . ." But that was not it. "Yes," he said grimly, "I follow Copernicus."

The Dane might not have heard. He was looking away, toward the door, where on a hook there hung a mildewed court uniform, complete with sash and feathered hat, a limp ghost of the previous householder, the late vice chancellor. Under the table Jeppe stirred, muttering. "I came to speak to you," Tycho said. Kepler waited, but there was nothing more. He looked at the Dane's big yellow feet clinging to the floorboards like a pair of purblind animals. In his time Tycho Brahe had determined the position of a thousand stars, and had devised a system of the world more elegant than Ptolemy's. His book on the new star of 1572 had made him famous throughout Europe.

"I have made," said Kepler, picking up his pen and looking at it with a frown, "I have made a small discovery regarding orbital motion."

"That it is invariable, after all?" Tycho suddenly laughed.

"No," Kepler said. "But the radius vector of any planet, it seems, will sweep out equal areas in equal times." He glanced at Tycho. "I regard this as a law."

"Moses Mathematicus," said Jeppe, and sniggered.

The rain was still coming down, but the clouds to the east had developed a luminous rip. There was a sudden beating of wings at the window. Kepler's steelpen, not to be outdone by the deluge outside, deposited with a parturient squeak upon his papers a fat black blot.

"Bells," said Tycho softly.

That night he was brought home drunk from dinner at the house of Baron Rosenberg in the city, and relieved himself in the fireplace of the main hall, waking everyone with his yelling and the stench of boiled piss. He kicked the dwarf and staggered away upstairs to his bed, from which Mistress Christine, gibbering in rage, had already fled. The household was no sooner settled back to sleep than the master reared up again roaring for lights and his fool and a meal of quails' eggs and brandy. At noon next day he summoned Kepler to his bedside. "I am ill." He had a mug of ale in his hand, and the bed was strewn with pastry scraps.

"You should not drink so much, perhaps," said Kepler mildly.

"Pah. Something has burst in my gut: look at that!" He pointed with grim pride to a basin of bloodied urine on the floor by Kepler's feet. "Last night at Rosenberg's my bladder was full for three hours, I could not leave the table for fear of seeming gross. You know what these occasions are."

"No," said Kepler, "I do not."

Tycho scowled, and took a swig of ale. He looked at Kepler keenly for a moment. "Be careful of my family, they will try to hinder you. Watch Tengnagel, he is a fool, but ambitious. Protect my poor dwarf." He paused. "Remember me, and all I have done for you. Do not let me seem to have lived in vain."

Kepler ascended laughing to his room. All he has done for me! Barbara was there before him, poking among his things. He edged around her to the table and plunged into his papers, mumbling.

"How is he?" she said.

"Eh? Who?"

"Who!"

"O, it's nothing. Too much wine."

She was silent for a moment, standing behind him with her arms folded, nursing enormities. "How can you," she said at last, "how can you be so . . . so . . ."

He turned to stare at her. "What."

"Have you thought, have you, what will become of us when he dies?"

"Good God, woman! He was dining with his fine friends, and drank too much as always, and was too lazy to leave his chair to pee, and injured his bladder. He will be over it by tomorrow. Permit me to know enough of doctoring to recognise mortal illness when—"

"You recognise nothing!" shrieking a fine spray of spit in his face. "Are you alive at all, with your stars and your precious theories and your laws of this and that and and and . . ." Fat tears sprang from her eyes, her voice broke, and she fled the room.

Tycho failed rapidly. Within the week Kepler was summoned again to his chamber. It was crowded with family and pupils and court emissaries, poised and silent like a gathering in the gloom on the fringes of a dream. Tycho was enthroned in lamplight upon his high bed. The flesh hung in folds on his shrunken face, his eyes were vague. He held Kepler's hand. "Remember me. Do not let me seem to have lived in vain." Kepler could think of nothing to say, and grinned uncontrollably, nodding, nodding. Mistress Christine plucked at the stuff of her gown, looking about her dazedly as if trying to remember something. The dwarf, blotched with tears, made to scramble on to the bed but someone held him back. Kepler noticed for the first time that Elizabeth Brahe was pregnant. Tengnagel skulked at her shoulder. There was a commotion outside the door of the chamber and Felix burst in, spitting Italian over his shoulder at someone outside. He strode to the bed and, thrusting Kepler away, took the Dane's hand in his own. But the Dane was dead.

He was buried, after an utraquist service, in the Teynkirche in Prague. The house on the Hradcany had an air of pained surprise, as if a wing had suddenly and silently collapsed. One morning it was discovered that the Italian had departed, taking Jeppe with him, no one knew to where. Kepler considered going too; but where would he go? And then a message came from the palace informing him that he had been appointed to succeed the Dane as imperial mathematician.

*　　*　　*

Everyone said the Emperor Rudolph was harmless, if a little mad, yet when the moment had come at last for Kepler to meet him for the first time, a spasm of fright had crushed the astronomer's heart in its hot fist. That was ten months before the Dane's death. Kepler by then had been in Bohemia nearly a year, but Tycho's grand manner was impervious to hints. He only shrugged and began to hum when Kepler ventured that it was a long time to have held off from this introduction. "His majesty is . . . difficult."

They trundled up the Hradcany and turned in between the high walls leading to the gate. Everywhere about them lay the economy of snow: a great white and only the black ruts of the road, the no-colour wall. The sky was the colour of a hare's pelt. Their horse stumbled on packed ice, and a scolopendrine beggar scuttled forward and opened his mouth at them through the carriage window in speechless imprecation. On the wooden bridge before the gate they skated ponderously to a halt. The horse stamped and snorted, blowing cones of steam out of flared nostrils. Kepler put his head out at the window. The air was sharp as needles. The gateman, a fat fellow in furs, waddled forth from his box and spoke to the driver, then waved them on. Tycho flung him a coin.

"Ah," said the Dane, "ah, I detest this country." He fussed at the sheepskin wrap about his knees. They were in the palace gardens now. Black trees glided slowly past, bare limbs thrown up as if in stark astonishment at the cold. "Why did I ever leave Denmark?"

"Because . . ."

"Well?" staring balefully, daring him. Kepler sighed.

"I do not know. Tell me."

Tycho transferred his gaze to the smoky air outside. "We Brahes have ever been ill-used by royals. My uncle Jorgen Brahe saved King Frederick from drowning in the Sund at Copenhagen, and died himself in the attempt, did you know that?" He did. It was an oft-told tale. The Dane was working himself up into a fine fit of indignation. "And yet that young brat Christian was bold enough to banish me from my island sanctuary, my fabulous Uraniborg, granted to me by royal charter when he was still a snot-nosed mewler on his nurse's knee—did you know *that*?" O he did, he did, and more. Tycho had ruled on Hveen like a despotic Turk, until even the mild King Christian could no longer countenance it. "Ah, Kepler, the perfidy of princes!" and glared at the palace advancing to meet them through the icy light of afternoon.

They were left to wait outside the chamber of the presence. There were others there before them, dim depressed figures given to sighing, and a crossing and recrossing of legs. It was bitterly cold, and Kepler's feet were numb. His apprehension had yielded before a grey weight of boredom when the groom of the chamber, an immaculately costumed bland little man, approached swiftly and whispered to the Dane, and already there was a hot constriction in Kepler's breast, as if his lungs, getting wind a fraction before he did of the advent at last of the longed-for and dreaded moment, had snatched a quick gulp of air to cushion the shock. He needed to urinate. I think I must go and—will you excuse—?

"Do you know," said the Emperor, "do you know what one of our mathematici has told us: that if the digits of any double number be transposed, and the result of the transposition be subtracted from the original, or vice versa of course, depending on which is the greater value, then the remainder in all instances shall be divisible by nine. Is this not a wonderful operation? By nine, always." He was a short plump matronly man with melancholy eyes. A large chin nestled like a pigeon in a bit of soft beard. His manner was a blend of eagerness and weary detachment. "But doubtless you, sir, a mathematician yourself, will think it nothing remarkable that numbers should behave in what to us is a strange and marvellous fashion?"

Kepler was busy transposing and subtracting in his head. Was this perhaps a test to which all paying court for the first time were subjected? The Emperor, slack-jawed and softly panting, watched him with an unnerving avidity. He felt as if he were being slowly and ruminatively devoured. "A mathematician, I am that, your majesty, yes," smiling tentatively. "Nevertheless I admit that I cannot say what is the explanation of this phenomenon..." He was discussing mathematics with the ruler of the Holy Roman Empire, the anointed of God

80

and bearer of the crown of Charlemagne. "Perhaps your majesty himself can offer a solution?"

Rudolph shook his head. For a moment he mused in silence, a forefinger palping his lower lip. Then he sighed.

"There is a magic in numbers," he said, "which is beyond rational explanation. You are aware of this, no doubt, in your own work? May be, even, you put to use sometimes this magic?"

"I would not attempt," said Kepler, with a force and suddenness that startled even him, "I would not attempt to prove anything by the mysticism of numbers, nor do I consider it possible to do so."

In the silence that followed, Tycho Brahe, behind him, coughed.

Rudolph took his guest on a tour of the palace and its wonder rooms. Kepler was shown all manner of mechanical apparatuses, lifelike wax figures and clockwork dummies, rare coins and pictures, exotic carvings, pornographic manuscripts, a pair of Barbary apes and a huge spindly beast from Araby with a hump and a dun coat and an expression of ineradicable melancholy, vast dim laboratories and alchemical caves, an hermaphrodite child, a stone statue which would sing when exposed to the heat of the sun, and he grew dizzy with surprise and superstitious alarm. As they progressed from one marvel to the next they accumulated in their train a troupe of murmurous courtiers, delicate men and elaborate ladies, whom the Emperor ignored, but who yet depended from him, like a string of puppets; they were exquisitely at ease, yet through all their fine languor it seemed to Kepler a thread of muted pain was tightly stretched, which out of each produced, as a stroked glass will produce, a tiny note that was one with the tone of the apes' muffled cries and the androgynous child's speechless stare. He listened closely then, and thought he heard from every corner of the palace all that royal sorceror's magicked captives faintly singing, all lamenting.

They came into a wide hall with hangings and many pictures and a magnificent vaulted ceiling. The floor was a checkered design of black and white marble tiles. Windows gazed down upon the snowbound city, of which the tiled floor was a

81

curious echo, except that all out there seemed a jumble of wreckage under the brumous winter light. A few persons stood about, motionless as figurines, marvellously got up in yellows and sky blues and flesh tints and lace. This was the throne room. Cups of sticky brown liqueur and trays of sweet-meats were carried in. The Emperor neither ate nor drank. He seemed ill at ease here, and glanced at his throne, making little feints at it, as if it were a live thing crouching there that he must catch off guard and subdue before he might mount it.

"Do you agree," he said, "that men are distinguished one from another more by the influence of heavenly bodies than even by institutions and habit? Would you agree with this view, sir?"

There was something touching in this dumpy little man, with his weak mouth and haunted eyes, that avid attentiveness. And yet this was the Emperor! Was he perhaps a little deaf?

"Yes," said Kepler, "yes, I do agree; but casting horoscopes, all that, an unpleasant and begrimed work, your majesty." He paused. What was this? Who had said anything of horoscopes? But Rudolph, according to the Dane, had nodded assent to Kepler's plea for an imperial stipend; he must be made to understand that a few florins annually would not purchase another wizard to add to his collection. "Of course," he went on, "I believe that the stars do, yes, influence us, and that it is permissible a ruler be allowed once in a while to take advantage of such influence. But, if you will permit me, sir, there are dangers . . ." The Emperor waited, smiling vaguely and nodding, yet managing to convey a faint unmistakable chill of warning. "I mean, your majesty, there is," with deliberate emphasis, while Tycho Brahe raked together the ingredients of another cautionary cough, "there is a danger if the ruler should be too much swayed by those about him who make star magic their business. I am thinking of those Englishmen, Kelley and the angel-conjuror Dee, who lately, I am told, deceived yo—your court, with their trickery."

Rudolph had turned slowly away, still with that pained vacant smile, still nodding, and Tycho Brahe immediately jumped in and began to speak loudly of something else. Kepler was annoyed. What did they expect of him! He was no crawling

82

courtier, to kiss hands and curtsy.

The day waned, the lamps were lit, and there was music. Rudolph took to his throne at last. It was the only seat in the room. Kepler's legs began to ache. He had expected much of this day. Everything was going wrong. Yet he had done his best to be upright and honest. Perhaps that was not what was required. In this empire of impossible ceremony and ceaseless show Johannes Kepler fitted ill. The music of the strings sighed on, an unobtrusive creaking. "It was the predictability of astronomical events," the Dane was saying, "which drew me to this science, for I saw, of course, how useful such predictions would be to navigators and calendar makers, also to kings and princes . . ." but his efforts were not succeeding either, Rudolph's chin was sunk on his breast, and he was not listening. He rose and touched Kepler's arm, and walked with him to the great window. Below them the city was dissolving into the twilight. They stood in silence for a moment, gazing down upon the little lights that flickered forth here and there. All at once Kepler felt a rush of tenderness for this soft sad man, a desire to shield him from the world's wickedness.

"They tell us that you have done wonderful works," the Emperor murmured. "We care for such things. If there were time . . ." He sighed. "I do not like the world. More and more I desire to transcend these . . . these . . ." His hand moved in a vague gesture toward the room behind him. "I think sometimes I might dress in rags and go among the people. I do not see them, you know. But then, where should I find rags, here?" He glanced at Kepler with a faint apologetic smile. "You see our difficulties."

"Of course, certainly."

Rudolph frowned, annoyed not at his guest it seemed but with himself. "What was I saying? Yes: these tables which Herr Brahe wishes to draw up, you consider them a worthwhile venture?"

Kepler felt like a hamfisted juggler, diving frantically this way and that as the balls spun out of control. "They would contain, your majesty, everything that is known in our science."

"Facts, then, you mean, figures?"

"Everything that is known."

"Yes?"

"The Tychonic tables will be the foundation of a new science of the sky. Herr Brahe is a great and diligent observer. The material he has amassed is a priceless treasure. The tables must be made, they shall be, and those who come after us will bless the name of any who had a hand in their making."

"I see, I see, yes," and coughed. "You are an Austrian, Herr Kepler?"

"Swabia is my birthplace; but I was in Graz for some years before I—"

"Ah, Graz."

"But I was driven out. The Archduke Ferdinand—"

"Graz," Rudolph said again. "Yes, our cousin Ferdinand is diligent."

Kepler closed his eyes. His cousin, of course.

The music ceased, and a parting glass was distributed. Tycho took Kepler's arm, trying it seemed to crush it in his fist. They bowed, and backed off towards the doors that were drawing open slowly behind them. Kepler halted, frowning, and trotted forward again before the Dane could stop him, muttering under his breath. "Nines, nines of course! Your majesty, a moment. See, sire, it is because of the nines, or I mean the tens, because we count in tens, and therefore the result will always be divisible by nine. For if we computed by nines, now, it would be eight, divisible by eight that is, and so on. You see?" sketching a triumphantly gay figure eight on the air. But the Emperor Rudolph only looked at him, with a kind of sadness, and said nothing. As they went out Tycho Brahe, sucking his teeth, turned on Kepler savagely. "The wrong thing you say, always the wrong thing!"

In the lamplight at the gate a few absent-minded flakes of snow were falling. The horse's hoofs rang on the cold stones, and somewhere off to the left the watch called out. At Kepler's side the Dane snorted and struggled, trying to contain the unwieldy parcel of his rage. "Have you no sense of of of," he gasped, "no understanding of—of anything? Why, at times today I suspected that you were trying, *trying* to anger him."

Kepler said nothing. He did not need Tycho to tell him how

84

badly he had fared. Yet he could not be angry at himself, for it was not he had done the damage, but that other Kepler shambling at his heels, that demented other, whose prints upon his life were the black bruises that inevitably appeared in the places whereon Johannes the Mild had impressed no more than a faint thumb-print of protest.

"Well, it is no matter, in the end," said Tycho wearily. "I convinced him, despite your clumsiness, that you should work with me in compiling the tables. I am to call them the *Tabulae Rudolphinae*. He believes that those who come after us will bless his name!"

"Yes?"

"And he will grant you two hundred florins annually, though God knows if you will ever see it, he is not renowned either for generosity or promptness."

On the bridge the carriage halted, and Kepler gazed for a long time into the illusory emptiness outside. What would be his future, bound to a protector in need of protecting? He thought of that woebegone king immured in perpetual check in his ice palace. Tycho elbowed him furiously in the ribs. "Have you nothing to say?"

"O—thank you." The carriage lurched forward into the darkness. "He does not like the world."

"What?"

"The Emperor, he told me that he does not like the world. Those were his words. I thought it strange."

"Strange? *Strange?* Sir, you are as mad as he."

"We are alike, yes, in ways . . ."

That night he fell ill. An insidious fever originated in the gall, and, bypassing the bowels, gained access to the head. Barbara forced him to take a hot bath, though he considered total immersion an unnatural and foolhardy practice. To his surprise the measure brought him temporary relief. The heat, however, constricted his bowels; he administered a strong purgative, and then bled himself. He decided, after careful investigation of his excreta, that he was one of those cases whose gall bladder has a direct opening into the stomach. This was an interesting discovery, though such people, he knew, are short-lived as a rule. The sky was catastrophic at that time. But he had so much still to do! The Emperor sent good wishes for his recovery. That decided him: he would not die. The fever abated at last. He felt like one of those neatly parcelled flies that adorn spiders' webs. Death was saving him up for a future feast.

Was there a lesson for him in this latest bout of illness? He was not living as he knew he should. His rational self told him he must learn continence of thought and speech, must practise grovelling. He set himself diligently to work at the Rudolphine Tables, arranging and transcribing endless columns of observations from Tcyho's papers. In his heart the predictability of astronomical events meant nothing to him; what did he care for navigators or calendar makers, for princes and kings? The demented dreamer in him rebelled. He remembered that vision he had glimpsed in Baron Hoffmann's garden, and was again assailed by the mysteriousness of the commonplace. *Give this world's praise to the angel!* He had only the vaguest notion of what he meant. He recalled too the squabbling when he had come first to Tycho, the farce of that flight from Benatek and the ignominious return. Would it be likewise with Rudolph? He wrote to Mästlin: *I do not speak like I write, I do not write like I think, I do not think like I ought to think, and so everything goes on in deepest darkness.* Where did these voices come from, these strange sayings? It was as if the future had found utterance in him.

III

—

Dioptrice

Pausing in the midst of Weilderstadt's familiar streets, he looked about him in mild amaze. It was still here, the narrow houses, the stucco and the spires and the shingled roofs, that weathervane, all of it by some means still intact, unaware that his memory had long ago reduced it all to a waxwork model. The morning air was heavy with a mingled smell of bread and dung and smoke—that smell!—and everywhere a blurred clamour was trying and just failing to make an important announcement. The lindens in Klingelbrunner lane averted their sheepish gaze from the puddles of sticky buds they had shed during the night. Faces in the streets puzzled him, familiar, and yet impossibly youthful, until presently he realised that these were not his former schoolfellows, but their sons. There is the church, there the marketplace. Here is the house.

There was bedlam when the carriage stopped, the children tussling, the baby squealing in Barbara's lap; it seemed to Kepler a manifestation of the speechless uproar in his heart. The street door was shut, the upstairs shutters fastened. Had the magic of his long absence worked here at least, bundled it all up and disappeared it? But the door was opening already, and his brother Heinrich appeared, with his awkward grin, stooping and bobbing in a paroxysm of shyness. They embraced, both of them speaking at once, and Kepler stepped back with a quick glance at the starched tips of his winged lace collar. Regina, a young woman now, had the protesting baby in her arms, and Barbara was trying to get at Susanna to give her a smack, and Susanna, nimbly escaping, knocked over little Friedrich, who cut his knee on the step and after a moment of open-mouthed silence suddenly howled, and a black dog trotting by on the street came over and began to bark at them all in furious encouragement. Heinrich laughed, showing a mouthful of yellow stumps, and waved them in. The old woman at the fire looked over her shoulder and went off at once, muttering, into the kitchen. Kepler pretended he had not seen her.

"Well . . !" he said, smiling all around him, and patting his pockets distractedly, as if in search of the key somewhere on his person that would unlock this tangle of emotions. It was a little low dark house, sparsely furnished. There was a yellowish smell of cat, which presently was concentrated into an enormous ginger tom thrusting itself with a kind of truculent ardour against Kepler's leg. A black pot was bubbling on the fire of thorns in the open hearth. Kepler took off his hat. "Well!"

Heinrich shut the door and pressed his back to it, tongue-tied and beaming. The children were suddenly solemn. Barbara peered about her in surprise and distaste, and Kepler with a sinking heart recalled those stories he had spun her long ago about his forebear the famous Kaspar von Kepler and the family coat of arms. Regina alone was at ease, rocking the baby. Heinrich was trying to take her in without going so far as to look at her directly. Poor sad harmless Heinrich! Kepler felt an inner engine softly starting up; O God, he must not weep. He scowled, and stamped into the kitchen. The old woman his mother was doing something to a trussed capon on the table.

"Here you are," he said; "we have arrived."

"I know it." She did not look up from her work. "I am not blind yet, nor deaf." She had not changed. She seemed to him to have been like this as far back as he could remember, little and bent and old, in a cap and a brown smock. Her eyes were of the palest blue. Three grey hairs sprouted on her chin. Her hands.

*   *   *

Laughable, laughable—she had only to look at him, and his velvet and fine lace and pointed boots became a jester's costume. He was dressed only as befitted the imperial mathematician, yet why else had he carried himself with jealous care on the long journey hither, like a marvellous bejewelled egg, except to impress her? And now he felt ridiculous. Sunlight was spilling through the little window behind her, and he could see the garden, the fruit bushes and the chicken run and the broken wooden seat. The past struck him again a soft glancing blow. Out there had been his refuge from the endless rows and beatings, out there he had dawdled and dreamed, lusting for the future. His mother wiped her hands on her apron. "Well come then, come!" as if it were he who had been delaying.

She glanced at Barbara with a sniff and turned her attention to the children.

"This is Susanna," said Kepler, "and here, Friedrich. Come, say God bless to your grandma." Frau Kepler examined them as if they were for sale. Kepler was sweating. "Susanna is seven already, and Friedrich is three or is it four, yes, four, a big boy—and," like a fairground barker, "here is our latest, the baby Ludwig! His godfather, you know, is Johann Georg Gödelmann, Saxony's Ambassador to the court of Prague."

Regina stepped forward and displayed the infant.

"Very pale," the old woman said. "Is he sickly?"

"Of course not, of course not. You, ah, remember Regina? My . . . our . . ."

"Aye: the cabinetmaker's daughter."

And they all, even the children, looked at the young woman in silence for a moment. She smiled.

"We are on our way from Heidelberg," said Kepler. "They are printing my book there. And before that we were in Frankfurt, for the fair, the book fair, I mean, in . . . in Frankfurt."

"Books, aye," Frau Kepler muttered, and sniffed again. She bent over the fire to stir the bubbling pot, and in the awkward silence everyone abruptly changed their places, making little lunges and sudden stops, setting Kepler's teeth on edge. He marvelled at how well the old woman managed it still, the art of puppetry! Heinrich sidled forward and stood beside her. As she straightened up she fastened a hand on his arm to steady herself, and Kepler noted, with a pang that surprised him, his brother's embarrassed smile of pride and protectiveness. Frau Kepler squinted at the fire. "A wonder you could come to see us, you are so busy."

Heinrich laughed. "Now ma!" He rubbed a hand vigorously through the sparse hairs on his pate, grinning apologetically. "Johann is a great man now, you know. I say, you must be a great man now," as if Kepler were deaf, "with the books and all, eh? And working for the Emperor himself!"

Barbara, sitting by the table, quietly snorted.

"O yes," said Kepler, and turned away from his mother and her son standing side by side before him, feeling a sudden faint disgust at the spectacle of family resemblance, the little legs and hollow chests and pale pinched faces, botched prototypes of his own, if not lovely, at least completed parts. "O yes," he said, trying to smile but only wincing, "I am a great man!"

*　　　*　　　*

E everyone was morbidly hungry, and when the capon had been dispatched they started on the bean stew from the three-legged pot. Heinrich was sent to the baker's, and came back with a sack of loaves, and buns for the children, and a flagon of wine. He had dallied in the wine shop, and his grin was crookeder than before. He tried to make Barbara take a drink, but she shook her head, turning her face away from him. She had not spoken a word since their arrival. The baby was sprawled asleep in her lap. The old woman squatted on a stool beside the fire, picking at her bowl of stew and mumbling to herself and sometimes grinning furtively. The children had been put to sit under Regina's supervision at the kitchen table. Kepler suddenly recalled a sunny Easter Sunday long ago, when his grandfather was still alive, one of those days that had lodged itself in his memory not because of any particular event, but because all the aimless parts of it, the brilliant light, the scratchy feel of a new coat, the sound of bells, lofty and mad, had made together an almost palpable shape, a great air sign, like a cloud or a wind or a shower of rain, that was beyond interpreting and yet rich with significance and promise. Was

92

that . . . happiness? Disturbed and puzzled, he sat now sunk in thought, watching shadows move on the wine's tensed meniscus in his cup.

He had been at Maulbronn then, the last of his many schools. Chance, in the form of the impersonal patronage of the Dukes of Württemberg, had given him a fine education. At fifteen he knew Latin and Greek, and had a grasp of mathematics. The family, surprised by the changeling in their midst, said that all this learning was not good, it would ruin his health, as if his health had ever been their only concern. The truth was they saw his scholarship as somehow a betrayal of the deluded image the Keplers had of themselves then of sturdy burgher stock. That was the time of the family's finest flourishing. Grandfather Sebaldus was the mayor of Weilderstadt, and his son Harry, Kepler's father, temporarily back from his profligate wanderings, was running an inn at Ellmendingen. It was a brief heyday. The inn failed, and Harry Kepler and his family moved back to Weil, where the mayor had become entangled in the shadowy litigations which were eventually to ruin him. Before long Harry was off again, this time to the Low Countries to join the Duke of Alba's mercenaries. Johannes was never to see him again. Grandfather Sebaldus became his guardian. A red-faced fat old reprobate, he considered Johannes a fancified little get.

The house had been crowded then. His brother Heinrich was there, a clumsy inarticulate boy, and their sister Margarete, and Christoph the baby whom no one expected would live, and Sebaldus's four or five adult sons and daughters, the renegade Jesuit Sebald the younger, locked in an upstairs room and raving with the pox, Aunt Kunigund, whose loony husband was even then secretly poisoning her, and poor doomed Katharine, lover of beautiful things, now a wandering beggar. They were all of them infected with the same wild strain. And what a noise they made, packed together in that stinking little house! All his life Kepler had suffered intermittently from tinnitus, the after-echo of those years, he believed, still vibrating in his head. His bad eyesight was another souvenir, left him by the frequent boxings which every inmate of the house, even the youngest, inflicted on him when there was nothing worthier at hand to punish. Happiness?

Where in all that would happiness have found a place?

*   *   *

Reeling a little, with a mug of wine in his fist and wearing a moist conspiratorial smile, Heinrich came and crouched beside his brother's chair. "This is a party, eh?" he wheezed, laughing. "You should come see us more often."

Of his surviving siblings, Kepler loved only Heinrich. Margarete was a bore, like the pastor she had married, and Christoph, a master pewterer in Leonberg, had been an insufferable prig even as a child. Still, they were innocent souls: could the same be said of Heinrich? He had the look of a happy harmless beast, the runt of the litter whom the farmer's fond-hearted wife has saved from the blade. But he had been to the wars. What unimaginable spectacles of plunder and rape had those bland brown eyes witnessed in their time? From such wonderings Kepler's mind delicately averted itself. He had peculiar need of *this* Heinrich, a forty-year-old child, eager and unlovely, and always hugely amused by a world he had never quite learned how to manage.

"You've printed up a book then—a storybook, is it?"

"No, no," said Kepler, peering into his wine. "I am no good at stories. It is a new science of the skies, which I have invented." It sounded absurd. Heinrich nodded solemnly, squaring his shoulders as he prepared to plunge into the boiling sea of his brother's brilliance. ". . . And all in Latin," Kepler added.

"Latin! Ha, and here am I, who can't even read in our own German."

Kepler glanced at him, searching in vain for a trace of irony in that awestruck smile. Heinrich seemed relieved, as if the Latin exonerated him.

"And now I am writing another, about lenses and spyglasses, how they may be used for looking at the stars—" and then, quietly: "—How is your health now, Heinrich?"

But Heinrich pretended he had not heard. "It's for the Emperor, is it, all these books you're writing, he pays you to write them, does he? I saw him one time, old Rudolph—"

"The Emperor is nothing," Kepler snapped, "an old woman unfit to rule." Heinrich was an epileptic. "Don't talk to me about that man!"

Heinrich looked away, nodding. Of all the ills with which he had been cursed, the falling sickness was the one he felt most sorely. Their father had tried to beat it out of him. Those scenes were among the earliest Kepler could remember, the boy stricken on the floor, the drumming heels and foam-flecked mouth, and the drunken soldier kneeling over him, raining down blows and screeching for the devil to come forth. Once he had tried to sell the child to a wandering Turk. Heinrich ran away, to Austria and Hungary, and on up to the Low Countries; he had been a street singer, a halberdier, a beggar. At last, at the age of thirty-five, he had dragged himself and his devil back here to his mother's house in Weilderstadt. "How is it, Heinrich?"

"Ah, not bad, not bad you know. The old attacks . . ." He smiled sheepishly, and rubbed a hand again on the bald spot on his skull. Kepler passed him his empty cup. "Let's have another fill of wine, Heinrich."

*   *   *

The children went out to the garden. He watched them from the kitchen window as they trailed moodily among the currant bushes and the stumps of last year's cabbages. Friedrich stumbled and fell on his face in the grass. After a moment he came up again in laborious stages, a tiny fat hand, a lick of hair with a brown leaf tangled in it, a cross mouth. How can they bear it, this helpless venturing into a giant world? Susanna stood and watched him with a complacent sneer as he struggled up. There was a streak of cruelty in her. She had Barbara's looks, that puffy prettiness, the small bright mouth and discontented eyes. The boy wiped his nose on his sleeve and waded after her doggedly through the grass. A flaw in the windowpane made him a sudden swimmer, and in the eyepiece of Kepler's heart too something stretched and billowed briefly. Just when he had given up all hope of children Barbara had

95

begun to flower with an almost unseemly abundance. He no longer had any trust, thought they would die too, like the others; the fact of their survival dazed him. Even yet he felt helpless and unwieldy before them, as if their birth had not ended the process of parturition but only transferred it to him. He was big with love.

He thought of his own father. There was not much to think of: a calloused hand hitting him, a snatch of drunken song, a broken sword rusted with what was said to be the blood of a Turk. What had driven *him*, what impossible longings had strained and kicked in *his* innards? And had *he* loved? What, then? The stamping of feet on the march, the brassy stink of fear and expectation on the battlefield at dawn, brute warmth and delirium of the wayside inn? What? Was it possible to love mere action, the thrill of ceaseless doing? The window reassembled itself before his brooding eyes. This was the world, that garden, his children, those poppies. I am a little creature, my horizons are near. Then, like a sudden drenching of icy water, came the thought of death, with a stump of rusted sword in its grasp.

". . . Well, are we?"

He jumped. "What?"

"*Ah!* do you ever listen." The baby in her arms put forth a muffled exploratory wail. "Are we to lodge in this . . . this house? Will there be room enough?"

"A whole family, generations, lived here once . . ."

She stared at him. She had slept briefly, sitting by the table. Her eyes were swollen and there was a livid mark on her jaw. "Do you ever think about—" "Yes." "—these things, worry about them, do you?"

"*Yes.* Do I not spend every waking hour worrying and arranging and—do I not?" A lump of self-pity rose in his throat. "*What more do you want?*"

Tears welled in her eyes, and the baby, taking its cue, began to bawl. The door to the front room had the look of an ear bent avidly upon them. Kepler put a hand to his forehead. "Let us not fight."

The children came in from the garden, and paused, catching the pulsations in the air. The baby howled, and Barbara rocked

96

him jerkily in a clockwork simulacrum of tenderness. Kepler turned away from her, frightening the children with his mad grin. "Well, Susan, Friedrich: how do you like your grandma's home?"

"There is a dead rat in the garden," Susanna said, and Barbara sobbed, and Kepler thought how all this had happened before somewhere.

*   *   *

Yes, it had all, all of it happened before. How was it he expected at each homecoming to find everything transformed? Was his self-esteem such as to let him think the events of his new life must have an effect, magical and redemptive, on the old life left behind him here in Weil? Look at him now. He had tricked himself out in imperial finery and come flouncing down upon his past, convinced that simply his elevation in rank would be enough to have caused the midden heap to sprout a riot of roses. And he had been hardly in the door before he realised that the trick had not worked, and now he could only stand and sweat, dropping rabbits and paper flowers from under his spangled cloak, a comic turn whom his glassy-eyed audience was too embarrassed to laugh at.

And yet Heinrich was impressed, and so too, according to him, was their mother. "She talks about you all the time—O yes! Then she wants to know why I can't be like you. I! Well, I tell her, you know, mam, Johann is—Johann!" slapping his brother on the shoulder, wheezing, with tears in his eyes, as if it were a rare and crafty joke he had cracked. Kepler smiled gloomily, and realised that after all that was it, what burned him, that to them his achievements were something that had merely happened to him, a great and faintly ludicrous stroke of luck fallen out of the sky upon their Johann.

He climbed the narrow stairs, yawning. Had the old woman put one of her cunning potions into the wine?—or the stew, perhaps! Chuckling and yawning, and wiping his eyes, he ducked into the little back bedroom. This house had been built for the Keplers all right, everything in miniature, the low ceil-

97

ings, the stools, the little bed. The floor was strewn with green rushes, and a basin of water and towels had been set out. Towels! She had not been wholly indifferent, then, to his impending visit. Afternoon sunlight was edging its way stealthily along the sill of the dingy window. Barbara was already asleep, lying on her back in the middle of the bed like a mighty effigy, a look of vague amazement on her upturned face. The baby at her side was a tiny pink fist in a bundle of swaddling. Susanna and Friedrich were crowded together in the truckle bed. Friedrich slept with his eyes not quite closed, the pupils turned up into his head and bluish moonlets showing eerily between the parted lids. Kepler leaned over him, thinking with resigned foreboding that someday surely he would be made to pay for the happiness this child had brought him. Friedrich was his favourite.

He lay for a long time suspended between sleep and waking, his hands folded on his breast. A trapped fly danced against the window pane, like a tiny machine engaged upon some monstrously intricate task, and in the distance a cow was lowing plaintively, after a calf, perhaps, that the herdsman had taken away. Strange, how comforting and homely these sounds, that yet in themselves were plangent with panic and pain. So little we feel! He sighed. Beside him the baby stirred, burbling in its sleep. The years were falling away, like loops of rope into a well. Below him there was darkness, an intimation of waters. He might have been an infant himself, now. All at once, like a statue hoving into the window of a moving carriage, Grandfather Sebaldus rose before him, younger and more vigorous than Johannes remembered having known him. There were others, a very gallery of stark still figures looking down on him. Deeper he sank. The water was warm. Then in the incarnadine darkness a great slow pulse began to beat.

*   *   *

Confused and wary, not knowing where he was, he strove to hold on to the dream. As a child, when he woke like this in

98

nameless fright, he would lie motionless, his eyelids quivering, trying to convince an imaginary watcher in the room that he was not really awake, and thus sometimes, by a kind of sympathetic magic, he would succeed in slipping back unawares into the better world of sleep. The trick would not work now.

That was what he had dreamed of, his childhood. And water. Why did he dream so often of water? Barbara was no longer beside him, and the truckle bed was empty. The sun was still in the window. He rose, groaning, and splashed his face from the basin. Then he paused, leaning thus and staring at nothing. What was he doing here, in his mother's house? And yet to be elsewhere would be equally futile. He was a bag of slack flesh in a world drained of essence. He told himself it was the wine and that troubled sleep, blurring his sense of proportion, but was not convinced. Which was the more real reality, the necessary certainties of everyday, or this bleak defencelessness? .

Early one summer morning when he was a boy he had watched from the kitchen a snail crawling up the window outside. The moment came back to him now, wonderfully clear, the washed sunlight in the garden, the dew, the rosebuds on the tumbledown privy, that snail. What had possessed it to climb so high, what impossible blue vision of flight reflected in the glass? The boy had trod on snails, savouring the crack and then the soft crunch, had collected them, had raced them and traded them, but never before now had he really looked at one. Pressed in a lavish embrace upon the pane, the creature gave up its frilled grey-green underparts to his gaze, while the head strained away from the glass, moving blindly from side to side, the horns weaving as if feeling out enormous forms in air. But what had held Johannes was its method of crawling. He would have expected some sort of awful convulsions, but instead there was a series of uniform small smooth waves flowing endlessly upward along its length, like a visible heartbeat. The economy, the heedless beauty of it, baffled him.

How closely after that he began to look at things, flies and fleas, ants, beetles, that daddy-longlegs feebly pawing the windowsill at twilight, its impossible threadlike limbs, the gauzy wings with fantastic maps traced on them—what were they *for*, these mites whose lives seemed no more than a form of clumsy dying? The world shifted and flowed: no sooner had he fixed a fragment of it than it became something else. A twig would suddenly put forth sticky malevolent wings and with a shove and a drugged leap take flight; a copper and crimson leaf lying on a dappled path would turn into a butterfly, drunken, a little mad, with two staring eyes on its wings and a body the colour of dried blood. His ailing eyesight increased the confusion. The limits of things became blurred, so that he was not sure where sentient life gave way to mere vegetable being. Sunflowers, with their faces pressed to the light, were they alive, and if not, what did it mean, being alive? Only the stars he knew for certain to be dead, yet it was they, in their luminous order, that gave him his most vivid sense of life.

He shook himself now like a wet dog. A huge yawn stopped him in his tracks, prising his jaws apart until their hinges crackled, and when Regina put her head into the room she found him teetering before her with mouth agape and eyes shut tight as if he were about to burst into violent song.

*　　*　　*

He peered at her through streaming tears and smiled.
"Mama sent me to wake you," she said.
"Ah."
Why was it, he wondered, that her candid gaze so pleased him always; how did she manage to make it seem a signal of support and understanding? She was like a marvellous and enigmatic work of art, which he was content to stand and contemplate with a dreamy smile, careless of the artist's intentions. To try to tell her what he felt would be as superfluous as talking to a picture. Her inwardness, which had intrigued Kepler when she was a child, had evolved into a kind of quietly splendid equilibrium. She resembled her mother not at all. She was tall and very fair, with a strong narrow face. Through her, curiously, Kepler sometimes glimpsed with admiration and regret her dead father whom he had never known. She would have been pretty, if she had considered being pretty a worth-

while endeavour. At nineteen, she was a fine Latin scholar, and even knew a little mathematics; he had tutored her himself. She had read his works, though never once had she offered an opinion, nor had he ever pressed her to.

"And also," she said, stepping in and shutting the door behind her, "I wanted to speak to you."

"O yes?" he said, vaguely alarmed. A momentary awkwardness settled between them. There was nowhere to sit save the bed. They moved to the window. Below them was the garden, and beyond that a little common with an elm tree and a duck pond. The evening was bright with sunlight and drifting clouds. A man with two children by the hand walked across the common. Kepler, still not fully awake, snatched at the corner of another memory. He had sailed a paper boat once on that pond, his father had gone there with him and Heinrich on a summer evening like this, long ago . . . And just then, as if it had all been slyly arranged, the three figures stopped by the muddy margin there and, a lens slipping into place, he recognised Heinrich and Susanna and the boy. He laughed. "Look, see who it is, I was just remem—"

"I am going to be married," Regina said, and looked at him quickly with an intent, quizzical smile.

"Married," he said.

"Yes. His name is Philip Ehem, he comes of a distinguished Augsburg family, and is a Representative at the court of Frederick the Elector Palatine . . ." She paused, lifting her eyebrows in wry amusement at the noise of this grand pedigree unfurling. "I wanted to tell *you*, before . . ."

Kepler nodded. "Yes." He felt as if he were being worked by strings. He heard faintly the children's laughter swooping like swifts across the common. There would be a scene with Barbara if they got their feet wet. It was one of her increasingly numerous obsessions, wet feet. Beyond Regina's head a berry-black spider dangled in a far corner of the ceiling. "Ehem, you say."

"Yes. He is a Lutheran, of course."

He turned his face away. "I see." He was jealous.

Ohow, how strange: to be shocked at himself; horrified but not surprised. Where before was only tenderness—suspiciously weighty perhaps—and sometimes a mild object-less craving, there suddenly stood now in his heart a full-grown creature, complete in every detail and even possessed of a past, blinking in the light and tugging hesitantly at the still unbroken birthcord. It had been in him all those years, growing unnoticed towards this sudden incarnation. And what was he supposed to do with it now, this unbidden goddess come skimming up on her scallop shell out of an innocent sea? But what else was there to do, save smile crookedly and scratch his head and squint at the window, pretending to be Heinrich, and say: "Well, married, yes, that's . . . that's . . ."

Regina was blushing.

"It will seem that we have come upon it suddenly, I know," she said, "and may be we have. But I—*we*—have decided, and so there seems no reason to delay." The colour deepened on her brow. "There is not," a rapid mumble, "there is not a *necessity* to hurry, as *she* will think, and no doubt say."

"She?"

"She, yes, who will make a great commotion."

The business was already accomplished in his head, he saw it before him like a tableau done in heraldic hues, the solemn bride and her tall grim groom, a pennant flying and the sky pouring down fat beneficent rays behind the scroll announcing *factum est!* and below, in a draughty underworld all to himself, Kepler inconsolabilis crouched with the hoof of a hunchbacked devil treading on his neck. He turned warily from the window. Regina had been watching him eagerly, but now she dropped her gaze and considered her hands clasped before her. She was smiling, amused at herself and embarrassed, but proud too, as if she had brought off some marvellous but all the same faintly ridiculous feat.

"I wanted to ask you," she said, "if you would—"

"Yes?" and something, before he could capture it, swooped out at her on the vibrating wings of that little word. She frowned, studying him with a closer attention; had she, O my

God, felt that fevered wingbeat brush her cheek?

"You do not . . . approve?" she said.

"I I I—"

"Because I thought that you would, I hoped that you would, and that you might speak to her for me, for us."

"Your mother? Yes yes I will speak to her, of course," lunging past her, talking as he went, and, pausing on the stairs: "Of course, speak to her, yes, tell her . . . tell her what?"

She peered at him in perplexity from the doorway. "Why, that I plan to marry."

"Ah yes. That you plan to marry. Yes."

"I think you do not approve."

"But of course I . . . of course . . ." and he clambered backwards down the stairs, clasping in his outstretched arms an enormous glossy black ball of sorrow and guilt.

*   *   *

Barbara was kneeling at the fireplace changing the baby's diaper, her face puckered against the clayey stink. Ludwig below her waved his skinny legs, crowing. She glanced over her shoulder at Kepler. "I thought as much," was all she said.

"You knew? But who is the fellow?"

She sighed, sitting back on her heels. "You have met him," she said wearily. "You don't remember, of course. He was in Prague, you met him."

"Ah, I remember." He did not. "Certainly I remember." How tactful Regina was, to know he would have forgotten. "But she is so young!"

"I was sixteen when I first married. What of it?" He said nothing. "I am surprised you care."

He turned away from her angrily, and opening the kitchen door was confronted by a hag in a black cap. They stared at each other and she backed off in confusion. There was another one at the kitchen table, very fat with a moustache, a mug of beer before her. His mother was busy at the iron stove. "Katharina," the first hag warbled. The fat one studied him a moment impassively and swigged her beer. The tomcat,

103

sitting to attention on the table near her, flicked its tail and blinked. Frau Kepler did not turn from the stove. Kepler silently withdrew, and slowly, silently, closed the door.

"Heinrich—!"

"Now they're just some old dames that come to visit her, Johann." He grinned ruefully and shoved his hands into the pockets of his breeches. "They are company for her."

"Tell me the truth, Heinrich. Is she ..." Barbara had paused, leaning over the baby with a pin in her mouth; Kepler took his brother's arm and steered him to the window. "Is she still at that old business?"

"No, no. She does a bit of doctoring now and then, but that's all."

"My God."

"She doesn't want for custom, Johann. They still come, especially the women." He grinned again, and winked, letting one eyelid fall like a loose shutter. "Only the other day there was a fellow—"

"I don't—"

"—Blacksmith he was, big as an ox, came all the way over from Leonberg, you wouldn't have thought to look at him there was anything—"

"I do not want to know, Heinrich!" He stared through the window, gnawing a thumbnail. "My God," he muttered again.

"Ah, there's nothing in it," said Heinrich. "And she's better value than your fancy physicians, I can tell you." Resentment was making him hoarse, Kepler noted wistfully: why had such simple loyalty been denied to *him*? "She made up a stuff for my leg that did more for it than that army doctor ever did."

"Your leg?"

"Aye, there's a weeping wound that I got in Hungary. It's not much."

"You must let me look at it for you."

Heinrich glanced at him sharply. "No need for that. She takes care of it."

Their mother shuffled out of the kitchen. "Now where," she murmured, "where did I leave that down, I wonder." She pointed her thin little nose at Barbara. "Have you seen it?"

104

Barbara ignored her.

"What is it, mother," Kepler said.

She smiled innocently. "Why, I had it just a moment ago, and now I have lost it, my little bag of bats' wings."

A crackling came from the kitchen, where the two hags could be seen, shrieking and hilariously shoving each other. Even the cat might have been laughing.

*   *   *

Regina came tentatively down the stairs. "You are not fighting over me, surely?" They looked at her blankly. Frau Kepler, grinning, scuttled back into the kitchen.

"What does she mean, bats' wings?" said Barbara.

"A joke," Kepler snapped, "a joke, for God's sake!"

"Bats' wings indeed. What next?"

"She's nobody's fool," Heinrich put in stoutly, trying not to laugh.

Kepler flung himself on to a chair by the window and drummed his fingers on the table. "We'll put up at an inn tonight," he muttered. "There is a place out toward Ellmendingen. And tomorrow we'll start for home."

Barbara smiled her triumph, but had the good sense to say nothing. Kepler scowled at her. The three old women came out of the kitchen. There was a fringe of foam on the fat one's moustache. The thin one made to address the great man sunk in gloom by the window, but Frau Kepler gave her a push from the rear. "O! hee hee, your ma, sir, I think, wants to be rid of us!"

"Bah," Frau Kepler said, and shoved her harder. They went out. "Well," the old woman said, turning to her son, "you've driven them away. Are you satisfied now?"

Kepler stared at her. "I said not a word to them."

"That's right."

"You would be better off if they did not come back, the likes of that."

"And what do you know about it?"

"I know them, I know their sort! You—"

105

"Ah, be quiet. What do you know, coming here with your nose in the air. We are not good enough for you, that's what it is."

Heinrich coughed. "Now mam. Johann is only talking to you for your own good."

Kepler considered the ceiling. "These are evil times, mother. You should be careful."

"And so should you!"

He shrugged. When he was a boy he had nursed the happy notion of them all perishing cleanly and quickly some night, in an earthquake, say, leaving him free and unburdened. Barbara was watching him, Regina also.

"We had a burning here last Michaelmas," said Heinrich, by way of changing the subject. "By God," slapping his knee, "the old dame fairly danced when the fire got going. Didn't she, mam?"

"Who was it?" said Kepler.

"Damned old fool it was," Frau Kepler put in quickly, glaring at Heinrich. "Gave a philtre to the pastor's daughter, no less. She deserved burning, that one."

Kepler put a hand over his eyes. "There will be more burnings."

His mother turned on him. "Aye, there will! And not only here. What about that place where you are, that Bohemia, with all those papists, eh? I've heard they burn people by the bushel over there. *You* should be careful." She stumped off into the kitchen. Kepler followed her. "Coming here and preaching to me," she muttered. "What do you know? I was healing the sick when you were no bigger than that child out there, cacking in your pants. And look at you now, living in the Emperor's pocket and drawing up magic squares for him. I dabble with the world, *you* keep your snout turned to the sky and think you're safe. Bah! You make me sick, you."

"Mother . . ."

"Well?"

"I worry for you, mother, that's all."

She looked at him.

*   *   *

106

All outside was immanent with a kind of stealthy knowingness. He stood for a while by the fountain in the marketplace. The stone gargoyles had an air of suppressed glee, spouting fatly from pursed green lips as if it were an elaborate foolery they would abandon once he turned his back. Grandfather Sebaldus used to insist that one of these stone faces had been carved in his likeness. Kepler had always believed it. Familiarity rose up all round him like a snickering ghost. What did he know? Was it possible for life to go on, his own life, without his active participation, as the body's engine continues to work while the mind sleeps? As he walked now he tried to weigh himself, squinting suspiciously at his own dimensions. looking for the telltale bulge where all that secret life might be stored. The murky emotions called forth by Regina's betrothal were only a part of it: what other extravagances had been contracted for, and at what cost? He felt somehow betrayed and yet not displeased, like an old banker ingeniously embezzled by a beloved son. A warm waft of bread assailed him as he passed by the baker's shop; the baker, all alone, was pummelling a gigantic wad of dough. From an upstairs window a servant girl flung out an exclamation of dirty water, barely missing Kepler. He glared up, and for a moment she goggled at him, then covered her mouth with her fingers and turned laughing to someone unseen behind her in the room, the son of the house, Harry Völiger, seventeen and prodigiously pimpled, creeping toward her with trembling hands ... Kepler walked on, brooding over all those years of deceptively balanced books.

He gained the common. The evening rested here, bronzed and quietly breathing, basking like an exhausted acrobat in the afterglow of marvellous exploits of light and weather. The elm tree hung intent above its own reflection in the pond, majestically listening. The children were still here. They greeted him with sullen glances, wishing not to know him: they had been having fun. Susanna slowly ambled away with her hands clasped behind her, smiling back in a kind of blissful idiocy at a file of confused and comically worried ducklings scrambling at her heels. Friedrich tottered to the water's edge carrying a mighty rock. His shoes and stockings were soaked, and he had managed to get mud on his eyebrows. The rock struck the water with a flat smack. "Look at the crown, papa, look look!—did you see it?"

"That's the king, all right," said Heinrich. He had come to fetch the children back. "He jumps up when you throw something in, and you can see his crown with all the diamonds on it. That right, Johann? I told him that."

"I don't want to go home," the child said, working one foot lovingly into the mud and plucking it out again with a delicious sucking sound. "I want to stay here with Uncle Heinrich and my grandma." His eyes narrowed thoughtfully. "They have a pig."

The surface of the pond smoothed down its ruffled silks. Tiny translucent flies were weaving an invisible net among the reflected branches of the elm, and skimmers dashed out from the shallows on legs so delicate they did not more than dent the surface of the water. Myriad and profligate life! Kepler sat on the grass. It had been a long day, busy with small discoveries. What was he to do about Regina? And what of his mother, dabbling still in dangerous arts? What was he to do. He remembered, as if the memory might mean something, Felix the Italian dancing with his drunken whores in a back lane on Kleinseit. The great noisome burden of things nudged him, life itself tipping his elbow. He smiled, gazing up into the branches. Was it possible, was this, was *this* happiness?

IV

———

Harmonice Mundi

David Fabricius: in Friesland

Honoured friend! you may abandon your search for a new theory of Mars: it is established. Yes, my book is done, or nearly. I have spent so much pains on it that I could have died ten times. But with God's help I have held out, and I have come so far that I can be satisfied and rest assured that the *new astronomy* truly is born. If I do not positively rejoice, it is not due to any doubts as to the truth of my discoveries, but rather to a vision that has all at once opened before me of the profound effects of what I have wrought. My friend, our ideas of the world & its workings shall never be the same again. This is a withering thought, and the cause in me of a sombre & reflective mood, in keeping with the general on this day. I enclose my wife's recipe for Easter cake as promised.

You, a colleague in arms, will know how things stand with me. Six years I have been in the heat & clamour of battle, my head down, hacking at the particular; only now may I stand back to take the wider view. That I have won, I do not doubt, as I say. My concern is, what manner of victory I have achieved, and what price I & our science, and perhaps all men, will have to pay for it. Copernicus delayed for thirty years before publishing his majestic work, I believe because he feared the effect upon men's minds of his having removed this Earth from the centre of the world, making it merely a planet among planets; yet what I have done is, I think, more radical still, for I have transformed the very shape of things—I mean of course I have demonstrated that the conception of celestial form & motion, which we have held since Pythagoras, is profoundly mistaken. The announcement of this news too will be delayed, not through any Copernican bashfulness of mine, but thanks to my master the Emperor's stinginess, which leaves me unable to afford a decent printer.

My aim in the *Astronomia nova* is, to show that the heavenly

111

machine is not a divine, living being, but a kind of clockwork (and he who believes that a clock has a soul, attributes to the work the maker's glory), insofar as nearly all the manifold motions are caused by a simple magnetic & material force, just as all the motions of the clock are caused by a simple weight. Yet, and most importantly, it is not the form or appearance of this celestial clockwork which concerns me primarily, but *the reality of it*. No longer satisfied, as I believe astronomy has been for milleniums, with the mathematical representation of planetary movement, I have sought to explain these movements *from their physical causes*. No one before me has ever attempted such a thing; no one has ever before framed his thoughts in this way.

Why, sir, you have a son! This is a great surprise to me. I put aside this letter briefly, having some pressing matters to attend to—my wife is ill again—and in the meantime from Wittenberg one Johannes Fabricius has written to me regarding certain solar phenomena, and recommending himself to me through my friendship for you, his father! I confess I am amazed, and not a little disturbed, for I have always spoken in my letters to you as to a younger man, and indeed, I wonder if I have not now and then fallen into the tone of a master addressing a pupil! You must forgive me. We should sometime have met. I think I am short of sight not only in the physical sense. Always I am being met with these shocks, when the thing before my nose turns out suddenly to be other than I believed it to be. Just so it was with the orbit of Mars. I shall write again and recount in brief the history of my struggle with that planet, it may amuse you.

Vale
Johannes Kepler

Hans Geo. Herwart von Hohenburg: at München

Entshuldigen Sie, my dear good sir, for my long delay in plying to your latest, most welcome letter. Matters at court devour my time & energies, as always. His Majesty becomes daily more capricious. At times he will forget my name, and look at me with that frown, which all who know him know so well, as if he does not recognise me at all; then suddenly will come an urgent summons, and I must scamper up to the palace with my star charts & astrological tables. For he puts much innocent faith in this starry scrying, which, as you know well, I consider a dingy business. He demands written reports upon various matters, such as for instance the nativity of the Emperor Augustus and of Mohammed, and the fate which is to be expected for the Turkish Empire, and, of course, that which so exercises everyone at court these days, the Hungarian question: his brother Matthias grows ever more brazen in his pursuit of power. Also there is the tiresome matter of the so-called Fiery Trigon and the shifting of the Great Conjunction of Jupiter & Saturn, which is supposed to have marked the birth of Christ, and of Charlemagne, and, now that another 800 years have passed, everyone asks what great event impends. I ventured that this *great event* had already occurred, in the coming of Kepler to Prague: but I do not think His Majesty appreciated the witticism.

In this atmosphere, the New Star of three years past caused a mighty commotion, which still persists. There is talk, as you would expect, of universal conflagration and the Judgment Day. The least that will be settled for, it seems, is the coming of a great new king: *nova stella, novus rex* (this last a view which no doubt Matthias encourages!). Of course, I must produce much wordage on this matter also. It is a painful & annoying work. The mind accustomed to mathematical demonstrations, on contemplating the faultiness of the foundations of astrology, resists for a long, long time, like a stubborn beast of burden, until, compelled by blows & invective, it puts its foot into the puddle.

My position is delicate. Rudolph is fast in the hands of wizards & all manner of mountebank. I consider astrology a political more than a prophetical tool, and that one should take care, not only that it be banished from the senate, but from the heads of those who would advise the Emperor in his best interests. Yet what am I to do, if he insists? He is virtually a hermit now in the palace, and spends his days alone among his toys and his pretty monsters, hiding from the humankind which he fears and distrusts, unwilling to make the simplest of decisions. In the mornings, while the groom puts his Spanish & Italian steeds through their paces in the courtyard, he sits gloomily watching from the window of his chamber, like an impotent infidel ogling the harem, and then speaks of this as his *exercise*! Yet, despite all, he is I confess far from ineffective. He seems to operate by a certain Archimedian motion, which is so gentle it barely strikes the eye, but which in the course of time produces movement in the entire mass. The court functions somehow. Perhaps it is just the nervous energy, common to all organisms, which keeps things going, as a chicken will continue to caper after its head has been cut off. (This is treasonous talk.)

My salary, need I say, is badly in arrears. I estimate that I am owed by now some 2,000 florins. I have scant hope of ever seeing the debt paid. The royal coffers are almost exhausted by the Emperor's mania for collecting, as well as by the war with the Turks and his efforts to protect his territories against his turbulent relatives. It pains me to be dependent upon the revenues from my wife's modest fortune. My hungry stomach looks up like a little dog to the master who once fed it. Yet, as ever, I am not despondent, but put my trust in God & my science. The weather here is atrocious.

Your servant, sir,
Joh: Kepler

Dr Michael Mästlin: at Tübingen

Greetings. That swine Tengnagel. I can hardly hold this pen, I am so angry. You will not credit the depths of that man's perfidy. Of course, he is no worse than the rest of the accursed Tychonic gang—only louder. A braying ass the fellow is, vain, pompous & irredeemably stupid. I will *kill* him, God forgive me. The only bright spot in all the horrid darkness of this business is that he still has not been paid, nor is he ever likely to be, the 20,000 florins (or 30 pieces of silver!) for which he sold Tycho Brahe's priceless instruments to the Emperor while the Dane was not yet cold in his grave. (He receives 1,000 florins annually as interest on the debt. This is twice the amount of my salary as Imperial Mathematician.) I confess that, when Tycho died, I quickly took advantage of the lack of circumspection on the part of the heirs, by taking his observations under my care, or, you may say (and certainly *they* do), purloining them. Who will blame me? The instruments, once the wonder of the world, are scattered across half of Europe, rusted and falling to pieces. The Emperor has forgotten them, and Tengnagel is content with his annual 5 per cent. Should I have let the same fate befall the mass of wonderfully precise & invaluable observations which Tycho devoted his lifetime to gathering?

The cause of this quarrel lies in the suspicious nature & bad manners of the Brahe family, but, on the other hand, also in my own passionate & mocking character. It must be admitted, that Tengnagel all along has had good reason for suspecting me: I was in possession of the observations, and I did refuse to hand them over to the heirs. But there is no reason for him to hound me as he does. You know that he became a Catholic, in order that the Emperor might grant him a position at court? This shows the man's character for what it is. (His lady Elizabeth goads him on—but no, I shall not speak of her.) Now he is Appellate Counsellor, and hence is able to impose his conditions on me with imperial force. He forbade me to print anything based upon his father-in-law's observations before I had completed the Rudolphine Tables; then he offered me freedom to print, provided I put his name with my own on the title pages of my works, so that he might have half the honours with none of the labour. I agreed, if he would grant me one quarter of that 1,000 florins he has from the Emperor. This was a shrewd move on my part, for Tengnagel, of course, true to his nature, considered the sum of 250 per annum too high a price to pay for immortal fame. Next, he got it into his thick head that he would himself take on the mighty task of completing the Tables. You will laugh with me, magister, for of course this is a nonsense, since the Junker has neither the ability for the task, nor the tenacity of purpose it will require. I have noticed it before, that there are many who believe they could do as well as I, nay, better, had they the time & the interest to attend the trifling problems of astronomy. I smile to hear them blowing off, all piss & wind. Let them try!

Luckily Tengnagel was vain enough to promise the Emperor that he would complete the work in four years: during which time he has sat upon the material like the dog in the manger, unable to put the treasure to use, and preventing others from doing so. His four years are now gone, and he has done nothing. Therefore I am pressing ahead with my *Astronomia nova*, the printing of which has at last begun at Vogelin's in Heidelberg. Good enough. But now the dolt insists that the book shall carry a preface written & signed by him! I dare not think what twaddle he will produce. He claims he fears I have used Tycho's observations only in order to disprove the Dane's theory of the world, but I know all he cares for is the clinking of coins. Ach, a base & poisonous fool.

K

Helisaeus Röslin, physician-in-ordinary to Hanau-Lichtenberg: at Buchsweiler in Alsace

A ve. I have your interesting & instructive *Discurs von heutiger Zeit Beschaffenheir*, which provokes in me, along with much speculation, many pleasant & wistful memories of those fraternal debates which engaged us in our student days together at Tübingen. I intend presently to reply with a public *Antwort* on those of my points on the Nova of 1604 which you challenge with such passion & skill, but first I wish to say a few words to you in private, not only in honour of our long friendship, but also in order to clarify certain matters which I may not air in print. For my position here in Prague grows more precarious daily. The royal personage no longer trusts anyone, and is particularly watchful concerning that science which you so energetically defend, and by which he puts much store. I would prefer to say *pseudo-science*. Please destroy this letter immediately you have read it.

I would grant in you, my dear Röslin, the presence of an *instinctus divinus*, a special illumination in the interpretation of celestial phenomena, which, however, has nothing to do with astrological rules. After all, it is true that God sometimes allows even pure simpletons to announce strange & wonderful things. No one should deny that clever & even holy things may come out of foolery & godlessness, as out of unclean & slimy substances comes the pretty snail or the oyster, or the silk-spinner out of caterpillar dirt. Even from the stinking dung heap the industrious hen may scrape a little golden grain. The majority of astrological rules I consider to be dung; as to what may be the grains worth retrieving from the heap, that is a more difficult matter.

The essence of my position is simply stated: that the heavens do something in people one sees clearly enough, but what specifically they do, remains a mystery. I believe that the *aspects*, that is the configurations which the planets form with one another, are of special significance in the lives of men. However, I hold that to speak of good & bad aspects is nonsensical. In the heavens it is not a question of good or bad: here only the categories harmonic, rhythmic, lovely, strong, weak & unarranged, are valid. The stars do not compel, they do not do away with free will, they do not decide the particular fate of an individual; but they impress on the soul a particular character. The person in the first igniting of his life receives a character & pattern of all the constellations in the heavens, or of the form of the rays flowing on to the earth, which he retains to the grave. This character creates noticeable traces in the form of the flesh, as well as in manners & gestures, inclinations & sympathies. Thus one becomes lively, good, gay; another sleepy, indolent, obscurantist; qualities which are comparable to the lovely & exact, or the extensive & unsightly configurations, and to the colours & movements, of the planets.

But upon what are based these categories, lovely & unlovely, strong & weak, et cetera? Why, upon the division of circles made by the knowable, that is constructable, regular polygons, as for instance is set out in my *Mysterium cosmographicum*; that is, the harmonic primordial relationships foreshadowed in the divine being. Thus all animated things, human & otherwise, as well as all the vegetable world, are influenced from heaven by the appropriate geometric instinct pertaining to them. All their activities are affected, individually shaped & guided by the light rays present here below and sensed by all these objects, as well as by the geometry & harmony which occurs between them by virtue of their motion, in the same way as the flock is affected by the voice of the shepherd, the horses on a wagon by the driver's shout, and the dance of the peasant by the skirl of the bagpipes. *This* is what I believe, and none of your monkeyshine will convince me otherwise.

I trust this frank German talk has not offended you, my dear Röslin. You live in my affections always, though sometimes I may snap & snarl, as if the habit of

> your friend and colleague,
> Johannes Kepler

Frau Katharina & Heinrich Kepler: at Weilderstadt
(To be read in their presence by G. Raspe, notary. Fee enclosed.)

Loved ones: I write to say that we have arrived home safely & well. Friedrich has a cough, but otherwise remains strong. Preparations for our dear Regina's wedding are already well advanced: she is wonderfully capable in matters such as these. Her intended husband is a fine & honourable man, and well set up. He came this week to pay us his respects. Of course, he has been here before, but not as a betrothed. I find him somewhat formal, and wonder if he may not prove inflexible. Everything was most polite. I have no doubt that Regina will be well treated by him, and will be happy, perhaps. They move to Pfaffenhofen in the Upper Palatinate after the wedding. There is talk of plague there.

We are still in our rooms in the old Cramer Buildings, and I think must remain here for the present. The quarters are satisfactory, for we are on the bridge, and so have the benefit of the river. The building is of stone, therefore there is less danger of fires breaking out, a thing I have always feared, as you know. Also we are situated in a good part of the city. At Wenzel College in the Old Town, where we lived before, things were very different: the streets there are bad, ill-paved and always strewn with every kind of filth, the houses are bad, roofed with straw or wattles, and there is a stink that would drive back the Turk. Our landlord here, though, is an unmannerly ruffian, and I have many differences with him, which upsets my digestion. Barbara tells me not to mind him. Why is it, I wonder, that people behave so badly toward each other? What is to be gained by fretting & fighting? I think there are some in the world who must sustain themselves by making their fellow men suffer. This is as true for the landlord who hounds his tenants, as it is for the infidel torturing his slaves to death: only the degree of evil differs, not the quality. These are the things I

119

think about, when my duties at court and my scientific studies allow me time to think at all. Not that I do much scientific work now, for my health is not good, with frequent fevers and an inflammation of the bowel, and my mind for the most part prostrate in a pitiful frost. But I do not complain. God is good.

We move in the midst of a distinguished society here in Prague. The Imperial Counsellor and First Secretary, Johann Polz, is very fond of me. His wife & his whole family are conspicuous for their Austrian elegance and their distinguished & noble manners. It would be due to their influence, if on some future day I were to make progress in this respect, though, of course, I am still far away from it (there is a difference between being a renowned mathematician and being great in society!). Yet notwithstanding the shabbiness of my household and my low rank, I am free to come & go in the Polz house as I please — and they are considered to belong to the nobility! I have other connections. The wives of two imperial guards acted as godmothers at Susanna's baptism. Stefan Schmid, the Imperial Treasurer; Matthäus Wackher, the Court Barrister; and His Excellency Joseph Hettler, the Baden Ambassador, all stood for our Friedrich. And at the ceremonies for little Ludwig, the Counts Palatine Philip Ludwig & his son Wolfgang Wilhelm von Pfalz-Neuburg were present. So you see, we are beginning to rise in the great world! All the same, I do not forget my own people. I think of you often, and worry for your well-being. You must take care of each other, and be kind. Mother, think on my warnings when last we spoke. Heinrich, cherish your mother. And in your prayers remember

your son & brother,
Johann

(Herr Raspe, for your eyes only: watch Frau Kepler's doings, as I requested, and keep me informed. I shall pay you for these services.)

Signor Prof. Giorgio Antonio Magini: at Bologna

It is as if one had woken up to find two suns in the sky. That is only, of course, a way of putting it. Two suns would be a miracle, or magic, whereas *this* has been wrought by human eye and mind. It seems to me that there are times when, suddenly, after centuries of stagnation, things begin to flow all together as it were with astonishing swiftness, when from all sides streams spring up and join their courses, and this great confluence rushes on like a mighty river, carrying upon its flood all the broken & pathetic wreckage of our misconceptions. Thus, it is not a twelvemonth since I published my *Astronomia nova*, changing beyond recognition our notion of celestial workings: and now comes this news from Padua! Doubtless you in Italy are already familiar with it, and I know that even the most amazing things can come to seem commonplace in only a little time; for us, however, it is still new & wonderful & somewhat frightening.

Word was brought to me first by my friend Matthäus Wackher, Court Barrister & Privy Counsellor to His Majesty, who had it from the Tuscan Ambassador lately arrived here. Whackher came to see me at once. The day was bright and blustery, with a promise of spring, I will remember it always, as one remembers only a handful of days out of a lifetime. I saw, from the window of my study, the Counsellor's carriage come clattering over the bridge, and old Wackher with his head stuck out at the window, urging the driver on. Does excitement such as his that day send out before it palpable emanations? For even as I watched him coming, I felt nervous stirrings within me, though I knew nothing of what he had to tell me. I ran down and met the carriage arriving at my door. Herr Wackher was already babbling at me before I could grasp it. Galileus of Padua had turned upon the night sky a two-lensed *perspicillum*—a common Dutch spyglass, in fact—and by means of its 30-times magnification, *had discovered four new planets.*

I experienced a wonderful emotion while I listened to this curious tale. I felt moved in my deepest being. Wackher was full of joy & feverish excitement. At one moment we both laughed in our confusion, the next he continued his narrative and I listened intently—there was no end to it. We clasped hands and danced together, and Wackher's little dog, which he had brought with him, ran about in circles barking shrilly, until, overcome by our hilarity and quite beside itself, it jumped up and clasped me amorously about the leg, as dogs will, licking its lips and insanely grinning, which made us laugh the harder. Then we went inside and sat down, calmer now, over a jug of ale.

Is the report true? And if so, of what type are these newly discovered heavenly bodies? Are they companions of fixed stars, or do they belong to our solar system? Herr Wackher, though a Catholic, holds to the view of the misfortunate Bruno, that the stars are suns, infinite in number, which fill the infinite space, and Galileo's discovery, he believes, is proof of it, the four new bodies being companions of fixed stars: in other words, that it is another solar system that the Paduan has found. To me, however, as you know, an infinite universe is unthinkable. Also I consider it impossible that these are planets circling our sun, since the geometry of the world set forth in my *Mysterium* will allow of five planets in the solar system, and no more. Therefore I believe that what Galileo has seen are *moons circling other planets*, as our moon circles the earth. This is the only feasible explanation.

Perhaps you, closer to the scene of these discoveries, already have heard the correct explanation—perhaps even you have witnessed the new phenomena! Ah, to be in Italy. The Tuscan envoy, de Medici, who gave this news to Wackher, has presented to the Emperor a copy of Galileo's book. I hope soon to get my hands on it. Then we shall see!

Write, tell me all the news!
Kepler

George Fugger, legatus imperatorius: *at Venice*

Lest silence & delay should make you believe that I agree with all you have to say in your latest letter, and since your position is peculiarly relevant in these matters, Galileo being in the employ of the Venetian Republic, I thought it prudent to interrupt my present studies and write to you straightway. Believe me, my dear Sir, I am deeply touched by your remarks regarding the claims to pre-eminence as between the Paduan & myself. However, I am not running a foot-race with him, that I should want for cheering & partisan broadcasting. Certainly, it is true what you say, that he urgently requires in these discoveries & claims of his the blessing of the Imperial Mathematician; and perhaps indeed this is, as you maintain, the only reason he has approached me. But why not? Some dozen years ago, before I was famous, and my *Mysterium* had just been published, it was *I* approaching *him*. True, he did not at that time make any great effort on my behalf. Perhaps he was too much taken up with his own work, perhaps he did not think much of my little book. Yes, I know his reputation for arrogance & ingratitude: what of it? Science, Sir, is not like diplomacy, does not progress by nods & winks & well-wrought compliments. It has always been my habit to praise what, in my opinion, others have done well. Never do I scorn other people's work because of jealousy, never do I belittle others' knowledge when I lack it myself. Likewise I never forget myself when I have done something better, or discovered something sooner. Certainly, I had hoped for much from Galileo when my *Astronomia nova* appeared, but the fact that I received nothing will not prevent me now from taking up my pen so that he should be armed against the sour-tempered critics of everything new, who consider unbelievable that which is unknown to them, and regard as terrible wickedness whatever lies beyond the customary bounds of Aristotelian philosophy. I have no wish to *pull out his feathers*, as you put it, but only to acknowledge what is of value, and question that which is doubtful.

No one, Excellency, should allow himself to be misled by the brevity & apparent simplicity of Galileo's little book. The *Sidereus nuncius* is highly significant & admirable, as even a glance through its pages will show. It is true that not everything in it is wholly original, as he claims—the Emperor himself has already turned a spyglass upon the moon! Also, others have surmised, even if they have not provided proof, that the Milky Way would, on closer inspection, dissolve into a mass of innumerable stars gathered together in clusters. Even the existence of planetary satellites (for this is, I believe, what his *four new planets* are, in fact) is not so amazing, for does not the moon circle the earth, and hence why should not the other planets have their moons? But there is a great difference between speculating on the existence of a myriad of invisible stars, and noting their positions on a map; between peering vacantly through a lens at the moon, and announcing that it is composed not of the *quinta essentia* of the schoolmen, but of matter much like that of the earth. Copernicus was not the first to hold that the sun sits at the centre of the world, but he *was* the first to build around that concept a system which would hold good mathematically, thus putting an end to the Ptolemaic age. Likewise Galileo, in this pamphlet, has set down clearly & calmly (and with a calm precision from which, I ruefully admit, I could learn much!) a vision of the world which will deliver such a blow to the belly of the Aristotelians that I think they will be winded for a long time to come.

The *Sidereus nuncius* is much talked about at court, as by now I suppose it is everywhere. (Would that the *Astronomia nova* had attracted such attention!) The Emperor graciously let me glance through his copy, but otherwise I had to contain myself as best I could until a week ago, when Galileo himself sent me the book, along with a request for my opinion on it, which I suppose he wishes to publish. The courier returns to Italy on the 19th, which leaves me just four days in which to complete my reply. Therefore I must close now, in the hope that you will forgive my haste—and also that you will not take amiss my response above to your touching & much appreciated gestures of support for me. In these matters of science, it is a question, you see, not of the individual, but of the work. I do not like

Galileo, but I must admire him.

By the way, I wonder, during your recent time in Rome, did you see or hear anything of Tycho's dwarf, and his companion, the one called Felix? I would have news of them, if you know any.

                    I am, Sir, your servant,
                        Johannes Kepler

Dr Johannes Brengger: at Kaufbeuren

Everything darkens, and we fear the worst. In the little world of our house, a great tragedy has befallen, which, in the morbid confusion of our grief, we cannot help but believe is in some way connected with the terrible events in the wider world. I think there are times when God grows weary, and then the Devil, seizing his chance, comes flying down upon us with all his fury & cruel mischievousness, wreaking havoc high & low. How far away now, my dear Doctor, seem those happier days when we corresponded with such enthusiasm & delight on the matter of our newborn science of optics! Thank you for your latest letter, but I fear I am unable at present to engage the interesting questions which you pose—another time, perhaps, I shall turn my mind upon them, and reply with the vigour they demand. I have not the heart for work now. Also much of my time is consumed by duties at court. The Emperor's eccentricities have come to seem more & more like plain insanity. He immures himself in the palace, hiding from the sight of his loathed fellow men, while in the meantime his realm falls asunder. Already his brother Matthias has dispossessed him of Austria, Hungary & Moravia, and is even now preparing to take over what is left. Throughout last summer and into the autumn, a congress of princes was held here in the city, which urged reconciliation between the brothers. Rudolph, however, despite his whimsy & his peculiarities, displays an iron stubbornness. Thinking to curb both Matthias & the princes, and also perhaps to set aside the religious freedoms wrested from him in the Royal Charter by the Lutheran Representatives here, he plotted with his kinsman Leopold, Bishop of Passau & brother to the poisonous Archduke Ferdinand of Styria, my old enemy. Leopold, of course, as vile & treacherous as the rest of his family, turned his army against us here, and has occupied part of the city. Bohemian troops massed against him, and frightful excesses by both sides are reported. Matthias, it is said, is now on his way here with an Austrian army, at the request of the Representatives—and of Rudolph himself! There can be only one result of all this, that the Emperor will lose his throne, and so I have begun to look elsewhere for a refuge. Certain influential people have urged me to come to Linz. For my own part, I cannot help but look with longing toward my native Swabia. I have sent a petition to the Duke of Württemberg, my sometime patron, but I have scant faith in him. Hard it is to know that one is not wanted in one's homeland! Also I have been offered Galileo's old chair at Padua, following his departure for Rome. Galileo has himself recommended me. The irony of this does not escape me. Italy—I do not relish the thought. Linz would seem, therefore, the most promising prospect. It is a narrow & provincial town, but there are people there whom I know, as well as a special friend. My wife would be happy to leave Prague, which she has never liked, and return to her native Austria. She has been most ill, with Hungarian fever & epilepsy. She bore these afflictions with fortitude, and all might have been well with her, had not our three children shortly thereafter been seized with the small-pox. The eldest one and the youngest survived, but Friedrich, our darling son, succumbed. He was six. It was a hard death. He was a fair child, a hyacinth of the morning in the first days of spring, our hope, our joy. I confess, Doctor, I fail sometimes to understand the ways of God. Even as the boy lay on his death bed, we could hear from across the city the noise of battle. How may I adequately express to you my feelings? Grief such as this is like nothing else in the world. I must close now.

Kepler

Frau Regina Ehem: at Pfaffenhofen

O, my dear Regina! in the face of these disasters which have befallen us, words are inapt, and silence the truest expression of feelings. Nevertheless, however things stand with me, you must have an account of these past weeks. If I am clumsy, or seem heartless or cold, I know you will understand that it is sorrow & shame which prevent me from expressing adequately all that I feel.

Who can say when was the real beginning of your mother's illness? Hers was a life crowded with difficulties & sadness. It is true, she never wanted for material things, however much she would blame me for my lack of success in the great world of society which it was ever her dream of entering. But to have been twice a widow by the age of 22, surely that was hard, as was the loss of our firstborn infants, and now our beloved Freidrich. Lately she had taken to secret devotions, and was never to be seen without her prayer book. Also her memory was not what it had been, and sometimes she would laugh at nothing at all, or suddenly cry out as if stricken. Her envy also had increased, and she was forever bemoaning her lot, comparing herself to the wives of councillors & petty court officials, who seemed to move in far greater splendour than she, the wife of the Imperial Mathematician. All this was in her mind only, of course. What could I do?

Her illness of last winter, that fever & the falling sickness, frightened me greatly, but she was very brave & strong, with a determination which astonished all who knew her. The child's death in February was a terrible blow. When I returned from a visit to Linz at the end of June, I found her ill again. The Austrian troops had brought diseases into the city, and she had contracted spotted typhus, or *fleckfieber*, as they call it here. She might have fought back, but her strength was gone. Stunned by the deeds of horror of the soldiery & the sight of the bloody fighting in the city, consumed by despair of a better future and

128

by the unquenchable yearning for her darling lost son, she finally expired, on the 3rd day of this month. As a clean smock was being put on her, at the end, her last words were to ask, Is this the dress of salvation? She remembered you in her final hours, and spoke of you often.

I am gnawed by guilt & remorse. Our marriage was blighted from the start, made as it was against our wills and under a calamitous sky. She was of a despondent & resentful nature. She accused me of laughing at her. She would interrupt my work to discuss her household problems. I may have been impatient when she went on asking me questions, but I never called her a fool, though it may have been her understanding that I considered her such, for she was very sensitive, in some ways. Lately, due to her repeated illnesses, she was deprived of her memory, and I made her angry with my reminders & admonitions, for she would have no master, and yet often was unable to cope herself. Often I was even more helpless than she, but in my ignorance persisted in the quarrel. In short, she was of an increasingly angry nature, and I provoked her, I regret it, but sometimes my studies made me thoughtless. Was I cruel to her? When I saw that she took my words to heart, I would rather have bitten off my own finger than give her further offence. As for me, not much love came my way. Yet I did not hate her. And now, you know, I have no one to talk to.

Think of me, my dear child, and pray for me. I have transferred to this inn—you remember the Golden Griffin?—for I could not abide the house. The nights are the hardest, and I do not sleep. What shall I do? I am a widower, with two young children, and all about is the turbulent disorder of war. I shall visit you, if possible. Would that you could come to see me here, but the perils would be too great. I sign myself, as in the old days,

Papa

Post scriptum. I have opened your mother's will. She left me nothing. My regards to your husband.

Johannes Fabricius: at Wittenberg

Greetings, noble son of a noble father. You must forgive me
for my long delay in replying to your numerous most
welcome & fascinating letters. I have been these past months
much taken up with business, both private & public. No doubt
you are aware of the momentous events that have occurred in
Bohemia, events which, along with all their other effects,
have led to my virtual banishment from Prague. I am here at
Kunstadt briefly, at the house of an old acquaintance of my late
wife, a good-hearted widow woman who has offered to care
for my motherless children until I have found quarters and
settled in at Linz. Yes, it is Linz I am bound for, where I am to
take up the post of district mathematician. You see how low I
am brought.

The year that has passed has been the worst I have ever
known; I pray I shall never see another such. Who would
believe that so many misfortunes could befall a man in so short a
time? I lost my beloved son, and then my wife. You would say,
this were enough, but it seems that when disasters come, they
come in dreadful armies. It was the entry of the Passau troops to
Prague that brought the diseases which took from me my little
son & my wife; then came the Archduke Matthias & his men,
and my patron & protector was toppled from his throne:
Rudolph, that poor, sad, good man! I did my best to save him.
Both sides in the dispute were much influenced by star pro-
phecies, as soldiers & statesmen always are, and, as Imperial
Mathematician & Court Astronomer, my services were
eagerly sought. Although in truth my best interests would
have been served had I thrown in my lot with his enemies, I was
loyal to my lord, and went so far as to pretend to Matthias that
the stars favoured Rudolph. It was to no avail, of course. The
outcome of that battle was determined before it began. Following his abdication in May, I remained at Rudolph's side. He had
been good to me, despite all, and how could I abandon him?
The new Emperor is not hostile to me, and only last month

went so far as to confirm me in my post of mathematicus. Matthias, however, is no Rudolph; I shall be better off in Linz.

I shall be better off: so I tell myself. At least in Upper Austria there are people who value me & my work. That is more than can be said of my fellow countrymen. Perhaps you know of my efforts to return to Germany? Recently I turned again to Frederick of Württemburg, begging him to grant me, if not a professorship of philosophy, at least some humble political post, in order that I might have some peace & a little space in which calmly & quietly to pursue my studies. The Chancellor's office was not unsympathetic, and even suggested I might be put in line for the chair of mathematics at Tübingen, since Dr Mästlin is old. The Consistory, however, took a different view. They remembered that, in a former petition, I had been honest enough to warn that I could not unconditionally subscribe to the Formula of Concord. Also they dragged out the old accusation that I lean toward Calvinism. The end of it all is that I am finally rejected by my native land. Forgive me, but I hereby consign them all to the pits of Hell.

I am 41, and I have lost everything: my family, my honoured name, even my country. I face now into a new life, not knowing what new troubles await me. Yet I do not despair. I have done great work, which some day shall be recognised for its true value. My task is not yet finished. The vision of the harmony of the world is always before me, calling me on. God will not abandon me. I shall survive. I keep with me a copy of that engraving by the great Dürer of Nuremberg, which is called Knight with Death & the Devil, an image of stoic grandeur & fortitude from which I derive much solace: for this is how one must live, facing into the future, indifferent to terrors and yet undeceived by foolish hopes.

I enclose an old letter which I found unposted among my papers. It concerns matters of scientific interest, and you should have it, for I fancy it will be some little time before I have the heart to turn again to such speculations.

Your colleague,
Joh: Kepler

Johannes Fabricius: at Wittenberg

Ah, my dear young sir, how happy I am to hear of your researches into the nature of these mysterious solar spots. Not only am I filled with admiration for the rigour & ingenuity of your investigations, but also I am carried back out of these hateful times to a happier period of my own life. Can it be only five years ago? Lucky I, who was the first in this century to have observed these spots! I say this, not in an attempt to steal your fire, if I may put it thus (nor even do I mean to join the tiresome controversy between Scheiner & Galileo over the priority of the discovery), but only to convince myself that there was a time when I could happily, and, one might say, in innocence, pursue my scientific studies, before the disasters of this terrible year had befallen me.

I first observed the phenomenon of solar spots in May of 1607. For weeks I had been earnestly observing Mercury in the evening sky. According to calculations, that planet was to enter into lower conjunction with the sun on May 29th. Since a heavy storm arose in the evening of the 27th, and it seemed to me this aspect would be the cause of such disturbance in the weather, I wondered if perhaps the conjunction should be fixed earlier. I therefore set to work to observe the sun on the afternoon of the 28th. At that time I had rooms at Wenzel College, where the Rector, Martin Bachazek, was my friend. A keen amateur, Bachazek had built a little wooden tower in one of the college lofts, and it was to there that he & I retired that day. Rays of the sun were shining through thin cracks in the shingles, and under one of these rays we held a piece of paper whereon the sun's image formed. And lo! on the shimmering picture of the sun we espied a little daub, quite black, approximately like a parched flea. Certain that we were observing a transit of Mercury, we were overcome with the greatest excitement. To prevent error, and to make sure it was not a mark in the paper itself, we kept moving the paper back & forth so that the light moved: and everywhere the little black spot appeared with the light. I drew up a report immediately, and had my colleague endorse it. I ran to the Hradcany, and sent the announcement to the Emperor by a valet, for of course this conjunction was of great interest to His Majesty. Then I repaired to the workshop of Jost Bürgi, the court mechanic. He was out, and so, with one of his assistants, I covered a window, letting the light shine through a small aperture in a tin plate. Again the little daub appeared. Again I sought verification for my report, and had Bürgi's assistant sign it. The document lies before me on my desk, and there is the signature: *Heinrich Stolle, watchmaker-journeyman, my hand*. How well I remember it all!

Of course, I was wrong, as so often; it was not a transit of Mercury I had witnessed, as you know, but a *sunspot*. Have you, I wonder, a theory as to the origin of this phenomenon? I have witnessed it often since that day, yet I have not decided to my own satisfaction what is the explanation. Perhaps they are a form of cloud, as in our own skies, but wonderfully black and heavy, and therefore easily to be seen. Or maybe they are emanations of burning gas rising from the fiery surface? For my own part, they are of the utmost interest not in their cause, but in that, by their form & evident motion, they prove satisfactorily the rotation of the sun, which I had postulated without proof in my *Astronomia nova*. I wonder that I could do so much in that book, without the aid of the telescope, which in your work you have put to such good use.

What should we do without our science? It is, even in these dread times, a great consolation. My master Rudolph grows stranger day by day: I think he will not live. Sometimes he seems not to understand that he is no longer emperor. I do not disabuse him of this dream. How sad a place the world is. Who would not rather ascend into the clear & silent heights of celestial speculation?

Please do not take my bad example to heart, but write to me soon again. I am, Sir,

yours,
Johannes Kepler

Frau Regina Ehem: at Pfaffenhofen

Life, so it used to seem to me, my dear Regina, is a formless & forever shifting stuff, a globe of molten glass, say, which we have been flung, and which, without even the crudest of instruments, with only our bare hands, we must shape into a perfect sphere, in order to be able to contain it within ourselves. That, so I thought, is our task here, I mean the transformation of the chaos without, into a perfect harmony & balance within us. Wrong, wrong: for our lives contain us, *we* are the flaw in the crystal, the speck of grit which must be ejected from the spinning sphere. It is said, that a drowning man sees all his life flash before him in the instant before he succumbs: but why should it be only so for death by water? I suspect it is true whatever the manner of dying. At the final moment, we shall at last perceive the secret & essential form of all we have been, of all our actions & thoughts. Death is the perfecting medium. This truth—for I believe it to be a truth—has manifested itself to me with force in these past months. It is the only answer that makes sense of these disasters & pains, these betrayals.

I will not hold you responsible, dear child, for our present differences. There are those about you, and one in particular, I know, who will not leave in peace even a bereaved & ailing man in his hour of agony. Your mother was hardly cold in her grave when that first imperious missive from your husband arrived, like a blow to the stomach, and now *you* write to me in this extraordinary fashion. This is not your tone of voice, which I remember with tenderness & love, this is not how you would speak to me, if the choice were yours. I can only believe that these words were dictated to you. Therefore, I am not now addressing you, but, through you, another, to whom I cannot bring myself to write directly. Let him prick up his ears. This squalid matter shall be cleared up to the satisfaction of all.

How can you insinuate that I am delaying in the payment of these monies? What do I care for mere cash, I, who have lost that

134

which was more precious to me than an emperor's treasury of gold, I mean my wife & my beloved son? That my lady Barbara chose not to mention me in her will is a profound hurt, but yet I intend to carry out her wishes. Although I have not the heart at the moment to investigate thoroughly how matters stand, I know in general the state of Frau Kepler's fortune, or what remains of it. When her father died, and the Mühleck estates were divided, she possessed some 3,000 florins in properties & goods. She was therefore not so rich as we had been led to believe—but that is another matter. I went with Frau Kepler to Graz at that time, when Jobst Müller had died, and spent no little time & pains in converting her inheritance into cash. Styrian taxes then were nothing less than punitive measures against Lutherans, and we suffered heavy losses in transferring her monies out of Austria. That is why there is not now those thousands which some people think I am trying to appropriate. Our life in Bohemia had been difficult, the Emperor was not the most prompt of paymasters, and inevitably, despite Frau Kepler's extreme parsimony, calls were made from time to time upon her capital. There were her many illnesses, the fine clothes which she insisted upon, and then, she was not one to be satisfied with beans & sausages. Do you imagine that we lived on air?

Also, after my marriage, I succeeded, against great opposition, in being appointed guardian of my wife's little daughter, our dear Regina, because I loved the child, as she was then, and because I feared that among her mother's people she would be exposed to the danger of Catholicism. I had been promised by Jobst Müller, 70 florins per annum for the child's maintenance: I was never paid a penny of that allowance, nor, of course, was I permitted to touch Regina's own considerable fortune. Therefore, I am fully justified in deducting from the inheritance a just & suitable recompense. I have two children of my own to care for. My friends & patrons, the House of Fugger, will oversee the transfer to you of the remaining sum. I trust you will not accuse *them* of suspect dealing?

Johannes Kepler

Dr Johannes Brengger: at Kaufbeuren

I have received today, from Markus Welser in Cologne, the first pages in proof of my *Dioptrice*. The printing has been delayed, and even now, when it has finally started, there is a problem with the financing of the project, and I fear it will be some long time before the work is completed. I finished it in August, and presented it at once to my patron, the Elector Ernst of Cologne, who unfortunately has proved less enthusiastic & less prompt than the author, and seems not to be in any hurry to give to the world this important work which is dedicated to him. However, I am glad to see even these few pages in print, since in my present troubled state I am grateful for the small diversion which they provide. How far away already seem those summer months, when my health looked to be improving, and I worked with such vigour. Now I am subject once more to bouts of fever, and consequently I have no energy, and am sore in spirit. Worries abound, and there are rumours of war. Yet, looking now afresh at the form of this little book, I am struck by the thought that perhaps, without realising it, I had some intimation of the troubles to come, for certainly it is a strange work, uncommonly severe & muted, wintry in tone, precise in execution. It is not like me at all.

It is a book that is not easy to understand, and which assumes not only a clever head, but also a particularly intellectual alertness & an extraordinary desire to learn the causes of things. In it I have set about clearing up the laws by which the Galilean telescope works. (I might add, that in this task I have had scant help, as you would expect, from him whose name is given to the new instrument.) It may be said, I believe, that between this book, and my *Astronomia pars optica* of 1604, I have laid the foundations of a new science. Whereas, however, the earlier book was a gay & speculative venturing upon the nature of light and the working of lenses, the *Dioptrice* is a sober setting out of rules, in the manner of a geometry manual. O, that I could send you a copy, for I am eager to hear your opinion. Damn these penny-pinchers! It is composed of 141 rules, schematically divided into definitions, axioms, problems & propositions. I begin with the law of refraction, the expression of which, I confess, is not much less inexact than previously, although I have managed not too badly by virtue of the fact that the angles of incidence dealt with are very small. I have also set out a description of total reflection of light rays in a glass cube & three-sided prism. As well, of course, I have gone more deeply than ever into the matter of lenses. In Problem 86, in which I demonstrate how, with the help of two convex lenses, visible objects can be made larger & distinct but inverted, I believe I have defined the principle upon which the astronomical telescope is based. Also, by treating of the suitable combinations of a converging lens with a diverging lens in place of a simple object lens, I have shown the way toward a large improvement upon the Galilean telescope. This will not please the Paduan, I think.

So you see, my dear Doctor, how far ahead I have pressed in our science. I think, indeed, that I have gone as far as it is possible to go, and I confess, with some regret, that I am losing interest in the subject. The telescope is a wonderfully useful instrument, and will no doubt prove of great service to astronomy. For my part, however, I grow tired rapidly of peering into the sky, no matter how wonderful the sights to be seen there. Let others map these new phenomena. My eyesight is bad. I am, I fear, no Columbus of the heavens, but a modest stay-at-home, an armchair dreamer. The phenomena with which I am already familiar are sufficiently strange & wonderful. If the new stargazers discover novel facts which will help to explain the true causes of things, fair enough; but it seems to me that the real answers to the cosmic mystery are to be found not in the sky, but in that other, infinitely smaller though no less mysterious firmament contained within the skull. In a word, my dear friend, I am old-fashioned; as I am also,

yours,
Kepler

Georg Fugger: at Venice

L et me yet again offer you my warm & sincerest thanks for
your loyal support of me & my work. I thank you also for
your kind words regarding my *Dissertatio cum nuncio sidero*, and
your efforts to promote in Italy the views expressed in that little
work. Yet, once more, I must protest at your too enthusiastic
championing of me against Galileo. I do not oppose him. My
Dissertatio does not, as you put it, *rip the mask from his face*. If you
read my pamphlet with attention, you will clearly see that I
have, with reservations, given my blessing to his findings.
Does this surprise you? Are you, perhaps, disappointed? How,
you will ask, can I be warm toward someone who will not even
deign to write to me directly? But as I have said before, I am a
lover of truth, and will welcome it & celebrate it, whatever
quarter it may come from. Sometimes I suspect that those who
concern themselves in this squabble over the reliability of
Galileo's findings, may in fact care less for the objective truth,
than they do for getting hold of ammunition to use against an
arrogant & clever man, and who is not subtle nor sly enough to
put on a false humility in order to please the general. That
young clown Martin Horky, Magini's assistant, in his so-
called *Refutation*, had the gall to quote me—no, to misquote
me, in support of his imbecile gibes against Galileo. I lost no
time in terminating my acquaintance with the young pup.

Still, I confess Galileo is difficult to love. You know, in all
this time he has written to me only one letter. For the rest, for
news of his further discoveries, and even for word of his reactions to my *Dissertatio* (which after all was an open letter directed to him!), I must depend on second-hand accounts from the
Tuscan Ambassador here, and other suchlike. And then, how
secretive & suspicious the Paduan is! When he does send me a
crumb, he hides it inside the most impossible & unnecessary of
disguises. For instance, last summer he sent, again through the
ambassador, the following message: *Smaismirmilmepoet-*

aleumibunenugttaurias. At first I was amused: after all, I myself sometimes play with anagrams & word games of this sort. However, when I set about deciphering the code, I was nearly driven out of my mind. The best I could manage was a bit of barbaric Latin verse that made no sense. It was not until last month—when Galileo had heard that the Emperor himself was curious—that the solution was furnished at last: hidden in that jumble was the announcement of the discovery of what appear to be two small moons circling Saturn! Now has come another puzzle, which seems to speak of a *red spot in Jupiter which rotates mathematically*. A red spot, I ask myself, or a red herring? How is one to respond to this kind of foolery? I shall scald the fellow's ears with my next letter.

And yet, what a splendid & daring scientist he is! O, that I could journey to Italy to meet this Titan! I will not have him sneered at, you know, in my presence. You mention how Magini & the dreadful Horky (nice name for him), and even you yourself, were delighted with the passage in the *Dissertatio* in which I mention that the principle of the telescope was set out 20 years ago by della Porta, and also in my own work on optics. But Galileo has not claimed the *invention* of the instrument! Besides, these anticipations were purely theoretical, and cannot diminish Galileo's fame. For I know what a long road it is from the theoretical concept to its practical achievement, from the mention of the Antipodes in Ptolemy to Columbus's discovery of the New World, and even more from the two-lensed instruments used in this country to the instrument with which Galileo has penetrated the skies.

Let me state, then, clearly and without equivocation, that my *Dissertatio* is not the masterpiece of irony which so many take it to be (would that I possessed such subtlety!), but an open & express endorsement of Galileo's claims. Thank you for the oranges. Though I regret to say the packaging was damaged, and they had all gone bad.

Your servant, Sir,
Joh: Kepler

Professor Gio. A. Magini: at Bologna

Excellent news, my dear sir: the Elector Ernst of Cologne, who is my patron, and who has been here throughout the summer for the Council of princes, returned last week from a brief visit to Vienna and brought with him a telescope, the very one which Galileo had himself presented to the Archduke of Bavaria. Thus the mean-spirited Paduan is frustrated in his jealousy by the kindness of my friends & patrons. Perhaps there is justice in the world, after all.

I have had much trouble with this Galilei (his father, I think, was a finer mind: have you read him?). With his usual imperiousness, he sends through his countrymen here at court, demands that I should support him in his claims regarding Jupiter, for it seems he is not content with my *Dissertatio*, and would have me repeat myself in ever more forceful affirmations of his genius—and yet, despite my many pleas, he would not send me an instrument with which to verify his claims to my own satisfaction. He says the expense & difficulty of manufacture prevents him, but I know that he has already distributed telescopes to all & sundry. What does he fear, that he excludes me? I confess I am led to suspect that his enemies may have something, when they say he is a braggart & a charlatan. I urged him to send me the names of witnesses, who would testify that they had seen what, in the *Sidereus nuncius*, he claims to be the case. He replied that the Grand Duke of Tuscany & one other of that numerous Medici clan would vouch for him. But I ask, what good are these? The Grand Duke of Tuscany, I do not doubt, would vouch for the sanctity of the Devil, if it suited him. Where are the *scientists* who will corroborate the findings? He says he holds them incapable of identifying either Jupiter or Mars, or even the moon, and so how can they be expected to know a new planet when they see it!

Anyway, it is all over now, thanks to the Elector Ernst. From August 30th, when he returned from Vienna, I have been, with the aid of the telescope, witnessing these wonderful new phenomena with my own eyes. Wishing, unlike the Paduan, to have the support of reliable witnesses, I invited to my house Ursinus the young mathematician, along with some other notables, that we might, individually, and by secret recording, at last provide indisputable proof of Galileo's claims. To avoid error, and also to preclude any charges of complicity, I insisted that we each draw in chalk on a tablet what we had seen in the telescope, the observations afterwards to be compared. It was all very satisfactory. We got in some good wine, and a hamper of food—game pies & a string of excellent sausage—and spent a very convivial evening, though I confess that the wine, combined with my poor eyesight, led me to a strange & peculiarly coloured view of the phenomena. However, all of the results matched up, more or less, and in the following days I was able myself to check them repeatedly. He was right, that Galilei!

Ah, with what trepidation did I apply my face to that splendid instrument! How would it be, if these new discoveries should only go to prove that I was wrong in my dearly held assumptions as to the true nature of things? I need not have feared. Yes, Jupiter possesses moons; yes, there are many more stars in heaven than are visible to the unaided eye; yes, yes, the moon is made of matter similar to that of the earth: but still, the shape of reality is as it has always seemed to me. The earth occupies the most distinguished place in the universe, since it circles the sun in the middle place between the planets, and the sun in turn represents the middle place at rest in a spherical space enclosed by the fixed stars. And everything is regulated according to the eternal laws of geometry, which is one & eternal, a reflection of the mind of God. All this I have seen, and am at peace—no thanks, however, to Galileo.

These are strange & marvellous times in which we live, that such transformations are wrought in our view of the nature of things. Yet we must hold fast to that, that it is only our vision which is being expanded & altered, not the thing itself. Curious, how easy it is for us little creatures to confuse the opening of our eyes with the coming into being of a new creation: like children conceiving the world remade each morning when they wake.

Your friend, Sir,
Johannes Kepler

Frau Katharina & Heinrich Kepler: at Weilderstadt

Unwholesome & frightening reports have come to me, never mind by what channels, regarding your conduct, my mother. I have already spoken to you on this matter, but it seems I must do so again, and forcefully. Do you not know what is being said about you in Weil & roundabout? Even if you do not worry for your own safety, have a thought at least for your family, for my position and that of your sons & daughter. I know that Weil is a small place, and that tongues will wag whether the scandal is real, or thought up by evil minds, but all the more reason, then, to have a care. Daily now we hear of more & more burnings in Swabia. Do not deceive yourself: no one is immune to the threat of these flames.

The woman Ursula Reinbold, the glazier's wife, has put it about that once, after taking a drink at your house, she became ill with awful fluxions, and holds that you had poisoned her with a magic draught. I know she is unbalanced, and has a bad reputation, and that the illness was probably brought on by an abortion—but it is with just such people as this that stories begin, which in time take on the semblance of truth in the general mind. Others, hearing of the Reinbold woman's charge, bethink themselves that they also have cause to complain against you. There is a kind of madness which takes hold of people at times such as this, when the stars are unpropitious. What wrong, anyway, did you do the glazier's wife? She says you abused her, and now seemingly she nurses a deep hatred of our family. I am told too that Christoph has been in some way involved with her—what is the young fool about, that he consorts with the likes of her?

There is more. Beutelspacher the schoolmaster says that he also had a drink of you, and that it was this drink which caused his lameness. (What *is* this drink, in which you seem to have soused the entire town?) Bastian Meyer says you gave his wife a

142

lotion, and after she had applied it she fell into a lingering illness & died. Christoph Frick the butcher says he suddenly felt pains in his thigh one day when he passed you by in the street. Daniel Schmid the tailor blames you for the death of his two children, because you would come into his house without cause, and whisper invocations in a strange language over the cradle. Schmid also claims that, when the children were ill, you taught his wife a prayer, to be uttered at full moon under the open sky in the churchyard, which would cure them, though they died all the same. And, wildest of all, I am told that you, Heinrich, have testifed that our mother had ridden a calf to death, and then wanted to prepare a roast from the carcase! *What is going on?* O and yes, mother, something else: a gravedigger at Eltingen says that on a visit to your father's grave, you asked the fellow to dig up the skull, so that you could have it mounted in silver & presented to me as a drinking vessel. Can this be true? Have you gone mad? Heinrich, what do you know of these matters? I am beside myself with worry. Should I come to Swabia and investigate for myself, I wonder. The business is growing serious. I pray you, mother, keep to the house, speak to no one, and above all cease this doctoring & giving of potions. I am sending this letter directly to Herr Raspe, as I shall do with all letters in future, for I am told that previously, despite my directions, you have gone to Beutelspacher, of all people, to have my letters read.

Have a care, now, I say, and pray for him who is

your loving son,
Johann

(Herr Raspe: My thanks for these informations. What am I to do? They will burn her, sure as God! Enclosed, the usual fee.)

143

H. Röslin: at Buchsweiler in Alsace

Several thoughts occur to me, following your latest letter, but the majority of them I must keep to myself, for fear of angering you further. I am sorry to note the hostility of your reaction to my *Antwort auff Röslini discurs*: believe me, my friend, it was not meant as an attack *ad hominem*. My tongue, I fear, has at times a rough & uncouth edge to it, especially when I am wrought, or even when I am only excited by the subject in hand, which last is the case on this occasion. I wished in my pamphlet to define as clearly as possible my attitude to astrology. I thought I had neither condemned nor condoned this science, of which you are such an ardent champion. Did I really say, in my last letter, that it was *monkeyshine*? What comes over me, to say such things! Please, I apologise. I shall try here, as briefly & concisely as possible, to make amends and show you my true opinion in the matter.

In fact, you will be interested to hear that I am at this very time engaged in the composition of another *Answer*, this time to an attack upon astrologers! Feselius, physician-in-ordinary to the dedicatee of your own *Discurs*, has produced a weighty attack upon the whole of astrology, which he altogether repudiates. Now, will it surprise you to know that I am about to weigh in, in my latest *Antwort*, with a defence against this broadside? For of course, contrary to what you seem to think, I do not hold all of that science to be worthless. Feselius, for instance, claims that the stars & planets were put up by God only as signs for determining time, and therefore astrologers, in scrying by the stars, impute a wrong intention to the Lord. Also he argues that Copernicus's theory is contrary to reason & to Holy Scripture. (I think, in this last, you agree with him? Forgive me, my friend, I can never resist a jibe.) All this, of course, is nonsense. Feselius is a foolish & pompous fellow, and I intend to dispatch him with a quick thrust of my sword. I mention him merely to show you that I am not wholly unsympathetic to your views.

144

I am interested in your contention that there is, behind the visible world, another world of magic which is hidden from us except in a few instances where we are allowed to witness magical actions at work. I cannot agree. Do you not see, Röslin, that the magic of, say, the so-called magic square is simply that numbers may be disposed in such a way as to produce wonderful configurations—but that this is the whole of it? No effects of this *magic* extend into the world. The real mystery & miracle is not that numbers have an effect upon things (which they do not!), but that they can express the nature of things; that the world, vast & various & seemingly ruled by chance, is amenable in its basic laws to the rigorous precision & order of mathematics.

It seems to me important that, not only is innate instinct excited by the heavens, but so also is the human intellect. The search for knowledge everywhere encounters geometrical relations in nature, which God, in creating the world, laid out from his own resources, so to speak. To enquire into nature, then, is to trace geometrical relationships. Since God, in his highest goodness, was not able to rest from his labours, he played with the characteristics of things, and copied himself in the world. Thus it is one of my thoughts, whether all of nature & all heavenly elegance is not symbolised in geometry. (I suppose this is the basis of all my belief.) And so, instinctively or thinkingly, the created imitates the Creator, the earth in making crystals, planets in arranging their leaves & blossoms, man in his creative activity. All this doing is like a child's play, without plan, without purpose, out of an inner impulse, out of simple joy. And the contemplating spirit finds & recognises itself again in that which it creates. Yes, yes, Röslin: all is play.

Vale
Johannes Kepler

Dr Michael Mästlin: at Tübingen

I have your beautiful & affecting letter, for which much thanks, though I confess it has saddened me greatly. For a long time, though I wrote to you repeatedly, I heard not a word, now suddenly, as if you have been spurred to it by resentment & irritation, comes this strange valediction. Have I *reached such a high step & distinguished position* that I could, if I wished, *look down on you*? Why, sir, what is this? You are my first teacher & patron, and, so I would like to think, my oldest friend. How would I look down on you, why should I wish to do so? You say my questions have been sometimes too subtle for your knowledge & gifts to comprehend: yet I am sure, magister, if there have been things you did not understand, the fault was mine, that my style of expression has been clumsy & unclear, or that my thoughts themselves were senseless. So you *understand only your modest craft*? On that score, I say only this: you understood the work of Copernicus at a time when others, whose names subsequently have made a great noise in the world, had not yet heard tell of the Ermlander or his theories. Come, my dear Doctor, no more of this, I will not have it!

Ah but yet, there is something in the tone of your letter which will not be gainsaid. The fault in this matter, I believe, is in my character. For it has always been thus with me, that I find it hard, despite all my efforts, to make friends, and when I do, I cannot keep them. When I meet those whom I feel I might love, I am like a little dog, with a wagging tail & lolling tongue, showing the whites of my eyes: yet sooner or later I am sure to flare up & growl. I am malicious, and bite people with my sarcasm. Why, I even like to gnaw hard, discarded things, bones & dry crusts of bread, and have always had a dog-like horror of baths, tinctures & lotions! How, then, may I expect people to love me for what I am, since what I am is so base?

Tycho the Dane I loved, in my way, though I think he never knew it—certainly I never attempted to tell him, so busy was I in trying to bite the hand, his hand, that was feeding me. He was a great man, whose name will last forever. Why could I not have told him that I recognised greatness in him? We fought from the start, and there was no peace between us, even on the day he died. True, he was eager for me to found my work upon his world system instead of on that of Copernicus, which was something I could not do: but could I not have dissembled, lied a little for his sake, soothed his fears? Of course, he was arrogant, and full of duplicity & malice, and treated me badly. But now I see that was his way, as mine is mine. And yet I cannot fool myself, I know that if he were to be resurrected and sent back to me now, there would be only the old squabbling. I am not expressing myself well. I am trying to explain how it is with me, that if I growl, it is only to guard what I hold precious, and that I would far rather wag my tail and be a friend to all.

You think I consider myself a lofty personage. I do not. High honours & offices I have never had. I live here on the stage of the world as a simple, private man. If I can squeeze out a portion of my salary at court, I am happy not to have to live entirely on my own means. As for the rest, I take the attitude that I serve not the Emperor, but rather the whole human race & posterity. In this confident hope, I scorn with secret pride all honours & offices, and also those things which they bestow. I count as the only honour the fact that by divine decree I have been put near the Tychonic observations.

Forgive, then, please, any slights that have been offered you in ignorance by

your friend,
K

Hans Georg Herwart von Hohenburg: at München

*S*alve. This will, I fear, be but the briefest of scribbles, to wish you & your family all happiness of the season. The court is busy with preparations for the festivities, and consequently I am forgotten for the moment, and hence am allowed a little time to pursue my private studies undisturbed. Is it not strange, how, at the most unexpected of moments, the speculative faculty, having just alighted from a long & wearisome flight, will suddenly take wing again immediately, and soar to even loftier heights? Having lately completed my *Astronomia nova*, and looking forward to a year or two of much needed rest & recuperation, here I am now launching out again, with renewed fervour, upon those studies of world harmony, which I interrupted seven years ago in order to clear away the little task of founding a new astronomy!

Since, as I believe, the mind from the first contains within it the basic & essential forms of reality, it is not surprising that, before I have any clear knowledge of what the contents will be, I have already conceived the form of my projected book. It is ever thus with me: in the beginning is the shape! Hence I foresee a work divided into five parts, to correspond to the five planetary intervals, while the number of chapters in each part will be based upon the signifying quantities of each of the five regular or Platonic solids which, according to my *Mysterium*, may be fitted into these intervals. Also, as a form of decoration, and to pay my due respects, I intend that the initials of the chapters shall spell out acrostically the names of certain famous men. Of course, it is possible that, in the heat of composition, all of this grand design might be abandoned. But it will be no matter.

I have taken as my motto that phrase from Copernicus, in which he speaks of the marvellous symmetry of the world, and the harmony in the relationships of the motion & size of the planetary orbits. I ask, in what does this symmetry consist? How is it that man can perceive these relationships? The latter

148

question is, I think, quickly solved—I have given the answer just a moment ago. The soul contains in its own inner nature the pure harmonies as prototypes or paradigms of the harmonies perceptible to the senses. And since these pure harmonies are a matter of proportion, there must be present figures which can be compared with each other: these I take to be the circle and those parts of circles which result when arcs are cut off from them. The circle, then, is something which occurs only in the mind: the circle which we draw with a compass is only an inexact representation of an idea which the mind carried as really existing in itself. In this I take issue strenuously with Aristotle, who holds that the mind is a *tabula rasa* upon which sense perceptions write. This is wrong, wrong. The mind learns all mathematical ideas & figures out of itself; by empirical signs it only remembers what it knows already. Mathematical ideas are the essence of the soul. Of itself, the mind conceives equidistance from a point, and out of that makes a picture for itself of a circle, without any sense perceptions whatever. Let me put it thusly: If the mind had never shared an eye, then it would, for the conceiving of the things situated outside itself, demand an eye and prescribe its own laws for forming it. For the recognition of quantities which is innate in the mind determines how the eye must be, and therefore the eye is so, because the mind is so, and not vice versa. Geometry was not received through the eyes: it was already there inside.

These, then, are some of my present concerns. I shall have much to say of them in the future. For now, my lady wife desires that the great astronomer issue forth into the town to purchase a fat goose.

Fröhliche Weihnachten!
Johannes Kepler

David Fabricius: in Friesland

As I have delayed long in my promise of a further letter, so it is right all the same that I should sit down now, on this festival of redemption, to tell you of my triumph. As, my dear Fabricius, what a foolish bird I had been! All along the solution to the mystery of the Mars orbit was in my hands, had I but looked at things correctly. Four long years had elapsed, from the time I acknowledged defeat because of that error of 8 minutes of arc, to my coming back on the problem again. In the meantime, to be sure, I had gained much skill in geometry, and had invented many new mathematical methods which were to prove invaluable in the renewed Martian campaign. The final assault took two, nearly three more years. Had my circumstances been better, perhaps I would have done it more quickly, but I was ill with an infection of the gall, and busy with the Nova of 1604, and the birth of a son. Still, the real cause of the delay was my own foolishness & shortness of sight. It pains me to admit, that even when I had solved the problem, *I did not recognise the solution for what it was*. Thus we do progress, my dear Doctor, blunderingly, in a dream, like wise but undeveloped children!

I began again by trying once more to attribute a *circular* orbit to Mars. I failed. The conclusion was, simply, that the planet's path curves inwards on both sides, and outwards again at opposite ends. This *oval* figure, I readily admit, terrified me. It went against that dogma of circular motion, to which astronomers have held since the first beginnings of our science. Yet the evidence which I had marshalled was not to be denied. And what held for Mars, would, I knew, hold also for the rest of the planets, including our own. The prospect was appalling. Who was I, that I should contemplate recasting the world? And the labour! True, I had cleared the stables of epicycles & retrograde motions and all the rest of it, and now was left with only a single

150

cartful of dung, i.e. this oval—but what a stink it gave off! And now I must put myself between the shafts, and draw out by myself that noisome load!

After some preliminary work, I arrived at the notion that the oval was an egg shape. Certainly, this conclusion involved some geometrical sleight of hand, but I could not think of any other means of imposing an oval orbit on the planets. It all seemed to me wonderfully plausible. To find the area of this doubtful egg, I computed 180 sun–Mars distances, and added them together. This operation I repeated 40 times. And still I failed. Next, I decided that the true orbit must be somewhere between the egg shape & the circular, just as if it were a perfect ellipse. By this time, of course, I was growing frantic, and grasping at any straw.

And then a strange & wonderful thing occurred. The two sickle shapes, or moonlets, lying between the flattened sides of the oval and the ideal circular orbit, had a width at their thickest points amounting to 0.00429 of the radius of the circle. This value was oddly familiar (I cannot say why: was it a premonition glimpsed in some forgotten dream?). Now I became interested in the angle formed between the position of Mars, the sun, and the centre of the orbit, the secant of which, to my astonishment, I discovered to be 1.00429. The reappearance of this value—.00429—showed me at once that there is a fixed relation between that angle, and the distance to the sun, which will hold good for all points on the planet's path. At last, then, I had a means of computing the Martian orbit, by using this fixed ratio.

You think that was the end of it? There is a final act to this comedy. Having tried to construct the orbit by using the equation I had just discovered, I made an error in geometry, and failed again. In despair, I threw out the formula, in order to try a new hypothesis, namely, that the orbit might be an ellipse. When I had constructed such a figure, by means of geometry, I saw of course that the two methods produced the same result, and that my equations was, in fact, *the mathematical expression of an ellipse*. Imagine, Doctor, my amazement, joy & embarrassment. I had been staring at the solution, without recognising it! Now I was able to express the thing as a law, simple, elegant,

151

and true: *The planets move in ellipses with the sun at one focus.*
God is great, and I am his servant; as I am also,

your humble friend,
Johannes Kepler

V

Somnium

Already the light was failing when he arrived in Regensburg at last. A fine rain drifted slantwise through the November dusk, settling in a silver fur on his cloak, his breeches, the nag's lank mane. He crossed the Steinerne Brucke over the sullen surge of the Danube. Dim figures, faceless and intent, passed him by in the streets. There was an ominous hum in his ears, and his hands, clutching the greasy reins, trembled. He told himself it was fatigue and hunger: he could not afford to be ill, not now. He had come to accost the Emperor, to demand a settlement of what he was owed.

The lamps were lit in Hillebrand Billig's house. From a way off he spied the yellow windows and the taverner and his wife within. It was an image out of a dream, that light shining through the brown gloom and the rain, and folk attending his coming. The old horse clattered to a stop, coughing. Hillebrand Billig peered at him from the doorway. "Why, sir, we did not expect you until the morrow."

Always the same, too late or too early. He was not sure what day of the week it was.

"Well," stamping his numbed feet, tears in his eyes from the cold, "here I am!"

He was put to dry by the fire in the kitchen, with a platter of ham and beans and a pint-pot of punch, and a cushion for his seething piles. An elderly dog snoozed at his feet, gasping and growling in its sleep. Billig fussed around him, a large leather-clad man with a black beard. At the stove·Frau Billig stood

155

paralysed by shyness, smiling helplessly upon her saucepans. Kepler no longer remembered how or when he had come to know the couple. They seemed to have been always there, like parents. He smiled vacantly into the fire. The Billigs were twenty years younger than he. Next year would be his sixtieth.

"I am bound for Linz," he said. He had just remembered that. There was interest on some Austrian bonds to be collected.

"But you'll bide with us a while?" said Hillebrand Billig, and, with ponderous roguishness: "The rate here, you know, heh, is *cheap*." It was his only joke. He never tired of it. "Is that not so, Anna?"

"O yes," Frau Billig managed, "you will be very welcome, Herr Doctor."

"Thank you," Kepler murmured. "I must, yes, spend a few days here. I have to see the Emperor, he owes me moneys."

The Billigs were impressed.

"His majesty will soon be returning to Prague," said Hillebrand Billig, who prided himself on knowing about these matters. "The congress has finished its business, I hear."

"But I will catch him, all the same. Of course, as to whether he will be prepared to settle his account with me, that is another question." His majesty had larger matters on his mind than the imperial mathematician's unpaid salary. Kepler sat upright suddenly, slopping his punch. The saddlebags! He rose, making for the door. "Where is my horse, what has become of my horse?" Billig had sent it to the stables. "But my bags, my my . . . my bags!"

"The boy will bring them."

"O." Kepler, moaning, turned this way and that. All of his papers were in those satchels, including a stamped and sealed imperial order for the payment of 4,000 florins from the crown's debt to him. The merest tip of something unspeakable was shown him briefly with a grin and then whisked away. Aghast, he sat down again, slowly. "What?"

Hillebrand Billig leaned down to him, mouthing elaborately. "I say, I will go out myself and bring them in, your bags, yes?"

"Ah."

"Are you unwell, Doctor?"

"No no . . . thank you."

He was trembling. He remembered out of his childhood a recurring dream, in which a series of the most terrible tortures and catastrophes was unfolded leisurely before him, while someone whom he could not see looked on, watching his reactions with amusement and an almost friendly attention. Just now that vision, whatever to call it, had been like that, the same slick flourish and the sense of muffled gloating. That was more, surely, than simply fear for his possessions? He shivered. "Eh?" Frau Billig had spoken. "Beg pardon, ma'am?"

"Your family," she said, louder, smiling nervously and plucking at her apron; "Frau Kepler, and the children?"

"O, they are very well, very well. Yes." A faint spasm, almost a pain, passed through him. It took him a moment to identify it. Guilt! As if by now he were not familiar with *that*. "We have lately had a wedding, you know."

Hillebrand Billig returned then, with rain in his beard, and set down the saddlebags on the hearth.

"Ah, good," Kepler mumbled, "very kind." He put up his feet on the bags, offering his toes to the blaze: let the chilblains suffer a little too, and serve them right. "Yes, a wedding. Our dear Regina has gone from us." He looked up into the Billigs' puzzled silence. "But what am I saying? I mean of course *Susan*." He coughed, raking up an oyster. His head hummed. "The match was made in heaven, when Venus whispered in the ear of my young assistant, Jakob Bartsch, a stargazer also, and a doctor of medicine." And when the goddess had become discouraged, seeing what a timid specimen was this Adonis, Kepler himself had taken up her task. Pangs of guilt then, too. Such bullying! He wondered if he had done right. There was much of her mother in that girl. Poor Bartsch. "Young Ludwig, my eldest boy, also is going for medicine." He paused. "And neither have I been idle: another little one, last April, a girl," leering sheepishly at the fire. Frau Billig rattled the pots on the stove: she disapproved of his young wife. So had Regina. *It would be a marriage*, she had written to him, *if my Herr Father had no child*. A curious way of putting it. He had read

157

much into that letter, too much. Foolish and sinful dreams. She was only hinting again about that damned inheritance. And he had replied that she might mind her own business, that he would marry when, and whom, he liked. But ah, Regina, what I could not say was that she reminded me of you.

Three times the name Susanna had occurred in his life, two daughters, one dead in infancy, one married now, and then at last a wife. Someone had been trying to tell him something. Whoever it was, was right. He had chosen her out of eleven candidates. Eleven! The comedy of it struck him only afterwards. He could no longer remember them all. There had been the widow Pauritsch of Kunstadt, who had tried to use his motherless children in plying her case, and that mother and daughter, each one eager to sell him the other, and fat Maria with her curls, the Helmhard woman who was built like an athlete, and that titled one, what was her name, a very Gorgon: all with advantages, their houses, their rich fathers, and he had chosen a penniless orphan, Susanna Reuttinger of Eferding, despite universal opposition. Even her guardian, the Baroness von Starhemberg, had considered her too lowly a match for him.

She was twenty-four the first time he met her, at the Starhembergs' house in Linz: a tall, slightly ungainly and yet handsome girl, with fine eyes. Her silence unnerved him. She spoke hardly a word that first day. He had thought she would laugh at him, a fussy middle-aged little man with weak sight, his beard already streaked with grey. Instead she attended him with a kind of tender intensity, leaning down to him her solemn grey eyes and downturned mouth. It was not that she much resembled Regina, but there was something, an air of ordered self-containment, and he was pierced. She was a cabinetmaker's daughter, like you, like you.

"Anna Maria we have called the baby," he said, and Anna Billig consented to smile. "A pretty name, I think."

Seven children Susanna had borne him. The first three had died in infancy. He wondered then if he had married another Barbara Müller née Müller. She saw him think it, watching him with that sad, apprehensive gaze. Yet he suspected, and was filled with wonder at the notion, that she was not hurt by it, but only concerned for him and *his* loss, his sense of betrayal.

She asked so little! She had brought him happiness. And now he had abandoned her. "Yes," he said, "a pretty name."

He closed his eyes. Waves of wind washed against the house, and beyond the noise of the rain he fancied he could hear the river. The fire warmed him. Trapped gas piped a tiny tune deep in his gut. This brute comfort made him think again of his childhood. Why? There had been precious few log fires and mugs of punch in old Sebaldus's house. But he carried within him a vision of lost peace and order, a sphere of harmony which had never been, yet to which the idea of childhood seemed an approximation. He belched, and laughed silently at the spectacle of himself, a sodden old dolt dozing in his boots, maundering over the lost years. He should fall asleep, with blubber mouth agape and dribbling, that would complete the picture. But that other roaring fire up his backside kept him awake. The dog yelped, dreaming of rats.

"Well, Billig, you tell me the electoral congress is finished its business?"

"Aye, it has. The princes have left already."

"And about time for them to finish, they have had six months at it. Has the young rake's succession been assured?"

"They do say so, Doctor."

"I must be quick then, eh, if I am to have satisfaction of his father?"

The Billigs laughed with him, but weakly. His heartiness, he saw, did not fool them. They were itching to know the real reason why he had fled home and family to come on this lunatic venture. He would have liked to know, himself. Satisfaction, was that what he was after? The promise of 4,000 florins was still in his bag, with the seal unbroken. This time most likely he would receive another, equally useless piece of parchment to keep it company. Three emperors he had known, poor Rudolph, the usurper Matthias his brother, and now the wheel of his misfortune had come full circle and his old enemy Ferdinand of Styria, scourge of the Lutherans, wore the crown. Kepler would never have gone near him, were it not for that unsettled debt. It was ten months to the day since he had last accosted him.

*　　*　　*

Cold it had been that morning, the sky like a bruised gland and a taste of metal in the air, and everything holding its breath under an astonishment of fallen snow. Soiled white boulders of ice lolled on the river. In the dark before dawn he had lain awake, listening in fright to the floes breaking before the bow, the squeaking and the groans and the sudden flurries of cracks like distant musket-fire. They docked at first light. The quayside was deserted save for a mongrel with a swollen belly chasing the slithering hawser. The bargemaster scowled at Kepler, his oniony breath defeating even the stink seeping up from the cargo of pelts in the hold. "Prague," he said, with a contemptuous wave, as if he had that moment manufactured the silent city rising behind him in the freezing mist. Kepler had haggled over the fare.

He had come from Ulm with the first printed copies of the *Tabulae Rudolphinae*. On the way that time also he had paused at Regensburg, where Susanna was lodging at the Billigs'. It was Christmas, and he had not seen her and the children for almost a year, yet he could not be idle. The Jesuits at Dillengen had shown him letters from their priests in China, asking for news of the latest astronomical discoveries, and now he set himself at once to composing a little treatise for the missionaries' use. The children hardly remembered him. He would stop, feeling their eyes on his back as he worked, but when he turned they would scurry off, whispering in alarm, to the safety of Anna Billig's kitchen.

He had wanted to continue on again alone, but Susanna would not have it. She was not impressed by his talk of snow-storms, the frozen river. Her vehemence startled him. "I do not care if you are *walking* to Prague: we shall walk with you."

"But . . ."

"But *no*," she said, and again, more softly this time: "But no, Kepler dear," and smiled. She was thinking, he supposed, that it was not good for him to be so much alone.

"How kind you are," he mumbled, "how kind." Always he believed without question that others were better than he,

160

more thoughtful, more honourable, a state of affairs for which the standing apology that was his life could not make up. His love for Susanna was a kind of inarticulate anguish choking his heart, yet it was *not enough*, not enough, like everything else that he did and was. Eyes awash, he took her hands in his, and, not trusting himself to speak further, nodded his soggy gratitude.

They lodged in Prague at The Whale by the bridge. The children were too cold to cry. The wharfinger's men rolled his precious barrel of books up from the quay, through the snow and the filth. Fortunately he had packed it with wadding and lined the staves with oilskin. The *Tables* were a handsome folio volume. Twenty years, on and off, he had devoted to that work! It contained the most of him, he knew, though not the best. His finest flights were in the *World Harmony* and the *Astronomia nova*, even the *Mysterium*, his first. He knew he had wasted too much time on the *Tables*. A year, two at the most, would have done it, when the Dane was dead and he had the observations, if he had concentrated. It might have made his fortune. Now, with everybody too busy at each other's throats to bother with such works, he would be lucky to recoup the cost of printing. Some there were who were interested still—but what did he care for converting the Chinee, and to popery at that? Sailors, though, would bless his name, explorers and adventurers. He had always liked the notion of those hardy seafarers poring over the charts and diagrams of the *Tabulae*, their piercing eyes scanning the bleached pages. It was they, not the astronomers, who made his books live. And for a moment his mind would range out over immensities, feel the blast of sun and salt wind, hear the gales howl in the rigging: he, who had not ever even seen the ocean!

He was not prepared for Prague, the new spirit that seemed abroad in the city. The court had returned from its Viennese seat for the coronation of Ferdinand's son as King of Bohemia; at first Kepler was charmed, imagining that the age of Rudolph had returned with it. He had been afraid, coming here, and not only of the ice on the river. The war was going well for the Catholic parties, and Kepler remembered how, thirty years before, Ferdinand had hounded the Protestant heretics out of

161

Styria. At the palace everything was bustle and an almost gay confusion, where he had expected stillness and stealth. And the clothes! The yellow capes and scarlet stockings, the brocades and the frogging and the purple ribbons; he had never seen such stuffs, even in Rudolph's time. He might have been among a spawn of Frenchmen. But it was in the clothes that he quickly saw how wrong he had been. There was no new spirit, it was all show, a frantic paying of homage not to greatness but to mere might. These reds and purples were the bloody badge of the counter-reformation. And Ferdinand had not changed at all.

If Rudolph had reminded Kepler, especially toward the end, of someone's mother come to her dotage, Ferdinand his cousin had the look of a dissatisfied wife. Pallid and paunchy, with delicate legs, he held himself off from the astronomer with a tensed preoccupied air, as if waiting for his taster to arrive and take a nibble before risking a closer approach. He was given to long unnerving silences, a trick inherited from his predecessors, dark pools in the depths of which swam the indistinct forms of suspicion and accusation. The eyes stared out like weary sentinels guarding that preposterous fat nose, their gaze blurred and pale, and Kepler felt not pierced but, rather, palped. He wondered idly if the imperial surliness might be due to a windy gut, for Ferdinand kept bringing up soft little belches, which he caught in his fingertips like a conjuror palming illusory baubles.

He managed the sickly shadow of a smile when Kepler arrived in his presence. The *Tables* pleased him: he had pretensions to learning. He summoned a secretary, and with a flourish dictated an order for 4,000 florins in acknowledgment of the astronomer's labours and to cover the expense of printing, even adding a memorandum to the effect that 7,817 florins were still owed. Kepler shifted from one foot to another, mumbling and simpering. Imperial magnanimity was always an ominous sign. Ferdinand dismissed him with a not unfriendly wave, but still he tarried.

"Your majesty," he said, "has been most kind, most generous. There is not only the matter of this ample grant. It betokens a noble spirit indeed, that he has maintained me in my position as mathematicus, though I profess a creed which is

162

anathema in his realm."

Ferdinand, startled and faintly alarmed, turned a poached eye on him. The title of imperial mathematician, which Kepler continued to hold since Rudolph's time, was by now no more than formal, but, in the midst of a confessional war, he meant to keep it. "Yes, yes," the Emperor said vaguely. "Well . . ." A pause. The secretary watched Kepler with brazen amusement, biting the tip of his pen. Kepler was wondering if he had made a tactical mistake. That was the kind of petitioning, oblique and well sugared with flattery, that Rudolph had expected: but this was Ferdinand. "Your religion," the Emperor said, "yes, it is, ah, an embarrassment. We understood that you were leaning toward conversion?" Kepler sighed; that old lie. He said nothing. Ferdinand's plump lower lip crept up to nibble a strand of his moustache. "Well, it is no great matter. Every man is entitled to profess as he . . . as he . . ." He caught Kepler's eager, harried gaze, and could not bring himself to finish it. The secretary coughed, and they both turned and looked at him, and Kepler was gratified to see how quickly he wiped the smirk off his foxy face. "But, no, it is no matter," the Emperor said, lifting a bejewelled hand. "The war, of course, makes difficulties. The army, and the people, look to us for guidance and example, and we must be . . . careful. You understand."

"Yes, of course, your majesty." He understood. There would be no place for him at Ferdinand's court. He felt, suddenly, immensely old and tired. A door at the far end of the hall opened, and a figure entered and came toward them, hands clasped behind him and head bent, considering his brilliant black hip-boots pacing the checkered marble. Ferdinand eyed him with something like distaste. "You are still here," he said, as if it were an ignoble trick that had been played on him. "Doctor Kepler, General von Wallenstein, our chief commander."

The general bowed. "I think I know you, sir," he said. Kepler looked at him blankly.

"He thinks he knows you," said Ferdinand; the idea amused him.

"I think, yes, I think we have had some contact," the general

163

said. "A long time ago—twenty years ago, in fact—I sent by devious routes a request to a certain stargazer in Graz, whose reputation I knew, to draw up a horoscope for me. The result was impressive: a full and uncannily accurate account of my character and doings. It was the more impressive, in that I had warned my agents not to divulge my name."

Tall windows on the left showed them a view down the Hradcany to the snowbound city. Kepler had stood once at just this spot, before this very view, with the Emperor Rudolph, discussing the plan for the *Tabulae Rudolphinae*. How slyly things rearrange themselves! Stargazer. He remembered. "Well, sir," he said, smiling tentatively, "it was not hard to find, you know, so eminent a name."

"Ah. Then you knew it was I." He shook his head, disappointed. "Even so, you did wonderfully well."

The Emperor grunted and turned morosely aside, abandoning them to each other with the air of a small boy whose ball has been taken from him by a bully. The toy had been not much prized, anyway.

"Come," said the general, and put a hand on Kepler's arm, "we must have a talk."

Thus began what was to be a brief and turbulent connection. Kepler admired the neatness of the thing: he had come here to seek an Emperor's patronage, and was given instead a general. He was not ungrateful to the arranging fates. He was in need of refuge. A year ago he had said his bitter last farewell to Linz.

* * *

Not that Linz had been the worst of places. True, that town had been his despair for fourteen years, he had thought he would feel nothing but relief at leaving. Yet when the day came, a sliver of doubt got under the quick of his expectations. After all, he had his patrons there, the Starhembergs and the Tschernembls. He had friends too, Jakob Wincklemann the lens grinder, for instance. In that old obscurantist's house by the river he had spent many a merry night drinking and dreaming. And Linz had given him Susanna. It pained him that he, the imperial mathematician, should be reduced again to teaching sums to brats and the blockhead sons of merchants at a district school, yet even in that there was something, an eerie sense of being given a second chance at life, as if it were Graz and the Stiftsschule all over again.

Upper Austria was a haven for religious exiles from the west. Linz was almost a Württemberg colony. Schwarz the jurist was there, and Baltasar Gurald the district secretary, Württembergers both. Even Oberdorfer the physician turned up briefly, a corpulent and troubled ghost, with his stick and his pale eye and poisonous breath, looking not a day older than when, twenty years before, he had officiated at the deaths of Kepler's children. To show that he held no grudge, Kepler invited the doctor to stand as sponsor at the christening of Fridmar, his second surviving child by Susanna. Oberdorfer embraced his friend with tears in his eyes, gasping out his appreciation, and Kepler thought what a spectacle they must be, this old fraud, and the grizzled papa, clasped in each other's arms and blubbering beside the baby's cot.

But then also there was Daniel Hitzler. He was the chief pastor in Linz. Younger than Kepler, he had been through the same Württemberg schools; along the way he had picked up the threads of the scandalous reputation left behind by his turbulent predecessor. Kepler was flattered, for Hitzler seemed to think him a very dangerous fellow. The pastor was a cold stick, who cultivated the air of a grand inquisitor. Little signs, however, gave him away. That black cloak was too black, the beard too pointedly pointed. Kepler had used to laugh at him a little, but liked him all the same, and felt no rancour toward him, which was curious, for Hitzler was the one who had had him excommunicated.

Kepler had known all along that it would come to this. In the matter of faith he was stubborn. He could not fully agree with any party, Catholic, Lutheran or Calvinist, and so was taken for an enemy by all three. Yet he saw himself at one with all Christians, whatever they might be called, by the Christian bond of love. He looked at the war with which God was rewarding a quarrelling Germany, and knew he was in the right. He followed the Augsburg Confession, and would not

165

sign the Formula of Concord, which he disdained as a piece of politicking, a formula of words merely, and nothing to do with faith.

Effects and consequences obsessed him. Was there a link between his inner struggles and the general confessional crisis? Could it be his private agonisings in some way provoked the big black giant that was stalking Europe? His reputation as a crypto-Calvinist had denied him a post at Tübingen, his Lutheranism had forced him out of Graz to Prague, from Prague to Linz, and soon those dreadful footfalls would be shaking the walls of Wallenstein's palace in Sagan, his last refuge. Through the winter of 1619, from his look-out in Linz, he had followed the Calvinist Frederick Palatine's doomed attempt to wrest the crown of Bohemia from the Hapsburgs. He shivered at the thought of his own connections, however tenuous, with that disaster. Had he helped to direct the giant's gimlet gaze, by allowing Regina to marry in the Palatinate, by dedicating the *Harmonice mundi* to James of England, father-in-law to the Winter King Frederick? It was as in a dream, where it slowly dawns that *you* are the one who has committed the crime. He knew that these were grossly solipsistic conceits, and yet . . .

Hitzler would not admit him to Communion unless he would agree to ratify the Formula of Concord. Kepler was outraged. "Do you require this condition of every Communicant?"

Hitzler stared at him out of an aquatic eye, perhaps wondering if he were wading into depths wherein he might be drowned by this excitable heretic. "I require it of *you*, sir."

"If I were a swineherd, or a prince of the blood, would you require it?"

"You have denied the omnipresence of the body of Christ and admitted that you agree with the Calvinists."

"There are some things, some things, mark you, on which I do not *disagree* with them. I reject the barbarous doctrine of predestination."

"You are set apart by your action in designating the Communion as a sign for that creed which was set down in the Formula of Concord, while at the same time contradicting this sign and defending its opposite." Hitzler fancied himself an orator. Kepler gagged.

"Pah! My argument, sir priest, is only that the preachers are become too haughty and do not abide by the old simplicity. Read the Church Fathers! The burden of antiquity shall be my justification."

"You are neither hot nor cold, Doctor, but tepid."

It went on for years. They met in Kepler's house, in Hitzler's, arguing into the night. They strolled by the river, Hitzler grave in his black cloak and Kepler waving his arms about and shouting, enjoying themselves despite all, and in a way playing with each other. When the Church representatives of Linz moved to dismiss Kepler from his post at the district school, and he was saved only by the influence of the barons, who approved his stand, Hitzler made no effort to help him, though he was a school inspector. The play ended there. What angered Kepler most was the hypocrisy. When he went out of the city, to the villages around, he was not refused Communion. There he found kind and simple priests, too busy curing the sick or delivering their neighbours' calves to bother with the doctrinal niceties of the Hitzlers. Kepler appealed his case to the Stuttgart Consistory. They sided against him. His last hope was to go in person to Tübingen and seek support from Matthias Hafenreffer, Chancellor of the university.

Michael Mästlin was greatly aged since Kepler had last seen him. He had a distracted air, as if his attention were all the time being called away to something more pressing elsewhere. As Kepler recounted his latest woes the old man would now and then bestir himself, furtively apologetic, striving to concentrate. He shook his head and sighed. "Such difficulties you bring upon yourself! You are no longer a student, arguing in the taverns and shouting rebellion. Thirty years ago I heard this talk from you, and nothing has changed."

"No," said Kepler, "nothing has changed, not I nor the world. Would you have me deny my beliefs, or lie and say I accept whatever is the fashion of the day, in order to be comfortable?"

Mästlin looked away, pursing his lips. In the college grounds below his window the tawny sunlight of late autumn was burnishing the trees. "You think me an old fool and an old pander," Mästlin said, "but I have lived my life honestly and not without honour, as best I could. I am not a great man, nor have I attained the heights which you have—O, you may sigh, but these things are true. Perhaps it is your misfortune, and the cause of your troubles, that you did great things and made yourself prominent. The theologians will not worry if I flout the dogmas, but you, ah, that is a different thing."

To that, Kepler had no reply. Presently Hafenreffer arrived. He had been Kepler's teacher here at Tübingen, and almost a friend. Kepler had never needed him before as he did now, and it made them shy of each other. If he could win the Chancellor to his side, and with him the theology faculty, the Consistory in Stuttgart would have to relent, for Tübingen was the seat of the Lutheran conscience. But Kepler saw, even before the Chancellor spoke, that his cause was lost. Matthias Hafenreffer also had aged, but with him the accumulation of years had been a refining process, honing him like a blade. He was what Hitzler played at being. His greeting was bland, but he bent on Kepler a keen glance. Mästlin was nervous of him, and began to fuss, calling plaintively for his servants. When none came, he rose himself and set out for his guests a jug of wine and a platter of bread, mumbling apologies for the poor fare. Hafenreffer smiled, eyeing the table. "A very suitable feast, Professor." Mästlin peered at him nervously, quite baffled. The Chancellor turned to Kepler. "Well, Doctor, what is all this I hear?"

"That man Hitzler—"

"He is enthusiastic, yes: but scrupulous also, and a fine pastor."

"He has denied me Communion!"

"Unless you ratify the Concord, yes?"

"In God's name, he is excluding me because of the frankness with which I recognise that in this one article, of the omnipresence of the body of Christ, the early Fathers are more conclusive than your Concord! I can name in my support Origen, Fulgentius, Vigilius, Cyril, John of . . ."

"Yes, yes, no doubt; we are aware of the breadth of your scholarship. But you incline to the Calvinist conception in the doctrine of Communion."

"I hold it self-evident that matter is incapable of transmutation. The body and soul of Christ are in Heaven. God, sir, is not an alchemist."

In the stillness there was the sense of phantom witnesses starting back, shocked, their hands to their mouths. Hafenreffer sighed. "So. That is clear and honest. But I wonder, Doctor, if you have considered the implication of what you say? I mean in particular the implication that by this . . . this doctrine, you diminish the sacrament of Communion to a mere symbol."

Kepler considered. "I should not say *mere*. Is not the symbol something holy, being at once itself and something other, greater? It is what may also be said, may it not, of Christ himself?"

That, he supposed afterwards, decided it. The affair dragged on for another year, but in the end Hitzler won, Kepler was excommunicated, and Hafenreffer broke with him. *If you love me*, the Chancellor wrote, *then eschew this passionate excitement*. It was sound advice, but ah, without passion he would not have been who he was. He packed his bags and set out for Ulm, where the *Tabulae Rudolphinae* were to be printed.

★   ★   ★

Elsewhere too the Keplers had been attracting the gigant's bloodshot glare. In the winter of 1616, after years of muttering and threats, the Swabian authorities moved officially to try his mother for a witch. She fled to Linz with her son Christoph. Kepler was appalled. "Why have you come? It will be taken for an admission of guilt."

"There has been worse already," Christoph said. "Tell him, mother."

The old woman looked away, sniffing.

"What worse?" Kepler asked, not really wanting to know. "What has happened?"

"She tried to bribe the magistrate, Einhorn," said Christoph, smoothing a wrinkle from his doublet.

Kepler groped behind him for a chair and sat down. Susanna laid a hand on his shoulder. Einhorn. All his life he had been hounded by people with names like that. "To *bribe* him? Why? How?"

Christoph shrugged. He was fifteen years younger than the astronomer, short and prematurely stout, with a low forehead and eyes of a peculiar violet tint. He had come to Linz chiefly to see his brother sweat over the bad news. "A wench," he said, "the daughter of this Reinbold woman, claims she suffered pains after our mother touched her on the arm. Einhorn was preparing a report of the matter for the chancery, and she offered him a silver cup if he would omit it. Didn't you, ma?"

"Jesus God," said Kepler faintly. "And what was the result?"

"Why, Einhorn was delighted, of course, since he is very thick with the Reinbold faction, and straightway reported the attempt to buy his silence, along with the other charges. It is a pretty mess."

"We are glad to see," Susanna said, "that the matter is not so serious as to trouble you greatly."

Christoph stared at her. She met him stoutly, and Kepler felt her fingers tighten on his shoulder. "Hush, hush," he murmured, patting her hand, "we must not fight."

Katharina Kepler spoke at last. "O no, he is not much put out, for he and your sister Margarete, and her holy husband the pastor, have sworn the three of them that they will desert me willingly if I am found in the wrong. So they told the magistrate. Isn't that a fine thing."

Christoph reddened. Kepler contemplated him sadly, but without surprise. He had never managed to love his brother.

"We have our own good names to think of," Christoph said, thrusting his chin at them. "What do you expect? She was warned. This past year alone in our parish they have burned a score of witches."

"God forgive you," Susanna said, turning away.

Christoph soon departed, muttering. The old woman stayed for nine months. It was a trying time. Old age nor her misfortunes had not dulled her sharp tongue. Kepler regarded her with rueful admiration. She had no illusions about the peril that she faced, yet he believed she was enjoying it all, in a queer way. She had never before had so much attention lavished on

170

her. She took a lively interest in the details of her defence which Kepler was busy assembling. She did not deny the evidence against her, only challenged the interpretations being put on it. "And I know," she said, "what they are after, that whore Ursula Reinbold and the rest of them, Einhorn too, they want to get their hands on my few florins when we lose the action. Reinbold owes me money, you know. I say we should ignore them, and they'll get tired of waiting."

Kepler groaned. "Mother, I have told you, the case has been reported to the ducal court of Württemberg." He did not know whether to laugh or be angry at the flicker of pride that brightened her ancient eyes. "Far from waiting, we must press for an early hearing. It is they who are delaying, because they know how weak is their case and want more evidence. Enough damage has been done already. Why, I too am accused of dabbling in forbidden arts!"

"O yes," she said, "yes, you have your good name to think of."

"For God's sake, mother!"

She turned her face away, sniffing. "You know how it began? It was because I defended Christoph against the Reinbold bitch."

"You told me, yes."

She meant to tell him again. "He was in some business with her tribe, and there was a dispute. And I defended him. And now he says he will abandon me."

"Well, I shall not abandon you."

He was writing off cannonades in all directions, to Einhorn and his gang, to acquaintances in the juridical faculty at Tübingen, to the court of Württemberg. The replies were evasive, and vaguely menacing. He was becoming convinced that the highest powers were conspiring to damage him through the old woman. And behind that fear was another, harder to face. "Mother," he ventured, squirming, "mother tell me, truly, swear to me, that . . . that . . ."

She looked at him. "Have you not seen me riding about the streets at night on my cat?"

The trial date was set for September, in Leonberg. Christoph, who lived there, appealed at once to the ducal court and had the proceedings transferred to the village of Güglingen. When Kepler and his mother arrived, the old woman was taken and put in chains with two keepers in an open room in the tower gate. The gaolers, merry fellows, enjoyed their job. They were being well paid, from the prisoner's own funds. Ursula Reinbold, seeing her prospective damages dwindling, demanded that the guard be reduced to one, while Christoph and his brother-in-law, Pastor Binder, reproached Kepler for allowing the expenses to mount alarmingly: he had insisted that her straw be changed daily, and that there should be a fire lit for her at night. The witnesses were heard, and the transcripts sent to Tübingen, where Kepler's friends in the law faculty decided that the evidence was such that the old woman should be questioned further under threat of torture.

It was a tawny autumn day when they led her to the chamber behind the courthouse. A breeze moved lazily over the grass, like a sweeping of invisible wings. Einhorn the magistrate was there, a wiry little man with a drop on the end of his nose, and various clerks and court officials. The party made a slow progress, for Frau Kepler was still suffering the effects of her chains. Kepler supported her, trying in vain to think of some comforting word. The strangest thoughts came into his head. On the journey from Linz he had read the *Dialogue on ancient and modern music* by Galileo's father, and now snatches of that work came back to him, like melodies grand and severe, and he thought of the wind-tossed sad singing of martyrs on their way to the stake.

They entered a low thatched shed. It was dark here after the sunlight, except in the far corner where a brazier stood throbbing, eager and intent, like a living thing. A tooth in Kepler's jaw suddenly began to ache. The air was stifling, but he felt cold. The place reminded him of a chapel, the hush, the shuffling of feet and the muffled coughs, the sense of rapt waiting. There was a hot smell, a mingling of sweat and burning coals, and something else, bitter and brassy, which was, he supposed, the stink of fear. The instruments were laid out on a low trestle table, grouped according to purpose, the thumbscrews and the gleaming knives, the burning rods, the pincers. Here were the tools of a craftsman. The torturer stepped forward, a fine tall

172

fellow with a bushy beard, who was also the village dentist.

"*Grüss Gott*," he said, touching a finger to his forehead, and bent a grave appraising eye upon the old woman. Einhorn coughed, releasing a sour waft of beer.

"I charge you, sir," he said, stumbling through the formula, "to present before this woman here arraigned the instruments of persuasion, that in God's grace she may bethink herself, and confess her crimes." He had a wide smudged upper lip, a kind of prehensile flap; the drop at the end of his nose glittered in the glare of the brazier. Not once during all the days of the hearing had he looked Kepler in the eye. He hesitated, that lip groping blindly for words, and then stepped back a pace, colliding with one of his assistants. "Proceed, man, proceed!"

The torturer in silence, lovingly, one by one displayed his tools. The old woman turned away.

"Look upon them!" Einhorn said. "See, she does not weep, even now, the creature!"

Frau Kepler shook her head. "I have wept so often in my life, I have no tears left." Suddenly, groaning, she fell to her knees in a grotesque parody of supplication. "Do with me as you please! Even if you pull one vein after another from my body, I would have nothing to admit." She clasped her hands and began to wail a *paternoster*. The torturer looked about uncertainly. "Am I required to pierce her?" he asked, taking up an iron.

"Leave it now," said Kepler, as if calling a halt to an unruly children's game. The sentence had been that she should be threatened only. A general snuffling and muttering broke out, and everyone turned away. Einhorn scuttled off. Thus years of litigation were ended. The absurdity of the thing overwhelmed Kepler. Outside, he leaned his head against the sunwarmed brick wall and laughed. Presently he realised that he was weeping. His mother stood by, dazed and a little embarrassed, patting his shoulder. The seraph's wings of the wind swooped about them. "Where will you go now?" Kepler said, wiping his nose.

"Well, I will go home. Or to Heumaden, to Margarete's house," where, within a twelvemonth, in her bed, with much complaining and crying out, she was to die.

"Yes, yes, go to Heumaden." He knuckled his eyes, peering

helplessly at the trees, the sky of evening, a distant spire. He realised, with amazement, and a sick heave, that he was, yes, it was the only word, disappointed. Like the rest of them, including even, perhaps, his mother, he had wanted something to happen; not torture necessarily, but *something*, and he was disappointed. "O God, mother."

"There now, hush."

By decree of the Duke of Württemberg she was declared innocent and immediately set free. Einhorn and Ursula Reinbold and the rest were directed to pay the trial costs. It was for the Keplers a great victory. Yet, mysteriously, there was a loss also. When Kepler returned to Linz he found his old friend Wincklemann the lens grinder gone. His house by the river was shuttered and empty, the windows all smashed. Kepler could not rid himself of the conviction that somewhere, in some invisible workshop of the world, the Jew's fate and the trial verdict had been spatchcocked together, with glittering instruments, by the livid light of a brazier. Something, after all, had happened.

*   *   *

Weeks passed, and months, and nothing was heard of the Jew. Kepler was drawn again and again to the little house on River Street. It was a pin-hole in the surface of a familiar world, through which, if only he could find the right way to apply his eye, he might glimpse enormities. He worked a ritual, walking rapidly twice or thrice past the shop with no more than a covert glance, and then abruptly stopping to rap on the door and wait, before giving himself up, with hands cupped about his face, to a long and inexplicably satisfying squint through the cracks in the shutters. The gloom within was peopled with vague grey shapes. If one of them someday should move! Stepping back then he would shake his head and depart slowly in seeming puzzlement.

He laughed at himself: for whose benefit was he performing this dumbshow? Did he imagine there was a conspiracy being waged against him, with spies everywhere, watching him?

174

The idea, with which at first he had mocked himself, began to take hold. Yet even in his worst moments of fright and foreboding he did not imagine that there was any human power behind the plot. Even random phenomena may make a pattern which, out of the tension of its mere existing, will generate effects and influences. So he reasoned, and then worried all the more. A palpable enemy would have been one thing, but this, vast and impersonal . . . When he made enquiries among the Jew's neighbours he met only silence. The locksmith next door, a flaxen-haired giant with a club foot, glared at him for a long moment, his jaw working, and then turned away saying: "We minds our own affairs down here, squire." Kepler watched the brute clump away into his shop, and he thought of the lens-grinder's wife, plump and young, until his mind averted itself, unable to bear the possibilities.

And then one day something shifted, with an almost audible clanking of cogs and levers, and there was, as it seemed, an attempt to make good his loss.

He recognised him a long way off by his walk, that laborious stoop and swing, as if at each pace he were moulding an intricate shape out of resistant air before him and then stepping gingerly into it. Kepler suddenly remembered a crowded hall at Benatek, and the summoner coming down from his master's table and saying silkily, as so often, *you ar wanted, sir*, the great head smiling up from its platter of dingy lace and one hand settling stealthily on the edge of the table like saurian jaws. But something was changed with him now. His gait was more tortured than of old, and he advanced with his face warily inclined, clutching jealously the stirrup strap of a piebald pony.

"Why, Sir Mathematicus, is it you?" palping the air with an outstretched hand. Second sight was all that was left him, his eye sockets were empty asterisks: he had been blinded.

It was sixteen years since they had last met, at Tycho's funeral in Prague. Jeppe had not aged. The blinding had drained his face of everything save a kind of childlike attentiveness, so that he seemed to be listening constantly past the immediate to something far away. He was dressed in beggar's rig. "A disguise, of course," he said, and snickered. He was on his way to Prague. He showed no sign of surprise at their meeting.

175

Perhaps for him, Kepler thought, in that changeless dark, time operated differently, and sixteen years was as nothing.

They went to a tavern on the wharf. Kepler chose one where he was not known. He gave it out that he also was passing through on his way elsewhere. He was not sure why he felt the need to dissemble. Jeppe's blank face was bent upon him intently, smiling at the lie, and he blushed, as if those puckered wounds were seeing him. It was quiet in the tavern. In a corner two old men sat playing a decrepit game of dominoes. The taverner brought two mugs of ale. He looked at the dwarf with curiosity and faint disgust. Kepler's shame increased. He should have invited the creature home.

"Tengnagel is dead, you knew that?" Jeppe said. "He did you some wrong, I think."

"Yes, we had differences. I did not hear he had died. What of his wife, the Dane's daughter?"

The dwarf smiled and shook his head, savouring a secret joke. "And Mistress Christine too, dead. So many of them dead, and only you and I still here, sir." In the tavern window suddenly there loomed the rust-red sail of a schooner plying upriver. The dominoes clattered, and one of the old men mumbled an oath.

"And what of the Italian?" Kepler asked.

It seemed for a moment the dwarf had not heard, but then he said:

"I have not seen him for many years. He took me to Rome when Master Tycho was dead. What times!" It was a garish tale. Kepler saw the pines and the pillars and the stone lions, the sunlight on marble, heard the laughter of painted whores. "He was a hard man in those days, given to duels and scuffles, a great gambler at the dice, spinning from one game to another with a sword at his side and his fool, your humble servant, sir, behind him." He reached out a hand, groping for his mug; Kepler stealthily slid it into his grasp. "You remember when we nursed him, sir, in the Dane's house? That wound never fully healed. He swore he could tell coming changes in the weather by it."

"We thought he would die," Kepler said.

The dwarf nodded. "You had regard for him, sir, you saw

176

his worth, as I did."

Kepler was startled. Was it true? "There was much life in him," he said. "But he is a scoundrel, for all that."

"O yes!" There was a pause, and Jeppe suddenly laughed. "I will tell you something to cheer you, all the same. You knew the Dane let Tengnagel marry his daughter because the wench was with child? But the brat was none of Tengnagel's doing. Felix had been there before him."

"And did the Junker know?"

"Surely. But he would not care. His only interest was to share in the Brahe fortune. You above all, though, sir, should appreciate the joke. What Tengnagel cheated you of is now inherited by the Italian's bastard."

"Yes," Kepler said, "it is a pretty notion," and laughed, but uneasily; between the cuckold and the cuckoo there was not much to choose. He felt a familiar unease; the dwarf knew too much. "Where is the Italian now?" he asked. "In prison, or on the run again?"

Jeppe called for more ale, and left Kepler to pay for it.

"Why, both, in a manner of speaking," he said. "He could never be at peace, that one. In Rome he might have been a gentleman, for he had friends and patrons, and was favoured even by the Pope, Her Holiness Clement, as he would have it. But he drank too much and diced too much, and spoke too freely, and made enemies. In a brawl one day over the score in a game of racquets he ran a player through the throat and killed him. We fled the city, and took sail for Malta, where he thought the Knights would give us shelter. They put him in prison. He was a turbulent guest, though, as you may imagine, and after a week they were glad to let him escape." A cat leaped with swift grace on to the counter where the taverner leaned, listening. Jeppe took a drink of ale and wiped his mouth on his sleeve. "For months we wandered through the Mediterranean ports, with the Vatican's spies on our heels. Then we heard talk of a papal pardon, and though I warned him it was a trick he would have nothing but to return to Rome. At Port' Ercole the customs men, Spanish louts, took him for a smuggler and threw him in the cells. When they let him go at last, our ship for Rome had sailed. He stood on the beach and watched it depart,

177

the red sail, I remember it. He wept for rage and for himself, beaten at last. His baggage had been already put aboard, and he had nothing left.''

They left the tavern. A raw wind was blowing off the river, and snowflakes whirled in the air. Kepler helped the dwarf to mount up. ''Farewell,'' Jeppe said, ''we shall not meet again, I think.'' The pony stamped and snuffled nervously, smelling the impending storm. Jeppe smiled, the blind face puckering. ''He died, you know, sir, on that beach at Port' Ercole, cursing God and all Spaniards. Old wounds had opened, and he had the fever. I held his hand at the end. He gave me a ducat to buy a Mass for him.''

Kepler looked away. Sorrow welled up in him, intense and amazing as tears in sleep, and as brief. ''There was much life in him,'' he said.

Jeppe nodded. ''I think you envied him that, sir?''

''Yes,'' with mild surprise, ''yes, I envied him that.'' He gave the dwarf a florin.

''Another Mass? You are kind, sir.''

''How will you live in Prague? Will you find a position?''

''O but I have a position.''

''Yes?''

''Yes,'' and smiled again. As he watched him ride slowly away through the snow, Kepler realised that he had not thought to ask who it was had blinded him. Maybe it was better not to know.

That night he had a dream, one of those involuntary great dark plots that now and then the sleeping mind will hatch, elaborate and enigmatic and full of inexplicable significance. Familiar figures appeared, sheepish and a little crazed, dream actors who had not had time to learn their parts. The Italian came forward, clad as a knight of the Rosy Cross. In his arm he carried a little gilded statue, which sprang alive suddenly and spoke. It had Regina's face. A solemn and complex ceremony was being celebrated, and Kepler understood that this was the alchemical wedding of darkness and light. He woke into the dim glow of a winter dawn. The snow was falling fast outside, the vague shadow of it moved on the wall by his bed. A strange happiness reigned in his heart, as if a problem that had been with him all his life had at last been decided; a happiness so firm and fine it was not dispelled even when he remembered that, six months before, in her twenty-seventh year, in the Palatinate, of a fever of the brain, Regina had died.

*   *   *

The after-image of that dream never entirely faded. Its silvery glimmer was mysteriously present in every page of his book of the harmony of the world, which he finished in a sudden frenzy in the spring of 1618. The empire was charging headlong into war, but he hardly noticed. For thirty years he had been accumulating the material and the tools for this, the final synthesis. Now, like a demented fisherman, he hauled in the lines of his net from all directions. He was entranced. Times he found himself at table, or walking the city wall in the rain, with only the vaguest recollection of how he had come there. Answering a remark of Susanna's, it would dawn on him that an hour had passed since she had spoken. At night the spinning coils of his brain blundered into a sack of sleep, and in the morning struggled out again enmeshed in the same thoughts, as if there had been no interruption. He was no longer a young man, his health was poor, and sometimes he pictured himself a thing of rags and straw dangling limply from a huge bulbous head, like those puppets he had coveted as a child, strung up by their hair in the dollmaker's shop.

The *Harmonia mundi* was for him a new kind of labour. Before, he had voyaged into the unknown, and the books he brought back were fragmentary and enigmatic charts apparently unconnected with each other. Now he understood that they were not maps of the islands of an Indies, but of different stretches of the shore of one great world. The *Harmonia* was their synthesis. The net that he was drawing in became the grid-lines of a globe. It seemed to him an apt image, for were not the sphere and the circle the very bases of the laws of world harmony? Years before, he had defined harmony as that which the soul creates by perceiving how certain proportions in the world correspond to prototypes existing in the soul. The

179

proportions everywhere abound, in music and the movements of the planets, in human and vegetable forms, in men's fortunes even, but they are all relation merely, and inexistent without the perceiving soul. How is such perception possible? Peasants and children, barbarians, animals even, feel the harmony of the tone. Therefore the perceiving must be instinct in the soul, based in a profound and essential geometry, that geometry which is derived from the simple divisioning of circles. All that he had for long held to be the case. Now he took the short step to the fusion of symbol and object. The circle is the bearer of pure harmonies, pure harmonies are innate in the soul, and so the soul and the circle are one.

Such simplicity, such beauty. These were the qualities which sustained him through exhaustion and the periodic bouts of rage before the intractability of the material. The ancients had sought to explain harmony by the mysticism of numbers, and had foundered in complexity and worthless magic. The reason why certain ratios produce a concord and others discord is not to be found in arithmetic, however, but in geometry, and specifically in the divisioning of the circle by means of the regular polygons. There was the beauty. And the simplicity was that harmonious results are produced only by those polygons which can be constructed with the compass and ruler alone, the tools of classical geometry.

Man he would show to be truly the *magnum miraculum*. The priests and the astrologers would have it that we are nothing, clay and ash and humours. But God had created the world according to the same laws of harmony which the swineherd holds in his heart. Do the planetary aspects influence us? Yes, but the Zodiac is no truly existing arc, only an image of the soul projected upon the sky. We do not suffer, but act, are not influenced but are ourselves the influences.

These were airy heights in which he moved. He grew dizzy. His eyesight was worsening, everything he looked on trembled as if under water or smoke. Sleep became a kind of helpless tumbling through black space. Alighting from some high leap of thought, he would find Susanna shaking him in alarm, as if he were a night-walker whom she had saved from the brink.

"What is it, what?" he mumbled, thinking of fire and flood, the children dead, his papers stolen. She held his face in her hands.

"O Kepler, Kepler . . ."

Now he went all the way back to the *Mysterium*, and the theory which through the years had been his happiness and his constant hope, the incorporation of the five regular solids within the intervals of the planets. His discovery of the ellipse law in the *Astronomia nova* had dealt a blow to that idea, but a blow not heavy enough to destroy his faith. Somehow the rules of plane harmony must be made to account for the irregularities in this model of the world. The problem delighted him. The new astronomy which he had invented had destroyed the old symmetries; then he must find new and finer ones.

He began by seeking to assign to the periods of revolution of the planets the harmonic ratios dictated by musical measurement. It would not work. Next he tried to discern a harmonic series in the sizes or volumes of the planets. Again he failed. Then he sought to fit the least and greatest solar distances into a scale, examined the ratios of the extreme velocities, and of the variable periods required by each planet to rotate through a unit length of its orbit. And then at last, by the nice trick of siting the position of observation not on earth but in the sun, and from there computing the variations in angular velocities which the watcher from the sun could be expected to see, he found it. For in setting the two extremes of velocity thus observed against each other, and in combined pairs among the other planets, he derived the intervals of the complete scale, both the major and the minor keys. The heavenly motions, he could then write, are nothing but a continuous song for several voices, perceived not by the ear but by the intellect, a figured music which sets landmarks in the immeasurable flow of time.

He was not finished yet, not by a long way. In the *Mysterium* he had asked what is the connection between the time a planet takes to complete its orbit, and its distance from the sun, and had not found a satisfactory answer. Now the question came back more urgent than ever. Since the sun governs planetary motion, as he held to be the case, then that motion must be connected with the solar distances, or else the universe is a senseless and arbitrary structure. This was the darkest hour of his long night. For months he laboured over the problem, wielding the Tychonic observations like the enormous letter wheels of a cabalist. When the solution came, it came, as always, through a back door of the mind, hesitating shyly, an announcing angel dazed by the immensity of its journey. One morning in the middle of May, while Europe was buckling on its sword, he felt the wing-tip touch him, and heard the mild voice say *I am here*.

It seemed a nothing, the merest trifle. It sat on the page with no more remarkable an air than if it had been, why, anything, a footnote in Euclid, one of Galileo's anagrams, a scrap of nonsense out of a schoolboy's bad dream, and yet it was the third of his eternal laws, and the supporting bridge between the harmonic ratios and the regular solids. It said that the squares of the periods of evolution of any two planets are to each other aș the cubes of their mean distances from the sun. It was his triumph. It showed him that the discrepancies in distance which were left over after the insertion of the regular polygons between the orbits of the planets were not a defect of his calculations, but the necessary consequences of the dominant principle of harmony. The world, he understood at last, is an infinitely more complex and subtle construct than he or anyone else had imagined. He had listened for a tune, but here were symphonies. How mistaken he had been to seek a geometrically perfected, closed cosmos! A mere clockwork could be nothing beside the reality, which is the most harmonic possible. The regular solids are material, but harmony is form. The solids describe the raw masses, harmony prescribes the fine structure, by which the whole becomes that which it is, a perfected work of art.

Two weeks after the formulation of that law the book was finished. He set about the printing at once, in a kind of panic, as if fire or flood, his greatest fears, or some other hobgoblin, might strike him down before he could make public his testament. Besides, the printing was a kind of work, and how could he simply stop? The trajectory he had long ago entered on would take time to run down, would sweep him through further books, the scrag-ends of his career. And even if he had been capable of rest, rest was not permissible, for then he would have had to face, in the dreadful stillness, the demon that has started up at his back, whose hot breath was on his neck.

For years the *World Harmony* had obsessed him, a huge weight pinning him down; now he was aware of a curious feeling of lightness, of levity almost, as if he had drunk again a dose of Wincklemann's drugged wine. That was the demon. He recognised it. He had known it before, the selfsame feeling, when, in the *Astronomia nova*, he had blithely discarded years of work for the sake of an error of a few minutes of arc, not because he had been wrong all those years—though he had—but in order to destroy the past, the human and hopelessly defective past, and begin all over again the attempt to achieve perfection: that same heedless, euphoric sense of teetering on the brink while the gleeful voice at his ear whispered *jump*.

★　　★　　★

Other and far less inviting precipices appeared under his feet. The world that once had seemed so wide was becoming narrower daily. The Palatinate's army had been crushed in the battle of Weisser Berg and Bohemia regained by the Catholics, but the war of the religions still raged. The Empire was ablaze and he was on the topmost storey. He could hear the flames roaring behind him, the crash of masonry and splintering timber as another staircase gave way. Before him there was only the shivered window and the sudden chill blue air. When in the autumn of 1619 the Elector Frederick and his wife Princess Elizabeth entered Prague to accept the crown offered him by the Bohemian Protestants, the *World Harmony* had been on the presses, and Kepler had had time to suppress only in a few final copies the dedication to James of England, the Princess's father. He had not needed that connection to mark him out as suspect. Even his attacks on the brotherhood of the Rosy Cross, and his dispute with the English Rosicrucian Robert Fludd, had won him no praise: the imperial parties, so he heard, were asking what he had to hide, that he should flaunt this too enthusiastic loyalty to his Catholic Emperor Ferdinand. He despaired, he was no good at politics. He was not even sure any longer who was fighting whom in the war. The Bohemian barons had not accepted the defeat of Weisser Berg, but they were a local disturbance: now there was talk of French and even Danish involvement. Kepler was baffled. Could these far-off kingdoms really care so much for religion and the fate of little Bohemia? It must be all a conspiracy. The Rosicrucians were to blame, or the Vatican.

Presently, as he knew it would, the old wheel turned: all Lutherans were ordered out of Linz. As the Emperor's mathematician, in title at least, Kepler could hope for immunity. He gave up his pilgrimages to Wincklemann's deserted shop, and stayed away from religious services. But the invisible plotters would not be thus easily put off. His library was confiscated by the Catholic authorities. He bitterly admired the accuracy of their aim; it was a hard blow to bear. And then, it was almost comic, Lutheranism threw up a tormentor of its own in the shape of Pastor Hitzler. Kepler felt himself backed into a corner, an old, puzzled rat.

The public turmoil was matched in the darkness of his heart, where a private war was raging. He could not tell what was the cause of battle, nor what the prize that was being fought for. On one side was all that he held precious, his work, his love for wife and children, his peace of mind; on the other was that which he could not name, a drunken faceless power. Was it still, he wondered, the demon that had risen up out of the closing pages of the *Harmonia mundi*, grown fat on the world's misfortunes? That was when he began to suspect a connection between his inner ragings and Europe's war, and feared for his sanity. He fled from the battlefield into the numbing grind of the *Tabulae Rudolphinae*. There, among the orderly marching columns of Tycho Brahe's lifework, he could hide. But not for long. Soon that manoeuvre was exhausted. Then he embarked on the first of his strange frantic wanderings. On the road he felt easier, the clash of battle within him stilled for a while by the pains and frustration of travel. It seemed to be what the demon wanted.

He used as excuse the moneys owed him by the crown. The printing of the *Tables* would be a costly business. He set out for Vienna and Ferdinand's court. After four months of haggling there he won a grudging part settlement of 6,000 florins. The

Treasury, however, cleverer and more careful than the Emperor, immediately transferred responsibility for the payment to the three towns of Nuremberg, Kempten and Memmingen. Once more Kepler set off, seeming to hear Vienna break out in general hilarity behind him. By the end of winter he had collected from the tight-fisted trinity of towns 2,000 florins. It would buy the paper for the *Tables*. The effort had exhausted him, and he turned wearily towards home.

When he got to Linz he found the city transformed into a military camp. The Bavarian garrison sent in by the Emperor was billeted everywhere. At Plank the printer's a squad of soldiers was sprawled at feed among the presses, their stink overlaying the familiar smells of ink and machine oil. All work had stopped. They watched him incuriously as he danced before them in helpless rage. He might have dropped into their midst from another planet. They were for the most part the sons of poor farmers. When the printing got under way at last they began to display a childlike interest in the work: few of them had ever seen a machine working before. They would gather about Plank's men in silent groups, staring and softly breathing like cattle at a stile. The sudden white flourish of a pulled proof never failed to call forth a collective sigh of surprise and pleasure. Later on, when the amazing fact had soaked into their understanding that Kepler was the sole cause of all this mighty effort, they turned their awed attention on to him. They would jostle to get near him at the benches or the readers' desk, trying to sift out of his talk of fonts and colophons and faces some clue to the secret of his wizardry. And occasionally they would pluck up courage enough to offer him a mug of beer or a twist of tobacco, grinning furiously at their boots and sweating. He grew accustomed to their presence, and ceased to heed them, except that now and then something spoke to him, at once faint and insistent, out of this warm noisome mass of life pressing at his back. Then he would fly into a rage again, and yell into their stunned faces, and stamp out of the shop, waving his arms.

In the spring the Lutheran peasantry revolted, sick of being harried, of being hungry, sick most of all of their arrogant Emperor. They swept across Upper Austria, delirious with success, unable to believe their own strength. By early summer

185

they were at the walls of Linz. The siege lasted for two months. The city had been ill-prepared, and was quickly reduced to horse meat and nettle soup. Kepler's house was on the wall, and from his workroom he could look down across the moats and the suburbs where the fiercest fighting took place. How small the protagonists looked from up here, and yet how vivid their blood and their spilled guts. The smell of death bathed him about as he worked. A detachment of troops was quartered in his house. Some among them he recognised from the printing house. He had thought his children would be terrified, but they seemed to regard it all as a glorious game. One morning, in the midst of a bitter skirmish, they came to tell him that there was a dead soldier in his bed.

"Dead, you say? No, no, he is wounded merely; your mama put him there to rest."

Cordula shook her head. Such a serious little girl! "He is *dead*," she said firmly. "There is a fly in his mouth."

Towards the end of June the peasant forces breached the wall one night and set fire to a section of streets before being repulsed. Plank's shop was destroyed, and with it all the sheets of the *Tables* so far printed. Kepler decided it was time to move. By October, the siege long since lifted and the peasants crushed, he had packed up everything that he owned and was on his way to Ulm, excommunicate and penniless, never to return.

In Ulm for a while he was almost happy. He had left Susanna and the children in Regensburg, and, alone once more after so many years, he felt as if time had magically fallen away and he was back in Graz, or Tübingen even, when life had not properly begun, and the future was limitless. The city physician Gregor Horst, an acquaintance from his Prague days, leased him a little house in Raben Alley. He found a printer one Jonas Saur. The work went well at first. He still imagined that the *Tables* would make his fortune. He spent his days in the printing house. On Saturday nights he and Gregor Horst would get quietly drunk together and argue astronomy and politics into the small hours.

But he could not be at rest for long. The old torment was rising once more in his heart. Saur the printer lived up to his name, and there were quarrels. Yet again Kepler turned his hopes toward Tübingen and Michael Mästlin; could Gruppenbach, who had printed the *Mysterium*, finish off for him the *Tables*? He wrote to Mästlin, and getting no reply he set out for Tübingen on foot. But it was February, the weather was bad, and after two days he found himself halted at a crossroads in the midst of turnip fields, exhausted and in despair, but not so far gone that he could not see, with wry amusement, how all his life was summed up in this picture of himself, a little man, wet and weary, dithering at a fork in the road. He turned back. The town council at Esslingen presented him with a horse, got from the town's home for the infirm. The beast bore him bravely enough to Ulm and then died under him. Again he saw the aptness of it, this triumphal entry, on a broken-down jade, into a city that hardly knew him. He made his peace with Jonas Saur, and at last, after twenty years, the *Tables* were hauled to completion.

Two kinsmen of Tycho Brahe called on him one day at his lodgings in Raben Alley, Holger Rosenkrands the statesman's son and the Norwegian Axel Gyldenstjern. They were on their way to England. Kepler considered. Wotton, King James's ambassador to Prague, had urged him once to come to England. Rosenkrands and Gyldenstjern would be happy to take him with them. Something held him back. How could he leave his homelands, however bad the convulsions of war? There was nothing for him but to go to Prague. He had the *Tables* at least to offer the Emperor. It was not likely it would be enough. His time was past. Even Rudolph in his latter days had grown bored with his mathematician. But he must go somewhere, do something, and so he took himself aboard a barge bound for the capital, where, unknown to both of them, Wallenstein awaited him.

*   *   *

Now, baking his chilblains at Hillebrand Billig's fire, he brooded on his time in Sagan. It had been at least a refuge, where for a while he had held still, the restlessness of his heart

187

feeding vicariously on his new master's doings. Wallenstein's world was all noise and event, a ceaseless coming and going to the accompaniment of distant cannonades and hoofbeats at midnight: as if he too were in flight from an inexorable demon of his own. Yet Kepler had never known a man who so fitted the shape and size of his allotted space. What emptiness could there be in *him*, that a stalking devil would seek for a home?

Billig was laboriously doing the tavern accounts at the kitchen table, licking his pencil and sighing. Frau Billig sat near him, darning her children's stockings. They might have been done by Dürer. A draught from the window shook the candle-light. There was the sound of the wind and the rain, the muffled roars of the Saturday night revellers in the tavern, the crackling of the fire, the old dog's snores, but beneath all a deep silence reigned, secret and inviolable, perhaps the silence of the earth itself. Why, dear Christ, did I leave home to come on this mad venture?

At first he had been wary of Wallenstein. He feared being bought for a plaything, for the general's obsession with astrology was famous. Kepler was too old and too tired to take up again that game of guesswork and dissimulation. For months he had held back, worrying at the terms Wallenstein was offering him, wanting to know what would be required of him in return. Conversation, said Wallenstein, smiling, your company, the benefit of your learning. The Emperor, with ill-concealed enthusiasm, urged him to accept the offered post, and took the opportunity to transfer on to Wallenstein the crown's considerable debt to its mathematician. Wallenstein made no protest; his blandness caused Kepler's heart to sink. Also the astronomer would be granted an annual stipend of 1,000 florins from the Sagan coffers, a house at Gitschin where the general had his palace, and the use of a printing press with sufficient paper for whatever books he might wish to publish, all this without condition or hindrance. Kepler dared to hope. Could it be, at last, could it be . . ?

It could not. Wallenstein indeed believed he had purchased a tame astrologer. In time, after many clashes, they had come to an arrangement whereby Kepler supplied the data out of which more willing wizards would work up the horoscopes and calendars. For the rest he was free to do as he wished. He saw no sign of the imperial debt being settled, nor of the printing works and the paper that had been promised. Things might have been worse. There was the house at least, and now and then he was even paid a little of his salary on account. If he was not happy, neither was he in despair. Hitzler's word came back to him: tepid. Sagan was a barbaric place, its people peculiar and cold, their dialect incomprehensible. There were few diversions. Once he travelled down to Tübingen and spent a gloriously tipsy month with old Mästlin, deaf and doddering now but merry withal. And one day Susanna came to him, with a look of mingled amusement and surprise, to announce that she was pregnant.

"By God," he said, "I am not so old then as I thought, eh?"

"You are not old at all, my dear, dear Kepler."

She kissed him, and they laughed, and then were silent for a moment, a little awkward, almost embarrassed, sharing an old complicity. What a happy day that had been, perhaps the best out of all the days of that amused and respectful, ill-matched and splendid marriage.

Wallenstein lost interest in him, even his conversation. Summonses to the palace grew rare, and then ceased altogether, and Kepler's patron became a stylised and intermittent presence glimpsed now and then in the distance, beyond a prospect of trees, or down the long slope of a hill on a sunlit evening, cantering among his aides, a stiff, rhythmically nodding figure, like a sacred effigy borne in brief procession on a feast-day. And then, as if indeed some mundane deity's memory had been jogged, workmen with a cart trundled up one day and dumped at Kepler's door a great lump of machinery. It was the printing press.

Now he could work again. There was money to be made from almanacs and navigational calendars. But he was ill that winter, his stomach was bad and he suffered much from gravel and the gout. His years were weighing heavily on him. He needed a helper. In a little book sent him from Strasburg he found on the dedication page a public letter addressed to him by the author, Jakob Bartsch, offering his humble services to the imperial astronomer. Kepler was flattered, and wrote inviting

189

the disciple to come to Sagan. Bartsch was a mixed blessing. He was young and eager, and wearied Kepler with his impossible enthusiasms. Kepler grew fond of him, all the same, and would have had fewer misgivings at his marrying into the family if Susanna, his daughter and Bartsch's bride, had not had so much of the Müller strain in her.

The young man willingly took over the drudgery of the almanacs, and Kepler was free to return to a cherished project, his dream of a journey to the moon. The larger part of that last year in Sagan he devoted to the *Somnium*. None of his books had given him such peculiar pleasure as this one. It was as if some old strain of longing and love were at last being freed. The story of the boy Duracotus, and his mother Fiolxhilda the witch, and the strange sad stunted creatures of the moon, filled him with quiet inner laughter, at himself, at his science, at the mild foolishness of everything.

"You will stay the night, then, Doctor?"

Frau Billig was watching him, her needle poised.

"Yes," he said, "certainly; and thank you."

Hillebrand Billig lifted his troubled head from his accounts and laughed ruefully. "Maybe you will help me with these figures, for I cannot manage them!"

"Aye, gladly."

They want to know what really has brought me here, O yes they do. But then, so do I.

When he finished the *Somnium* there had been another crisis, as he had known there would be. What was it, this wanton urge to destroy the work of his intellect and rush out on crazy voyages into the real world? It had seemed to him in Sagan that he was haunted, not by a ghost but something like a memory so vivid that at times it seemed about to conjure itself into a physical presence. It was as if he had mislaid some precious small thing, and forgotten about it, and yet was tormented by the loss. Suddenly now he recalled Tycho Brahe standing barefoot outside his room while a rainswept dawn broke over the Hradcany, that forlorn and baffled look on his face, a dying man searching too late for the life that he had missed, that his work had robbed him of. Kepler shivered. Was it that same look the Billigs saw now, on his face?

Susanna had stared at him in disbelief. He would not meet her eye. "But why, why?" she said. "What is to be gained?"

"I must go." There were the bonds to be seen to in Linz. Wallenstein was in disgrace, had been dismissed. The Emperor was sitting with the Diet in Regensburg, ensuring the succession of his son. "He owes me moneys, there is business to be finished, *I must go.*"

"My dear," Susanna said, trying if a joke would work, "if you go, I will expect to see the Last Judgment sooner than your return." But neither one smiled, and she let fall her hand from his.

He travelled south into wild winter weather. He took no notice of the elements. He was prepared to go on to Prague if necessary, to Tübingen—to Weilderstadt! But Regensburg was far enough. I know he will meet me here, I'll recognise him by the rosy cross on his breast, and his lady with him. Are you there? If I walk to the window now shall I see you, out there in the rain and the dark, all of you, queen and dauntless knight, and death, and the devil . . ?

"Doctor, Doctor you must go to bed now, and rest, you are ill."

"What?"

"You are shaking . . ."

Ill? Was he? His blood sizzled, and his heart was a muffled thunder in his breast. He almost laughed: it would be just like him, convinced all his life that death was imminent and then to die in happy ignorance. But no. "I must have been asleep." He struggled upright in his chair, coughing, and spread unquiet hands to the fire. Show them, show them all, I'll never die. For it was not death he had come here to meet, but something altogether other. Turn up a flat stone and there it is, myriad and profligate! "Such a dream I had, Billig, such a dream. *Es war doch so schön.*"

What was it the Jew said? Everything is told us, but nothing explained. Yes. We must take it all on trust. That's the secret. How simple! He smiled. It was not a mere book that was thus thrown away, but the foundation of a life's work. It seemed not to matter.

"Ah my friend, such dreams . . ."

The rain beat upon the world without. Anna Billig came and filled his cup with punch. He thanked her.

Never die, never die.

Note

The standard biographies are *Kepler*, by Max Caspar, translated and edited by C. Doris Hellman (London, 1959), and *Tycho Brahe*, by J.L.E. Dreyer (Edinburgh, 1890). I must also mention, once again, my indebtedness to, and admiration for, Arthur Koestler's *The Sleepwalkers* (London, 1959). Another work which provided me also with valuable insights into early 17th-century life and thought is *The Rosicrucian Enlightenment*, by Frances A. Yates (London, 1972).

For their help and encouragement, I wish to thank especially Don Sherman and Ruth Dunham, and my wife, Janet.

Johannes Kepler died in Regensburg on November the 15th, 1630.

JOHN BANVILLE

The Book of Evidence

"Freddie Montgomery is a gentleman first and a murderer second . . . He has committed two crimes. He stole a small Dutch master from a wealthy family friend, and he murdered a chambermaid who caught him in the act. He has little to say about the dead girl. He killed her, he says, because he was physically capable of doing so. She annoyed him. It made perfect sense to smash her head in with a hammer. What he cannot understand, and would desperately like to know, is why he was so moved by an unattributed portrait of a plain middle-aged woman that he felt compelled to steal it . . .

"I have read books that are as cleverly constructed as this one and I can think of a few – not many – writers who can match Banville's technical brilliance, but I have read no other novel that illustrates so perfectly a single epiphany. It is, in its cold, terrifying way, a masterpiece"
Maureen Freely, *Literary Review*

"Compelling and brutally funny reading from a master of his craft"
Patrick Gale, *Daily Telegraph*

"Banville must be fed up being told how beautifully he writes, but on this occasion he has excelled himself in a flawlessly flowing prose whose lyricism, patrician irony and aching sense of loss are reminiscent of *Lolita*"
Observer

"Completely compelling reading . . . not only entertains but informs, startles and disturbs"
Irish Independent

JOHN BANVILLE

Doctor Copernicus

Nicolas Koppernigk, better known as Copernicus, was the astronomer whose system of a sun-centred universe gave birth to the great Renaissance revolution in cosmology that was to shatter the medieval conception of the world and was to lead to the formulation of the image of the solar system that we know today. It may be difficult for us now to comprehend the profound shock which the publication of the Copernican world-picture caused in the astronomer's own day, but John Banville's novel captures the feel of that remote time, and his imaginative reconstruction makes Copernicus the man a real and palpable figure.

Set in a fascinatingly alien world as it is, the gripping human drama of this novel nevertheless transcends its context, making it at once a historical and a very modern novel.

JOHN ARDEN

Books of Bale

John Bale, a sixteenth-century English friar who converted to Protestantism while young, stands at the centre of John Arden's dazzling second novel. A complex individual caught up in momentous times, John Bale is captured supporting Henry VIII's repudiation of the Pope and, as Bishop of Ossory in Ireland, the harsh imposition of English religious policy upon his Catholic diocese.

We meet Bale through the reminiscences, letters and dreams of various associates and relatives, and see him as lover, playwright and instrument of colonial oppression. And, as his story is woven, the medieval world gives way to the modern, Catholicism is tyrannised by English Protestantism, and Elizabethan theatre is born.

Here is a novel of astonishing scope and vitality which ranges richly across a living tapestry of character and history.

"Historically cranky, gutsy, opinionated, and singularly refreshing as anything by Robert Graves"
Observer

"There are few novelists who can combine the concrete and the abstract with such assurance, and the combination makes *Books of Bale* both vigorous and pleasurable"
Irish Times

"A vivid, eccentric piece of period pastiche, gaining its vitality from theatrical obsession and not being afraid to broaden its stage lavishly"
Guardian

"A vigorously lifelike sprawl of a book"
Sunday Times

BRENDA MADDOX

Nora

Nora Joyce is commonly portrayed by the literary world as an illiterate, coarse chambermaid and no match for her husband's genius. This new and enthralling biography is the first full study of Nora's life before, with, and after James Joyce. Here she is revealed as devoted, passionate, eloquent, irreverent, long-suffering and a powerful influence upon her difficult and demanding husband.

In releasing Nora from the world of academic footnotes, Brenda Maddox has produced both a fine biography of a complex woman and a work which will inform and interest all Joyce readers and scholars.

"One of the finest biographies to have appeared for some years."
Irish Independent

"*Nora* is a brilliant biography that radically alters our understanding. With all respect for Ellman's monumental work, Maddox's biography of Joyce's wife can now be recommended as the first book to read about Joyce himself."
Newsweek

"Essential reading"
Anthony Burgess

"[A] remarkable portrait of what must be one of the strangest, most fruitful, evenly matched, and in the end for both parties most thoroughly satisfactory of literary marriages."
The Saturday Telegraph

BEN FORKNER ed.

The New Book of Dubliners

This collection of stories set in Dublin in this century, apart from containing James Joyce's story "Ivy Day in the Committee Room" taken from his celebrated collection of stories, *Dubliners*, contains stories by fourteen other writers. The editor's aim in this collection was to search out stories in which the special qualities of Dublin life enter into the narrative as an active force. Most of the writers in the collection were not Dubliners but came to Dublin from other regions and other cities of Ireland.

As the editor writes: "Dublin is surpassingly prodigal of public theatre of all sorts and there is far more than one type of stage in these stories . . . Whatever else binds these brilliantly varied stories together, they are bound most of all by the success with which they extend Joyce's achievement in *Dubliners* through almost a century of creative association between a single city and a single literary genre."

MOY McCRORY

Bleeding Sinners

"*Bleeding Sinners* deals with women's fertility; its pain and pleasure; its consequences in a world fettered by ignorance and fear. Its eleven short stories range from the frankly fantastic – as when a bored wife wakes up to find her husband has turned into a giant sprouting potato – to the naturalistic Belfast setting of the title piece . . . This is an extraordinary book about ordinary experience, beautifully written and observed"
Time Out

"Moy McCrory has a laser-sharp eye and knife-like pen . . . the story 'Drop Stars Fall in Unmarked Places' is a consciously literary poetic gem . . . by itself it makes *Bleeding Sinners* worth the price and marks Moy McCrory as a writer to watch"
Scotland on Sunday

"Her prose style is taut and muscular, her narrative skill tackles complex interwoven time-scapes with deceptive ease . . . this is a book which demands to be read"
Spare Rib

"McCrory writes revealingly about a raw world that cannot settle cosily into sistership. She can also be very witty"
Guardian

"Generous and compassionate, and to coin a phrase, bloody marvellous"
Irish Times

MICHEL TOURNIER

Gilles & Jeanne

"*Gilles & Jeanne* studies, clinically and voluptuously, the progress of the French ogre, Gilles de Rais, the original Bluebeard, who was burned in 1440 for sorcery, sodomy and the slow slaughter of scores of innocent children . . .

"*Gilles & Jeanne* is spare and pared down, telling the stories of Joan of Arc and Gilles de Rais in a series of brief narrative moments . . .

"The world of this tale is beautifully realised; the thick forests and bestial human life of the Vendée, the gold and aesthetic curiosity of Prelati's greedy Florence, the lost children of the woodcutter Perrault making their way to the distant castle . . . Tournier has been described as a French John Fowles. Both titillate the imagination before offering a moral scheme. Both deal in the romantic seductiveness of inflicted pain. But the Frenchman is more precise, has a tougher intellect and writes much better. This makes his text more shocking and the reader's moral trouble considerably greater."
A. S. Byatt, *Sunday Times*

"A brief, exciting narrative"
City Limits

"Tournier's totalitarian fable is written with his characteristic scholarly brilliance, which keeps the horror at a distance, but only just"
Tribune

A Selected List of Titles Available in Minerva

While every effort is made to keep prices low, it is sometimes necessary to increase prices at short notice. Mandarin Paperbacks reserves the right to show new retail prices on covers which may differ from those previously advertised in the text or elsewhere.

The prices shown below were correct at the time of going to press.

Fiction

☐	7493 9026 3	**I Pass Like Night**	Jonathan Ames	£3.99	BX
☐	7493 9006 9	**The Tidewater Tales**	John Barth	£4.99	BX
☐	7493 9004 2	**A Casual Brutality**	Neil Bissoondath	£4.50	BX
☐	7493 9018 2	**Interior**	Justin Cartwright	£3.99	BC
☐	7493 9002 6	**No Telephone to Heaven**	Michelle Cliff	£3.99	BX
☐	7493 9028 X	**Not Not While the Giro**	James Kelman	£3.99	BX
☐	7493 9011 5	**Parable of the Blind**	Gert Hofmann	£3.99	BC
☐	7493 9010 7	**The Inventor**	Jakov Lind	£3.99	BC
☐	7493 9003 4	**Fall of the Imam**	Nawal El Saadawi	£3.99	BC

Non-Fiction

☐	7493 9012 3	**Days in the Life**	Jonathon Green	£4.99	BC
☐	7493 9019 0	**In Search of J D Salinger**	Ian Hamilton	£4.50	BX
☐	7493 9023 9	**Stealing from a Deep Place**	Brian Hall	£3.99	BX
☐	7493 9005 0	**The Orton Diaries**	John Lahr	£4.99	BC
☐	7493 9014 X	**Nora**	Brenda Maddox	£5.99	BC

All these books are available at your bookshop or newsagent, or can be ordered direct from the publisher. Just tick the titles you want and fill in the form below. Available in:
BX: British Commonwealth excluding Canada
BC: British Commonwealth including Canada

Mandarin Paperbacks, Cash Sales Department, PO Box 11, Falmouth, Cornwall TR10 9EN.

Please send cheque or postal order, no currency, for purchase price quoted and allow the following for postage and packing:

UK	55p for the first book, 22p for the second book and 14p for each additional book ordered to a maximum charge of £1.75.
BFPO and Eire	55p for the first book, 22p for the second book and 14p for each of the next seven books, thereafter 8p per book.
Overseas Customers	£1.00 for the first book plus 25p per copy for each additional book.

NAME (Block Letters) ....

ADDRESS ....

....